Laura!

Tracey Richardson

Copyright © 2013 Tracey Richardson
All rights reserved.
ISBN: 1481128043
ISBN-13: 978-1481128049

DEDICATION

To my supporters who have encouraged me to keep on writing, and to Laura Boult, my great-grandmother without whom this book could not have been written.

Table of Contents

Table of Contents vi
Chapter 1. Louisiana 1
Chapter 2. New York – Now That's Entertainment! 14
Chapter 3. The Crossing 21
Chapter 4. Paris 26
Chapter 5. Françoise 34
Chapter 6. Dancing 43
Chapter 7. The Apartment 48
Chapter 8. A Trip Back Home 53
Chapter 9. The Baby 61
Chapter 10. It's War 67
Chapter 11. Randolph Visits 74
Chapter 12. Her Career 82
Chapter 13. The Dance Craze of '20's 89
Chapter 14. Marcelle de St Martin 93
Chapter 15. The Roaring Twenties in Paris 97
Chapter 16. The Movies 108
Chapter 17. The Great Depression 113
Chapter 18. The Winds of War 126
Chapter 19. The Flight from Paris 130
Chapter 20. The War Rages 138
Chapter 21. New York 141
Chapter 23. Marcella 149
Chapter 24. Henry 153
Chapter 25. Françoise 156
Chapter 26. The War on French Soil 163
Chapter 27. The Liberation of Paris 165
Chapter 28. Return to Paris by way of Louisiana 168

Chapter 29. Joyeux Noel en Paris 173
Chapter 30. Return to Show Business 184
Chapter 31. Randolph Passes Away 194
Chapter 32. Laura's European Tours 203
Chapter 33. Chez Laura! 208
Chapter 34. Laura's World Tours 211
Chapter 35. Laid to Rest 216
ABOUT THE AUTHOR 218

ACKNOWLEDGMENTS

Thank you to my friends and family who have encouraged me in my writing.

Chapter 1. Louisiana

Laura Celestina Boult was born February 27, 1875, in St Maurice, Louisiana, the seventh of eleven children of David Hammett Boult, Junior and Isabella McNeal Boult. By all accounts she was a beautiful happy baby. Her parents, although wealthy at one time, were very poor by the time she was born.

Laura was always tall for her age. She had long, thick, wavy, blond hair, and hazel eyes with flecks in them that sparkled when she was happy or when she was extremely angry. Laura was not particularly gifted in school but she learned to read and write easily enough. Her father was highly educated, having been sent up north to a boarding school with six of his brothers and sisters. Her mother, on the other hand, could barely read and write.

Laura's paternal grandfather, David Boult, had been a white dentist who came to Louisiana from Maryland. He had met and fallen in love with her paternal grandmother, Florestine Cordes. Florestine was of mixed race heritage on both sides – her father being a mixture of French and Negro and her mother being a mixture of Spanish and Negro. Florestine had grown up in New Orleans and had been educated there and in Maryland at a boarding school. After a tumultuous meeting in New Orleans the David and Florestine had married and moved to

Natchitoches Parish where they purchased an historical plantation in St. Maurice. There they had established their family and had thirteen children. Providence smiled on them in the beginning. Then they, like so many others, lost all they had worked for after the Civil War. By then most of their children were grown and they moved from their mansion into much a smaller house in Natchitoches. Laura's grandfather was in local politics and was active public life and served in many offices within the parish.

Laura's father, David Jr., was the third child of his parents' union. Nearly everyone in his family looked white or near white. David Jr. was one of the ones who looked white. He was a brunette with large dark brown eyes like his mother. David Jr. followed in his father's footsteps somewhat, except he did not practice dentistry. He was a farmer with a very large farm. Large farms were no longer referred to as plantations, just large farms. He had been very successful at running the farm then, he too, tried his hand at politics. No one knows how it happened, but things took a turn for the worse for him financial-wise. Maybe he took too much time away from watching over his farm but one year he found his financial fortunes slipping away. From then, it was a downhill slide. He used every opportunity at his disposal to provide for his very large family. His father had been an estate manager and had managed to bring in very lucrative amounts from this work, so David Jr. did the same. It was these funds that kept his family going.

Laura's mother, Isabella, was also half white. Isabella had been raised by her mother after Isabella's father, reported to be a white man, abandoned them. Isabella and her four sisters did not talk about their father. Isabella's mother had been a slave on Isabella's father's plantation, so Isabella and her sisters may have been the product of a master-slave relationship. The McNeal girls would never know because Isabella's mother was silent on the matter. Although all of Isabella's sisters did not look white, they were very light-skinned and they were all blonds with light colored eyes, some blue, some green, and one hazel like Laura's.

Laura's immediate family was an odd one. Half the children had dark hair and eyes like their father and the other half had inherited from their mother. But the one thing they all had in common was that they all looked white, except for her brother Charlie, who had pale white skin, dark blond wavy hair, thin lips, and a broad, unmistakably Negroid nose.

But no matter how light-skinned they were, no matter how blond their hair, no matter the color of their eyes, they were always thought of and considered to be Negro in the eyes of the whites around them. As Negros, they were always treated with disrespect and humiliated at every turn. They were called derogatory names to their faces and no one thought they should mind that at all. That was the way of white and Negro relations before the turn of the 20th century. That was just the way it was.

From the time Laura could remember, they lived in a huge, rambling house in St Maurice. St. Maurice was just a wide spot in the road and had it not been for the fact that it was on the Old Spanish Trace where it crossed the Red River, no one would have probably ever heard of it. When the parish was being formed in 1852, it was her grandfather, David Boult, who proposed that St. Maurice be the parish seat. At that time, with over 1,000 inhabitants, it was the largest city in the newly formed parish. However, another town, Winnfield was selected. By the time Laura was born, there were barely 100 people living in or around St. Maurice.

St. Maurice was far enough away from Natchitoches, the largest nearby town, that going into town was a major treat – one that did not happen every week - but not so far away that they could not get into town when they needed to. It was in this rural environment, in the red dirt of North Louisiana, that Laura grew up.

Laura was taken to a fair in Natchitoches when she was about eight years of age. There was a variety show with singing and dancing. The dancers performed a dance called the Cakewalk. With their backs arched, the dancers high-stepped and strutted to meet the band. Such prancing Laura had never seen before in her life. From that moment on, she was fascinated with performing. As soon as she got home she jumped off the wagon and ran to her play area in the side yard. She practiced the high stepping dance over and over until her mother made her come into the house because of the darkness. The next day she was at it again. She finally got the routine down pat. She excitedly showed the dance to her parents and all of her sisters and brothers. They thought she was cute trying to imitate the dancers she had seen on stage - but nothing more. All except her older sister Cora, who studied her intently as the child performed.

Several weekends later, Cora sneaked Laura out of the house and entered her in a contest at the local juke joint. Poor rural Negros needed a place to relax and socialize after a hard week's working on plantations and sharecropping. They flocked to these often unappealing, decrepit, ramshackle buildings where they could buy food, get a drink, dance, gamble, and generally let their hair down and let off steam. These juke joints were all over rural southern America. As time went on, Cora seemed to find every one near St. Maurice. Dance contests were all the rage and nearly every juke joint had them. They had prizes for all ages. Cora entered Laura in the 10 and under category. Laura usually got a silver coin and a cheap bracelet as her winnings. Cora continued to enter Laura in contests in juke joints all over the area and Laura continued to win.

One night as Laura was waiting her turn to perform, she saw a young boy and girl do a very, to her, silly dance. When they came off the makeshift performance stage (which was just a cleared area in the middle of the joint) she asked them what they called the dance. They told her it was called the buck-and-wing. She thought that was an extremely silly name. But the boy and girl won the contest doing that silly dance. Oddly enough, the next day, when Laura was out in the play yard practicing, she tried to do it. It was really hard to do. "Phooey, who needs that ole silly dance. I can do the Cakewalk," she said to herself, and she began to practice her Cakewalk routine.

The next time Cora entered her in a contest, the same boy and girl won with the same silly dance. Much to her own surprise, the next day Laura found herself practicing that silly dance again. But try as she might she could not get her feet working to do it.

The next time she went to a contest she saw the same boy and girl there. She decided to approach them. They told her their names were Freda and Mac and they were from Chicago. They were spending the summer down south with their mama's folks. "Can you show me how to do that dance?" Laura asked them. "I practiced it and practiced it and I just can't get it."

"Where did you try to do it?" Mac asked.

"Out in the yard," Laura answered.

"Well, first of all you have to do it on the porch or in the house," said Mac. "It won't work out in the yard. But here're some steps you can try." And he proceeded to show her a couple of the steps. Laura caught on right away.

Lordy be. They won again. "But that's the last time," Laura said to herself. "They're not going to beat me again," she vowed.

The next time Cora took her to a contest, Laura was ready for Freda and Mac. She did her Cakewalk but this time she added a few buck-and-wing steps she had stolen from Freda and Mac's act. But again the young couple from Chicago won in their age group. Then thankfully summer was over and Freda and Mac went back up north to Chicago. "Good," thought Laura to herself. "Maybe us local folks can win something now."

And she did. This time she won doing the silly buck-and-wing thrown in with her ever popular rendition of the Cakewalk. And much to her surprise, not only did people clap for her, they stood up and clapped. This was her first standing ovation and she loved it. She was hooked. Show business was now in her blood.

She read everything she could get her hands on about actors and entertainers. She would write little plays and skits and coerced her sisters and brothers and her best friend Lucille, who lived the next farm over, into taking roles in them. Sometimes Laura would act out multiple parts, always with singing and dancing in them. Laura had always loved playing in her mother's clothes and now she incorporated these dress-up routines into her little productions. Lucille was her partner in crime and every dance step Laura learned, she taught to Lucille. The only difference between Laura and Lucille was that Lucille could not manage to slip away to enter contests, but she loved to sing and dance as much as Laura did.

Laura's singing voice was developed in the Evergreen Baptist Church on State Route 477 in St. Maurice, on the edge of the huge plantation that her grandmother and grandfather had once owned. She sang soprano until she was a teenager when her voice deepened into a mellow alto, but she could sing all parts harmony, except for bass, of course. Some people cannot carry a tune in a water bucket. Laura was not one of those people. Her voice was not high and delicate but full and throaty and she could really belt out a song. Her friend Lucille on the other hand had to really stretch to make her thin thready soprano voice heard. The girls loved to sing duos and they were on lots of church and school programs doing just that.

When Laura was not doing her chores, she was practicing her dance steps. Her singing she practiced all the time, everywhere, except in the class room. For that she had to be quiet and still, which was not in her inherent nature. Her nature was to run and sing and dance.

Once a week her father would bring home a newspaper from Shreveport. Laura would go straight to the section with the advertisements for different shows. Shreveport was a day's ride away from St. Maurice and they only got to go about once a year. This year her parents were planning on taking them all to the state fair. One of her aunts lived in Shreveport and she was going to put them all up for two days.

Laura had Cora scour all the papers looking for dance contests. By now the two girls were partners and Laura shared half of her winnings with Cora. After taking out some money for candy for herself and Lucille, Laura gave the rest of her winnings to her mother. Her mother always used some of the money for Laura - fabric for a new dress, hair ribbons, some little thing to let Laura know that she was special for bringing in extra money.

Cora finally found a promising contest being held in Shreveport during the time they were going to be there. They started making preparations for Laura to enter. Her mother sewed her a new dress and trimmed it with a big ribbon sash that was long enough to tie into a big bow in the back. She even got a smaller matching ribbon for her long blond hair.

The contest was at a local juke joint but it wasn't being held in the evening like most others. It was being held during the afternoon. Her entire family attended. Laura got up and sang her best, danced the Cakewalk, and threw in some buck-and-wing steps for good measure. She did not win but she did get an honorable mention though, and for that she got money and a medal attached to a ribbon to pin on her dress. She was so proud. Her family all told her what a good job she did and there must have been something wrong with the judges to pick someone else to win the grand prize. Laura was happy to be an also-ran.

The day came when Laura's school days were over. Her parents did not send her back to the fall session when she was 13. She was expected to get a job. Her father found one for her at a two-bit roadhouse up the highway from where they lived. They set her younger brother Charlie the task of taking her to work in the wagon each day and picking her up in the evening. She worked a twelve hour day – from 7AM until 7 PM.

One day, as she was giving one of her impromptu Cakewalk performances out back of the roadhouse, she was stopped dead in her tracks by the too familiar voice of Misses, the wife of the roadhouse owner.

"Laura!" the high nasal female voice yelled at her.

"Yes Ma'am," Laura called as she ran back into the restaurant. She picked up a broom and started sweeping. This was her life for two years – working in the restaurant and entering contests when there were any.

One day Laura was a gangling, all elbows and knees teenager, the next she was a beautiful fully developed young woman, with the accoutrements required to turn the heads of all of the men she encountered, black and white alike. She was about five feet eight inches tall with luxurious honey blond hair that hung down almost to her waist. Because it was such a nuisance, she kept it pinned up into a bun in the back. Unless you knew her ancestry, you would have sworn she was all white.

Laura gravitated towards white men for her love interests. It was little wonder. They looked like the people she had been surrounded by all her life. Except for the field hands on her father's farm, and the hand full of dark-skinned Negroes who were lucky enough to attend the one room school where Laura attended grade school, Laura had never really been around dark-skinned Negroes that much. None of the Negro boys who buzzed around her were any darker than she was and she was related to most of them.

Marvin Johnson, a white boy, lived across the field from the Boults. Laura would sneak out of the house at night to see him. She got pregnant the first time she had sex with him. He was sixteen. She was fifteen. Marvin rented a room in a house and talked Laura into moving in with him. Her father pitched a fit and threatened to kill Marvin but eventually he gave in. She was tainted forever. He knew that no respectable Negro man would ever marry her now. The baby was born almost exactly nine months later. She named the baby after Marvin.

Within a year after having her first child she was pregnant again. She named that baby Christopher, but no one ever called him that. Everyone just called him Chris. By then Marvin had moved them to a three room house he had rented. It was not much more than a shack really. Laura did not do much dancing anymore. She was too busy taking care of two small children and Marvin did not like for her to go out to juke joints in the evening. He wanted her to stay home with him and the babies. But she sang all the time – making beds, scrubbing floors, changing diapers, washing clothes, and hanging them out on the line to dry – everything she did, she did with a song. People would stop in the road to listen to her sing.

When she got pregnant with the second child, Marvin constantly talked about what life would be like for his children. He did not want them to lead the harsh lives that Negros in Natchitoches Parrish were living. He wanted more for them. He decided to move to Florida where his brother was living. After the baby was born, he broke the news to Laura that he did not want her to accompany him and the boys. He wanted to raise the them as white and he thought that he would not be able to do so if she was with them. He told Laura point blank that he did not want her to have contact with the boys for fear it would become known that they had Negro blood in them. He left her with twenty dollars. That was all she had to her name. She could not even remain in the house they had shared together. She was forced to move out. She moved back in with her parents and went back to work at the roadhouse.

Laura was heartbroken – too heartbroken to sing anymore. She cried continually. One day she was sweeping out the restaurant in-between picking up dishes and taking them to the kitchen. Because she was not white, they would not let her wait on customers. A fella who ate at the restaurant nearly every day, Andrew Jones, was there having his dinner on night. "Smile," he said to her.

"Nobody is paying me to smile," she retorted. As soon as she said it, she regretted it because she knew he would tell Misses that she had been uppity with him, and Misses would hit her. It was not allowed for a Negro to be uppity to a white person. That could land you in jail. But Andrew did not tell Misses.

The following day, he said the same thing to her again. "Smile." This time she did not smart off at him but she did not smile either.

Each day when he came in to have his dinner, Andrew would wait until she came near and he would say, "Smile." Each day she would not smile.

Finally, after about two weeks of this, Andrew said, "I know you can smile. I've seen you smile. You're much prettier when you smile."

She replied, "I don't have anything to smile about."

"Why not?" he asked.

"Because my man left and took my babies with him," she answered sullenly.

"Oh," he said, truly sorry. "I didn't know. Who was your man? Big Jim?" he was referring to a dark-skinned Negro man who was always hanging around outside waiting for Laura to come out the back door.

"No. Big Jim is a pest I can't get rid of," said Laura. It's Marvin Johnson."

"Marvin Johnson?" asked Andrew incredulously. He had gone to school with Marvin and he knew how much Marvin hated and despised Negroes. Andrew was surprised that Marvin would take up with one. He reasoned that Laura must be something special.

From that day forward, Andrew would follow Laura around the room with his eyes. He finally got up the nerve to ask if he could call on her.

"What for?" was all she asked.

"'Cause I like you and want to see you, that's what for."

"What you want to see me for? You think because I was with Marvin, I'll be with you, too? Well you're wrong. I loved Marvin and he loved me. But he loved our boys more. That's why he left me behind. Because he wanted our boys to have a better life."

"No, Laura. I don't want to be with you that way. I just want to just come and sit and talk to you."

"About what?"

"About why you're so sad all the time. I'd like to make you smile if I can."

"No one can make me smile," she said sadly. "Not 'til I have my boys back with me again."

"Marvin isn't coming back, Laura. You may as well get over it. I talked to his sister Muriel and she said he's not ever coming back. He's in Florida somewhere."

Tears started rolling down Laura's face. "I can't get over it. Can't you see that? I'm empty without those boys."

Andrew reached out and took her in his arms. He kissed her on the cheek. Finally she stopped crying.

"Can I come to see you Sunday?" he asked quietly.

She nodded.

She moved in with him the following week. Her father did not say a word.

Hampton Thomas was born a year later. The year after that she had her fourth child – another little boy. She named him Randolph Andrew after his father.

Laura felt suffocated and guilty all at the same time. Andrew was head over heels in love with her and she felt nothing for him. She still loved Marvin.

Andrew was forever after her to have sex with him. She felt like she had to get away. If she stayed she would have a baby every year until finally her body would give out and she would die an early death. After the last child was born she resolved to leave Andrew but he gave her very little money. She felt trapped with him and the children.

She talked to her eldest sister Cora – the only person she felt she could confide in. Her parents had cut off all contact with her when she moved in with Andrew. Cora suggested that she move out. But where could she go? Her only alternative would be to move into a room somewhere. How could she do that to her children? As long as she was with Andrew, Hamp and Randolph had a room of their own and a backyard to play in. Andrew showered them with toys – including a tricycle, which the children dearly loved to ride.

Laura's friend Lucille had grown into a pretty and vivacious woman. Lucille's aunt lived in New York City in a place called Harlem. Lucille's aunt had told Lucille that she could get her a job in a fancy lady's house. So Lucille had left the red dust of Louisiana behind and moved to the big city.

Lucille worked for the fancy lady for about six months. She wrote to Laura that the ways and customs of the lady and her family were strange; they were forever doing queer things. Like trying to talk to Lucille, asking her questions about what she thought about this and that, about what she thought about Booker T. Washington and W.E.B. DuBois.

Lucille wrote, "I'm not smart like you. I barely know who Booker T. Washington is and I certainly don't know who this W.E.B. DuBois is, if there really is such a person with three initials. And if I did have thoughts about these two people who my fancy lady and her family want to talk about, at the most no good can come out of telling a white person what I'm thinking about. They would just use it against me."

Lucille liked to go out and party on Saturday nights. She wrote to Laura, "Last Saturday night I was out dancing at a club called The Pig's Foot. This fat white man came up to me and said I look pretty enough to be one of the girls on the stage. He wanted to know if I can sing and dance, that he wanted me to be in a show he was putting on. I asked around and found out he is legit. I auditioned for him and he gave me a job in the chorus. Girl, what I'm making compared to what I was getting as a maid is not to be believed. You've got to come to New York!"

Another time Lucille wrote to Laura, "You can out-sing and out-dance all of the girls in the chorus line put together and you're prettier, too. Please come to New York and share my good fortune with me. We can share my apartment. After I got the job at the nightclub I had to move out of the private home where I was working at. They needed the bed for the new maid. It's a right nice apartment, only two rooms though but it has an indoor toilet down at the end of the hall."

Laura did not know what an apartment was, but she knew that this was a way for her to get out of the living arrangement she had with Andrew.

Laura was pretty but having four children before the age of 21 had bloated her. She would need to drop some weight. She started practicing her dance steps daily. Slowly the weight started to come off. She ruminated on Lucille's offer for weeks before finally writing to her that she wanted to come to New York but that she had no money. Lucille sent her money for train fare.

Laura knew that she would never be able to take care of her two sons with what she would be making working at a small restaurant and because she did not know what life in the big city would bring, she felt she had no choice but to leave them behind. In her mind she was not abandoning them but providing for them.

Except for Hamp and Randolph Laura was not leaving much behind. Randolph was then two years old. By then Laura had talked to her mother and father and they thought her moving to New York City was better than remaining in St. Maurice, living out-of-wedlock with a white man and having a baby every year. They agreed to take Hamp and Randolph until Laura could get on her feet and send for them. Provided Andrew would let her parents have the boys. Andrew agreed.

Laura could sing and she loved to dance. She had started to believe that maybe there was a place where she could put her only two God-given talents to work for her. By now Lucille was working at a place called The Plantation, a club for whites only in New York City. Lucille wrote that the money was outstanding and no one asked where you came from or what you left behind. Laura anxiously looked forward to seeing all the wondrous things that Lucille wrote to her about – especially skyscrapers. Laura did not really believe that there were buildings so tall that you had to have a special little room to go to the top floor.

Laura's leaving did not phase Hamp, but Randolph cried terribly when she got on the wagon to drive away. It tore her heart out to see him cry so, but she knew that if she remained in Louisiana, alcohol and drugs would overcome her. That was the only way to get through the despair of having no hope.

Laura's younger brother Charlie drove her to Natchitoches in their father's wagon to catch the train to New York. It would be a two day journey, with Laura riding in the last car in the train, with no amenities, for most of the way. Not allowed to eat in the dining car south of the Mason-Dixon line, she had to provide her own food or be prepared to purchase food at the different train stations along the way. Isabella packed her a box lunch done up with string, containing fried chicken and biscuits. Laura was happy to see that she was not the only colored person eating from a box lunch on the trip north.

Laura arrived in New York, tired, disheveled, and needing to relieve herself when she encountered indoor plumbing for the first time in her life. She already liked city living.

Chapter 2. New York – Now That's Entertainment!

Laura arrived in New York in the dead of winter. In her purse was what was left of the one hundred dollars her mother had given here. It would have to provide her with food, shelter, and incidentals until she was able to find a job and get her first payday. Laura moved in with Lucille so the shelter part was covered. Lucille took Laura to the same nightclub where she worked when she first came to New York. The old stage manager had been let go and a new stage manager had taken over. He was a real hard-nose. Laura had a few pictures and she even had a newspaper clipping with her name in it from a Negro newspaper, but the stage-manager would not look at them. Because she had no experience he refused to even give her an audition. "Come back when you get some experience," he said to her as he turned and walked away.

Laura went to a restaurant Lucille told her about and asked for a job as a waitress. Assuming she was white, all they wanted to know was "have you waited tables before, and where?"

One day a man eating in the restaurant kept leering at her. That was nothing new to her. Finally, just as he was about to leave, he slid a dog-eared business card across the table to her. "Come to see me if you want to stop working as a waitress," was all that he said.

Laura kept the dog-eared card for two weeks. Finally, on her one day off that week, a Wednesday, she went to see Ernst Wilmont, the man whose name was on the card.

"Lift your skirt, Girlie, and let me see your legs," Wilmont said to her.

Laura was appalled. "Well, lift it! If you want a job as a showgirl you have to show your legs," he barked.

Laura lifted her skirt to her knees. She was beet red with shame and embarrassment.

"Can you tap?" Wilmont asked.

"What?" she asked. He showed her what he was talking about. He was clumsy at it but she got the picture.

Laura broke into a lively buck-and-wing routine she had taught herself.

"Do a step-heel, then heel-step." Wilmont said. Laura had no idea what he was talking about. He showed her a clumsy combination step. She imitated him, only her steps were light and graceful.

"Let me see you shuffle."

"What's a shuffle?" she asked. Again, he showed her and again, she imitated him, performing the steps with precision.

"Now do a shuffle-ball-change," he called out.

Laura was a fast learner, and she figured out on her own what that would look like.

She executed the steps to perfection, then added a lively shuffle step and ended in a buck-and-wing flourish.

"You'll do. You can tap pretty good." he said. He wrote something on a piece of paper and handed it to her. "Report to this rehearsal hall tomorrow morning at 10."

"What are you hiring me for?" she asked.

"We go on the road in seven days and I'm two girls short. You know of anyone interested?" Laura recommended her friend Lucille. When she told Lucille about the job, Lucille declined, citing her stable position at The Plantation.

Laura was put on the last row of the chorus with little hope of moving up, but the pay for the job was twice what Laura had been earning as a waitress. Laura was ecstatic, but what the hell was a "tap"? she wondered. She would soon find out from the other dancers that was the new name for the buck-and-wing, with a lot of flourishes added and she, along with other colored performers, were one of the first who knew how to do it. Only now you added little pieces of metal to your shoes to make the sounds louder. "What will folks think of next?" she wondered.

During those days, theater was an ensemble production. These ensembles would pack their trunks and board trains, often with the greater stars in their own private cars, to take their shows on the road. Traveling across country, they played whistle-stops and one-night-stands. These tours were very lucrative for the theater owners, the producers, and the performers.

To insure that his stars had lucrative routes and theaters along the way, particularly in the smaller towns, one noted showman, Charles Frohman instigated the creation of the "Syndicate". He and his company of directors and producers picked the theaters, the stars, the plays, and other assorted acts for the entire season, including the black stars and theaters. This syndicate controlled the success or failure for hundreds of theaters and thousands of performers throughout the country. They all made money – huge amounts of money. The ensemble that Laura was a part of was part of this syndicate. Laura packed her trunk and joined the throng.

After nine weeks of performing, Laura was moved from the third row of the chorus to the second row, and then to the first row. Each move toward the front of the stage got her a raise in pay. She got progressively better at dancing and singing until eventually she was given a one minute spot. One minute is a long time when you are tapping your heart out. The "spot" also came with a raise. She was now making four times what she had earned as a waitress. She was on the road in the mid-west for six months when they brought her back to New York.

Laura had a strong clear voice with a more than average range and was a better than average dancer, she was still required to work with voice, dancing, as well as acting coaches one hour a day during rehearsals. Although she had strong performance skills, even she noticed that her deliverance skills were weak – the ability to be heard in the back of the house. There was a trick to it and she had not yet mastered that trick. After several weeks of working with the voice coach, she finally learned how to project her voice into the back of the room. Her dancing improved also. She learned that all of the steps she had made up actually had names to them and by putting together the named steps, you could memorize the order of the steps and then recreate them at will. It was called choreography.

She paid attention to instructions, practiced every day, and again was moved up to the front row of the chorus line, occasionally being given speaking and featured dancing spots. All the time she earned excellent pay, sending a portion of it home for the upkeep of her boys.

Because she had learned her craft so well, she was put to work up and down the Broadway circuit - first at the Victoria at 42nd St and Seventh Ave, then at the Republic on 42nd. Then finally they put her in a show at The Casino. After it burned in 1905, they put her at the Lyric a few doors down from the Republic and after that opening a new show at the New Amsterdam a few doors further down.

She was one of the top chorus girls in the city. She could get a table at any of the restaurants that catered to the after-theater crowd, no matter how busy or crowded they were. Of all the restaurants in New York, the restaurant and jazz club run by minor mobster Joe Zelli, a transplanted Italian with a bent for all things Parisian, was her favorite and she was a favorite there, with them placing her at a choice table whenever she patronized the establishment.

She was not a star but she was well-known. It seemed that not a day went by that someone did not send a note backstage to her and she regularly received bouquets from stage-door johnnies.

All of the productions she was in followed the same formula – the Hero, Villain, and the Damsel in Distress. There was always some sort of conflict, which was resolved to the benefit of the Hero, and the Hero and the Damsel in

Distress got together in the end, all with singing and dancing. It was slap trap, but it was slap trap that worked.

The Shuberts - Lee, Jacob, and Samuel - were producers of the highest magnitude. Laura was working for them in their latest theatrical production at the New Amsterdam. And no one had a clue that she was a Negro. That was until her brother Charlie came to New York City. Down in Louisiana where there were a lot of mixed race people, he blended right in. But up north, with Europeans with their thin hawk noses, he stood out like a sore thumb. He could be mistaken for no one except someone with Negro blood in his ancestry.

Charlie was a gambler and a hustler and he had been down on his luck for some time. There was a floating crap game he wanted to get into and he was short of funds. He came to the theater looking for Laura so he could touch her for a loan. She was seen slipping him money by one of the Schubert brothers. She was called into the office of the brothers before the matinee the following day. They demanded to know what she was doing talking to "that Negro".

Laura explained that she knew him from back in Louisiana, that he worked on her father's plantation. It was not exactly a lie. Charlie had indeed worked on their father's farm, not as a field hand as she led them to believe, but as a clerk keeping track of the payroll, livestock, goods and supplies being bought, crops being sold, all mostly in his head, until the gambling and partying life called to him forever. Even though Laura swore she would never have cause to see Charlie again, they fired her anyway.

She drug herself home to her lavish apartment, knowing that she would have to give it up – the Shuberts would see to that. Because Laura was part of the tight circle that was theater in New York, it had meant that her living was secure. To be outside of this tight circle meant that she might have to stoop to the edges of respectability in order to put bread in her mouth and a roof over her head. Once it was known that Laura had passed for white, she would be neither white nor Negro. She would be ostracized by all segments of theater society.

Laura knew she had to act before the news about her ethnicity and her racial deceit spread throughout the theater district. She went up to Harlem looking for a theatrical booking agent she knew who hung out around the Alhambra Theater. She had heard that Daniel Frohman was putting together an all-colored revue that he was taking to Paris. They were going to play the Moulin Rouge. The cabaret, built in 1889 by Joseph Oller, who also owned the Paris Olympia theater, had as its trademark symbol a red windmill on the roof – hence the name Moulin Rouge – the Red Mill. Laura wanted the agent to ask for a job for her in the show. She might as well go to Paris, she reasoned, her career in New York was finished now that it was discovered that she was a Negro. Much to her amazement, she landed a singing and dancing role on her first audition.

Laura was told, with pride, that the theater was in Pigalle but their accommodations would be in Montmartre. Little did they know that she did not know the difference, nor would it have mattered if they had been housed in a slum. She was just glad to have been given an opportunity to get out of town before her reputation caught up with her. They would sail one week later to Le Harve on the *Amerique*, a ship of the French line Compagnie Générale Transatlantique. From there they would take a train to Paris.

Laura went to her apartment and made plans to move out. Although she told herself differently, in her heart she knew she would not be returning. She sold all her furniture and half of her clothes. Stripped to what a showgirl would consider the bare necessities, she packed her belongings into four steamer trunks. Laura had worked steadily since coming to New York and had saved her money, that she did not send home for the support of her boys She had been saving up to bring them to New York to live with her. She, therefore, had the funds of her own to pay for the shipping of her trunks to Paris and did not have to rely on the one trunk per chorus girl rule. Because they were going overseas, the producer generously allowed them two trunks, only because they would have to adhere to established, well-enforced dress codes on the ship. Stars and bit players were allowed to take more with them, but Laura was working this show as a regular showgirl. "My how the mighty do come down", she thought to herself. She had to pay for the shipping of the other two trunks herself.

As the cab took her from her apartment to the docks, with tears streaming down her face, she hummed the words to the recent George M. Cohen show, *Little Johnny Jones*, for which she had auditioned for a part in but did not get, "Give my regards to Broadway, Remember me to Herald Square. . ." It would be another year before that song would become a Broadway hit and the anthem of all who worked there. The year was 1905 and Laura was 30 years old. She felt as though she had already lived a lifetime.

Chapter 3. The Crossing

The crossing of the Atlantic from New York to Le Harve took eight days. The workings of a luxury ocean liner class ship is a magnificent thing – for the liner must carry everything to accommodate its' passengers onboard. The *Amerique* carried on board enough beef, pork, veal, chicken, turkeys, game birds, dairy products, and other food stuffs to feed first class, second class, and steerage passengers as well as the entire crew. The ship carried with it fresh water, coffee, tea, twenty-five hundred quarts of milk and cream, thousands of eggs, tons of butter, and almost everything else that could be imagined that a passenger might need. Bread was baked fresh onboard each day.

The person in charge of making sure that there was enough of everything to last throughout the trip was the chief steward. He was the keeper of all the foodstuffs, doling it out to the chief cooks as required to create the menus from which the passengers selected their meals. For first and second class passengers this consisted of four meals a day and for steerage class, three. Meals for the ship's crew was similarly segregated – officers had four meals a day while regular seamen had only three. At the very least the chief steward planned for twenty-four meals every day, with some of the meals, those of first class passengers, having as many as thirty dishes. Passengers' wishes and dietary restrictions were accommodated as much as possible.

Work began on passenger ships at 5 o'clock each morning with hot coffee and rolls being served to the crew and continued unabated until they were served breakfast beginning at 7:30. In between, the crew saw to the needs of the passengers.

It was the job of the cabin crews to change out all of the linens in every cabin in first and second class, each day. Altogether, bed linens, towels, and table linens for all classes of passengers and ranks of crew, numbered around 20,000 pieces per trip. The linens of the ship are not laundered on board but are bundled and laundered at the terminus of the line called "the works" where the laundry from the crossing before was laundered and awaited their pickup before the next crossing.

It was to these luxuries that Laura awakened on her first full day at sea. From the moment she went in to breakfast at 8 AM, throughout the day, the ship's cruise director found ways to keep the passengers busy, entertained, and segregated. There were physical activities, deck tennis, shuffleboard, cards, charades, shows, gambling, fancy and plain dinners, reading, and just plain relaxing on deck. Laura indulged in each and every one of these, she and the rest of her troupe - away from white passengers. In addition, the show's producer and director had arranged for a rehearsal room and there were rehearsals each day, which was kind of interesting, since there was great movement of the ship underneath their feet.

She went for a long walk after breakfast each morning. On two decks there was painted on the floor, a footpath guide such as those painted on the ground where athletes ran track. There were five "lanes". Laura supposed that it was expected that each walker would pick a lane and walk only in that lane. However, that was not the practical experience. Walkers were all over the place. There were the hardy walkers and ones with canes. There were the delicate walkers and ones with parasols. And every kind of walker in-between. During one of these walks, her hand accidentally brushed the hand of an old white man. You would have thought that she had scalded him with hot water. He jerked his hand back and wiped it hard on his pants, as if her blackness, of which there was none mind you, could somehow rub off on him. Laura was mortified that this would cause some sort of incidence. It did not. Everyone, except the old white man who she had accidentally brushed, went right on walking as if nothing had happened.

There was a fitness center with giant medicine balls and free weights. For this activity, Laura had three exercise dresses. These dresses stopped at mid-calf and were worn with long black stockings. All three of Laura's exercise dresses had sailor collars and when she wore them she looked like an 18 year old. Whites and Negros were kept segregated by only allowing each group in at certain times of the day.

After lunch she attended lectures and lessons – there were French language lessons, a lecture on French history, a lecture on Joan de Arc, a lecture on the Sun King Louis XIV, drawing and painting lessons, ballroom dancing lessons, and much, much more. There were all manner of classes and lectures to keep one occupied in the afternoons. Although all races were in the auditorium for the lectures and lessons, except for the ballroom lessons, whites were in one section and Negros were relegated to the back of the room.

One day she was part of a group that was given a guided tour by the ship's first officer. This tour involved all of the mechanical workings of the ships. There were more men and boys on the tour than women and girls. The only reason Laura signed up for the tour was because by the fifth day she was really starting to get bored. In the middle of the tour, she was called aside by one of the ship's officers. He begged her pardon profusely, but asked her, in the oh, so, politest of tones, if she would please leave the tour. Being used to worse treatment from whites, she merely smiled and went on her way to the observation deck, where she stood by herself by the railing for quite some time, all the while thinking, "I thought it was going to be different, but it's the same ole racist bull-shit."

Thank goodness they had rehearsals each day which took up two hours of the afternoon. After leaving rehearsals, they returned to their cabins and dressed for afternoon tea, which lasted for about an hour. Even though they were segregated in the dining room where the tea was served, they were expected to dress in the same manner as the white passengers. These teas required a special dress made of lawn or very thin cotton, usually trimmed with lace. Laura had brought five of these along in her "crossing trunks". Each of her tea dresses had dramatic lace inserts and contrasting linen panels with more lace and linen panels in the back of the dresses and on the sleeves. Each was worn with three inch deep satin ribbons which streamed down almost touching the floor. Each dress had its own matching hat – two being sailor hats with streamers, and the other three being fashionable hats of the day with ostrich plumbs and all. Laura did not like to brag but she thought her dresses to be prettier than the white girls', although they probably paid a lot more for theirs than she paid for hers.

After tea they all returned to their cabins again, where they took a nap or just rested. One of three dress codes applied each evening. There was a schedule that was left on the dresser by the cabin crew each evening for the next day's dinner activities.

Formal: That meant dressed to the nines! Since Laura loved dressing up, this was not a problem for her. She had brought along several formal gowns. However, closet space was very limited so her ball dresses were hung inside the cabin on a clothes line that the cabin steward had strung up for their benefit. Three of the seven nights at sea were designated formal nights when passengers were required to wear full evening dresses with trains. This meant matching shoes, purses, scarves, gloves, jewelry, and hair accessories.

Laura's newest and at the current time, most favored gown, was a floral scalloped affair. The scallops of the flowers created the neck opening. The front of the gown was a solid lace panel from neck opening to hem. The front of the gown was a floral cutout which overlapped the lace down the front. The shoulders were decorated with flowers, one bouquet on each shoulder. The sleeves were puffed and short. The waist was encircled with a satin scarf tied in a bow in front. The gown was trained at 36 inches.

The second gown was red and gold brocade floral, also trained at 36 inches. It had a low-cut draped bodice and back. There were solid gold skirt panel inserts. Although bustles were beginning to die out, this dress had one.

Semiformal: Two other of the seven nights at sea were designated as semi-formal. This to Laura meant a long gown but without a train. Laura had brought along several of these gowns that she had packed in her "crossing" trunks. One of the two she had with her in-cabin was a beautiful shade of mauve trimmed in darker mauve velvet. The other was a black lace gown trimmed in gold.

The first night and last night of the cruise were designated elegant casual which included just about everything else that Laura owned. She did not know what casual attire consisted of since she was formally dressed each time she went out in public. To Laura, dressing up was part of the fun of living.

On arising from their naps in the afternoon, the fashionable ladies onboard spent an hour dressing. Cocktails were at 7 and dinner at 8. Dinner lasted until 10, at which time they moved to the ballroom where most passengers danced until 1 or 2 in the morning. Negros had a separate ballroom. It was small and as there were only a few Negro passengers, the dance floor was usually half empty. Laura and the other girls in the show took the opportunity to show their fancy footwork. Usually the other few Negro passengers gave them a round of applause when they got off the dance floor.

If Paris was going to be anything like the crossing on the ship, Laura already knew that she was going to love it. Everything was so much more luxurious and over the top than in the states. And she, like all Negros, knew that there was a different attitude towards them in Europe, especially in Paris. She could not wait to start a new life free from racism. Her only regret was her boys. How she wished she could have them with her. But she knew that could not be.

Chapter 4. Paris

At long last, France! Laura could not believe she was actually there. How could this be? Nowhere in her daydreams of escaping the red dust of Northern Louisiana did she ever imagine herself in such a wonderful and magnificent place.

They took a train from Le Harve where they docked, into Paris. The train station, Gare St. Lazare, was old, extremely busy, and very dirty. But Laura did not notice any of this, she was so awed with the idea of being in the City of Lights. They were able to get taxi cabs bound for the hotel without any difficulty.

Laura settled herself into the hotel room in Paris. As soon as she got there she started thinking about looking for permanent arrangements. Laura had bought tour books which she read on the crossing and she set about trying to visit each monument and museum listed in the books – an impossible task but one she undertook anyway. She spent all of her free time getting to know the city and she liked what she saw. She reasoned, if she were not able to remain in Paris, at least she would be able to say that she had a good vacation there.

Laura had six major tourist attractions on her must-see list – Notre Dame, the Louvre, the Dome of les Invalides, the Arc de Triomphe, the Tour Eiffel, and Versailles.

The first stop was the Louvre. Located on the Right Bank of the Seine, the Louvre was begun as a fortress during the 12th century under the reign of Philip II. Until 1682, when Louis XIV enlarged the hunting chateau in Versailles and moved his court there, the Louvre Palace was considered the monarch's primary residence. After the Sun King and his entourage decamped, the Louvre began displaying the royal collections, including a collection of statues. During the French Revolution it became an official museum of the nation's treasures, opening with over 500 paintings. Under Napoleon, it was renamed the Musée Napoleon and the collections were enlarged with artwork taken from cities the French army had conquered. After Napoleon's defeat at Waterloo, many items that had been looted from other countries were officially returned. Even so, by the time Laura paid her first visit there, it housed over 35,000 artifacts – too many items to be seen in one, two, a dozen, or maybe even a lifetime of visits. Laura, a real history buff, visited at least once a month, during the entire time she was in Paris, for the rest of her life.

Next on her must-see list was the Tour Eiffel, jokingly referred to as "the iron asparagus". Built entirely of iron lattice work in 1889 on the Champ de Mars as the entrance to the World's Fair which was held that year, the tower was named after the man whose company built it. Contrary to popular belief, it was not designed by Gustave Eiffel but by Maurice Koechline and Emile Nougier, two senior engineers who worked for Eiffel's company, the Compagnie des Establissments Eiffel. The Tour Eiffel is one of the most, if not the most, recognized structures in the world. Laura went there on her second full day in Paris. She was mesmerized. Only she discovered, much to her dismay, that she was afraid of heights. She would not go past the second landing. That was high enough for her. From that vantage point she could see all of the city laid out before her.

On her day off, Laura went out to the Château de Versailles on the train and like so many before and after her, marveled at the decadence in which the monarchy had lived – surrounded by gold and plushness not to be imagined if you had not seen it with your own eyes. The court of Versailles was the center of political power in France when in 1682, Louis XIV forced his court to move there from Paris, until Louis XVI, his queen Marie Antoinette, their children, and his sister were forced to return to Paris in 1789. Laura trod the stairways where all of the members of the royal families who had lived there had walked before her. She was shocked at their lack of privacy in their royal bedchambers. People literally slept on the floors while the royal couples had intimate relations with each other. She absolutely could not believe her eyes when she walked through the royal gardens, admiring some of the 2,400 plus fountains and waterworks. She came back awed at all she had seen.

On Sunday, Laura visited Notre Dame de Paris for mass. One of the most beautiful cathedrals in the world, it has dramatic towers, beautiful stained glass windows, and exquisitely sculpted statuary. It, too, took Laura's breath away. The heartbeat of medieval Paris, the church was not built in one fell swoop. It took almost 200 years to complete, its' construction taking place from 1160 to 1345. Many died while working on the building project that was to become the magnificent Roman Catholic Marian cathedral located on the eastern half of the Île de la Cité. Originally conceived in the French Gothic tradition, the flying buttresses on the rear of the building, give it not only stability, but a definite air of grace and beauty. The many statues, gargoyles, and chimeras were put in place, not just for mere decoration, but in many cases to serve as supports and to drain off rain water before it could collect on the building and damage it.

Many oversaw the construction of the edifice over the two hundred plus years it took to complete it. This explains its' mix of styles and periods as evidenced by the differing styles at different heights of the west façade and the towers and the magnificent rose window contained therein. Between 1210 and 1220, the fourth architect of the project oversaw the construction of the level with the rose window and the great halls beneath the towers. Although rose windows, from the very simplest to the very ornate, predates the Medieval period, their use became almost de rigueur from then forward, being seen in various forms in almost all large European churches.

The North rose window, added between 1220 and 1250, set the pattern for the gigantic and complex window in the south transept and many other rose windows too come. The window is divided into segments by stone mullions in two bands radiating from a central roundel, each terminating in pointed arches and tracery. The window has at its center the Blessed Virgin Mary and Christ Child in Majesty, surrounded by prophets and saints. It is this window above all else in the cathedral that so mesmerized Laura and kept her returning each Sunday to view its magnificence.

Though several organs were installed in the cathedral over time, the first noteworthy organ was finished in the 18th century by François-Herni Clicquot. Some of Clicquot's original pipework in the pedal division was still existent in the organ during Laura's stay in Paris. The organ was almost completely rebuilt and expanded in the 19th century by Aristide Cavaillé-Coll and it is this organ that most people recognized as being "The Organ" of Notre Dame. With 111 stops, five 56-key manuals and a 32-key pedal board, the organ had 7,800 pipes, with 900 classified as historical. When Laura first began to visit there, it was entirely manual and its sound was stupendous, with its low bass register reverberating the teeth in her body.

Each time Laura would enter through those magnificent doors with the organ already playing, something spiritual would come over her and fill her spirit. Her prayers, which were so difficult for her to compose at home, came easily to her in this place. Laura attended mass each and every Sunday she was in Paris.

Chills went through Laura's body each time she heard the stupendous bells of the cathedral. There were five bells at Notre Dame. The greatest, the bourdon bell was nick-named Emmanuel, located in the South Tower. Emmanuel weighed just over 13 tons, and was tolled to mark the hours of the day and for various occasions and services, ringing in a resounding E ♭ tone. This bell was always rung first, at least 5 seconds before the rest. There were four additional bells on wheels in the North Tower, which were swing chimed. These bells were rung for various services and festivals, being rung manually when Laura was first became an attendee of the cathedral, and later automated.

After mass, Laura would usually go for a long walk, often on the Ile de la Cite, having lunch at some out-of-the-way bistro or restaurant. Reflecting and mediating on her day, she would talk to no one. Around 4 she would head back to the hotel. Rested and ready for all life had to throw at her for another week, she would leave for the theater by five, arriving there no later than six. She always made a point of being on time.

One Sunday, when Laura was just wandering around the city, she encountered Auguste Rodin's *Le Penseur*. The Thinker is a bronze statue on a marble pedestal. Intended to sit atop "The Doors of Hell", an ensemble piece based on Dante's Inferno, it was conceived as only one sculpture in a larger work. The Thinker, used by Dante to represent deep thinking and philosophy was originally entitled, and was always referred to by the creator, as *Le Poète* – the poet being Dante contemplating writing his epic poem. When the museum where the Dante's Inferno ensemble was supposed to be housed was not built, the pieces that had already been created were exhibited alone. The Thinker was first exhibited as an individual sculpture in 1905 at the Salon in Paris. When Laura first saw it, it was still in the Salon. The piece was later purchased for the people of Paris to enjoy after Gabriel Mourey, the editor of "Les Arts de la vie" began a subscription for its purchase. It was finally placed in the Musée Rodin, a museum dedicated to the art of Rodin, where Laura often went to contemplate her life and its strange twists and turns.

Among those sites that Laura took in just for the decadence of the spirit, were grands magazins, among them, Printemps, Le Bon Marché, and Galeries Lafayette, some of the original Bell Epoch department stores. They all soon became favorites of hers because they had everything a shopper could ask for – clothing, shoes, jewelry, home goods, and eating establishments. "Why shop anywhere else?" she reasoned.

Laura also shopped in smaller shops, but less frequently, but mostly she just faire du lèche-vitrine. Laura had a different goal in mind than the other members of her troupe. For them, Paris was maybe a one-time thing. They wanted to spend every penny they made in the shops. For Laura it was to be hers to enjoy for a lifetime. She did not recklessly spend all of the money she earned on the trip. She put herself on a daily budget. She indulged herself in sightseeing, but not in spending recklessly on Parisian clothing and gee-gaws. She went out to restaurants, but not to expensive ones, choosing instead to partake of her meals in small out of the way eating establishments. One of her favorites, George V, was on the Avenue des Champs-Élysées, known in France as La plus belle avenue du monde - the most beautiful avenue in the world.

As the show was only booked for 30 days, she had to begin to look out for her future right away. Each day, Laura would visit with different booking agents, looking for one who would represent her. Each of them made it clear that high kicks notwithstanding, they were mostly interested in younger women, preferably around the age of 18 or 20. At 30, Laura was considered a little long in the tooth. She was told time and again, if she only had a gimmick, or would consider taking off her clothes, they might be able to place her. Laura was not new to show business. She knew that taking off her clothes, stripping, would be the last whistle stop before beginning a life of prostitution. Before doing that, she vowed she would return to Louisiana and clean up white people's houses.

Laura had given herself four weeks to find a new show, or rather circumstances had given her that long. "Le Revue de Couleur", the show she was currently booked into, was due to close exactly 30 days after it opened. She was unsuccessful at landing anything more than a call-back audition. Two days before the revue closed, the troupe was given notification that they had been extended another 30 days. Laura felt like a great weight had been lifted off her shoulders. Surely she could find something within that time. After all she was an experienced Broadway showgirl, with all that entailed. She could prance around the stage with a fifty pound weight on her head and high-kick with the best of them.

The following day she received a telegram. Would she please come to the offices of theatrical agent Françoise Goldman at 10AM the next morning. He had a position to offer her.

Laura already had a wardrobe planned for the interview. She had started working on it when she was first informed that continental hemlines had gone up - going from the floor with full trains - to the ankles. Her audition dress was cut with a placket in the skirt that allowed her to perform a high kick without changing into rehearsal clothes. It was tight in the waistline but not so tight that she could not hit the highest note in her range with ease. The color of the dress brought out the highlights in her golden hair. Her hazel eyes sparkled. Her makeup was applied to perfection. She walked out of the door and into a new life.

Laura performed a dance routine that she had choreographed herself. She even brought her own sheet music for the pianist. She performed a series of tap steps, a flourish, a prance around the stage, and ended her routine with a high kick. Laura got the spot – the headliner in a revue entitled 'La Petite Cozettes de Couleur"- The Little Pretty Ones of Color - at the Follies-Bergère Theater. There were six other colored girls in the revue. Laura was not aware until the first rehearsal that they all had one thing in common. Although adequately endowed in the breast area, none of them were overly endowed. They were all to appear bare-breasted. She was not exactly snowed by this revelation. Over half the women at the Moulin Rouge appeared on stage bare-breasted. However, when told to remove her shirtwaist she ran off the stage embarrassed and angry. She was approached by the producer, Françoise Goldman.

Tall, about five feet 10, dark hair and dark eyes, with a smooth complexion that looked as if he had shaved, all except a small moustache, that morning - he was handsome personified.

"Mon petite," he began in French, then switched to English. "Why do you carry on so? It is natural, my dear. Look at the revue at the Moulin Rouge where you just left. Only the girls in the Colored Revue are covered, and look at them. They will soon be returning to America with no prospects in front of them. Maybe they will find work on Broadway, maybe they will not."

"But you, mon petite coquette, mon chérie, you are special. You will stay here in Paris and in two years' time you will have made enough money to return to America and retire forever. Rich powerful men will grovel at your feet and beg you to be their mistress for life. Some will even ask you to marry them. You will say 'no' of course, for French men cannot be trusted to be faithful, and you, mon chérie, deserve only the very best. Who knows, I might even be one of those rich powerful men who would ask you to be my wife. I know that I already have a strong attraction for you."

"Oh, you are bashful. Don't worry, mon petit, one day you will desire me as much as I desire you. For now, dry your eyes, come back inside, and take off your shirtwaist. I promise you, you will never have to take off more than that unless that is your wish. I will show you how to do it discretely so no man on earth will mind that you did not strip naked for him. I will show you how to drop a strap seductively, to step out of your tap pants only to be covered by other pants underneath, to take off your shirtwaist, only to be covered by an undergarment. There is a company in Germany that has invented a device called a brassiere that is perfect for dancers. I will send for several for you to use in the show. But for now, bear with me. Come. Please." He stretched out his hand to her.

She did not know why then, or even later when she thought about it, but she took his outstretched hand and together they walked back into the theater and she walked into fame and riches the likes of which she had never imagined.

Chapter 5. Françoise

Françoise was true to his word. He taught Laura how to drop a shoulder strap and make it as meaningful as if she had taken off the whole blouse. He taught her how to step out of her high-cut tap pants and immediately hide behind a giant fan. He taught her how to remove her bra with her back to the audience and turn and grab the curtain just as she would have been exposed. The audience, both men and women alike, roared, clapped, and begged for more. She would always give them one last curtain call, clad only in the drapery of the curtain as covering for her near-nakedness. Occasionally, she would let them sneak a split-second peak at her. They would clamor for more, which she would not give them.

Françoise was true to his word in another respect. Françoise had always proclaimed to all who would listen that he was a confirmed bachelor, and would always be one; that no one woman would ever be enough for him. And, oh, yes, that he loved no one but himself. His actions belying his words, he became one of the many men who fell in love with Laura. He showered her with flowers, clothing, and jewelry. Each Saturday night he ordered champagne, petit fois-gras sandwiches, and petits fours brought to her dressing room and there, among all of the brightest luminaries in Paris, he admired her as she held reign.

Françoise was a non-practicing Jew, meaning that he did not attend synagogue, did not observe the Laws of Kashrut, and did not observe the Jewish Sabbath. Among his favorite foods were bacon, ham, oysters, lobster, and escargot – all foods that were forbidden to Jews.

His parents, his father Yakim (whose birth name was Joachim), and his mother, Bethel, had come from Krakow, Poland to Paris as a young married couple. His father was a diamond merchant and had moved his mother from one small apartment to succeedingly larger ones and finally into a beautiful granite house in the 4th arrondissement, in an area known as the Pletzl – Yiddish for "little place". This area had been home to Jews since the 13th century.

Until the 17th century, there was also located in the arrondissement, in an area called le Marais, a neighborhood of the fashionably elite, government ministers, lesser barons, dukes, and earls. This neighborhood was full of grand mansions, lavish gardens, and beautiful places on which to rest the eyes. After the royal court removed to Versailles, this neighborhood began to deteriorate. Those who remained in Paris or who kept townhouses in the city, relocated to the Faubourg Saint-Germain area. By the beginning of the 20th century, in the 4th there was a mixture of slums, mansions, and everything in between, with almost the entire population being Jewish.

The Goldman family home was off the Rue des Rosier near Rue Malher and Rue des Hospitalieres-St-Gervais. It wasn't just a house, it was a small mansion. It had begun to deteriorate when they acquired it. Yakim had then spent a small fortune restoring it to its once glorious past. In this, the Goldman family home, were held parties of all sorts. There were birthday parties for the children and the adults, anniversary parties, parties during Hanukah, parties after religious observances and fasts – you name it and Françoise's parents thought it was a good idea to have a party because of it.

Françoise's sister, Jokima, was ten years older than Françoise and as they were not raised as contemporaries, they never grew close. She was a dutiful daughter and did as her parents wished, attending the schools they recommended and marrying the man they selected for her. In return for her obedience, her parents showered her with gifts – toys when she was a child, and clothes and all manner of exquisite accessories, including furs and especially jewelry (after all her father was a diamond merchant!) as an adult.

Jokima had two children of her own, a boy and a girl. Françoise would have loved to spoil his niece and nephew but Françoise's brother-in-law was very devout and very intolerant of Françoise and his high living ways. He did not encourage Jokima to seek out the society of her brother and he did not encourage Françoise's visits. So although Françoise had a fondness for the children and never missed sending presents on their birthdays, except for their bar and bat mitzvahs, and during Hanukkah, he rarely saw them.

The Goldman's second child - their only son - was a different matter from their dutiful daughter. It seemed to the parents that he was in constant rebellion against them from the day he was born. Françoise's father and mother were well known in their community and were known to be liberal thinkers. Perhaps that is why their only son rebelled against them, dropping out of the Sorbonne after his second year and going into show business.

The Goldman parents never disowned their son, in spite of his high-living ways and his renunciation of Judaism. In fact, they left him very well off when they passed away. Françoise accepted the money from the sale of his father's diamond business and with the proceeds from the sale he began investing in the stock market and real estate.

But for his own home, Françoise used money he had earned himself from the profits from theatrical shows he produced. The house he selected had been built by the original owner in 1620 by a minor duke to curry favor with Queen Mother Marie de Medici who sought to bring development to a vast marshy field. She had created a long tree-lined path that she named Cours de la Reine, later in 1709 renamed to Champs-Élysées, the place of the blessed dead in Greek mythology. At that time there were only six properties along the avenue. During the second empire the avenue became the home of some of the wealthiest Parisians, including the Rothchilds, the Péreire family, and many of Napoleon Bonaparte's relatives. The mansion sat about two blocks off the wide boulevard.

Having his choice of land, the duke chose a lot on the corner for his residence. Because of this foresight, this house was one of the few in the older section of Paris that not only had a large garden in the rear of the house but also a stable for horses.

Around 1838, Ignaz Hittorf was commissioned to help invigorate the area surrounding the thoroughfare by installing sidewalks, gas lamps, and fountains up and down the boulevard and environs. The house by then had seen its better days. It had been subdivided and turned into apartments, four on each of four floors. Because of its rundown condition, Françoise was able to acquire is for a fraction of its later worth.

Françoise moved into the house and combined two of the apartments together to form his personal residence. The others he rented out and set about a restoration project that lasted ten years. He had all of the apartments repainted and wallpapered from the first floor to the fourth. He had new rugs laid and modern bathrooms installed. He had the house wired for electricity and had modern gas heaters installed to heat the apartments during the winter and in the kitchen for cooking. The apartments in his mansion became a very much sought after residence. However, Françoise only rented to show people, his apartment house at one time being the residence of many great luminaries of the Parisian stage.

Françoise's very large residence suited his convenience very well, as he often had girls in his show who were between residences, so to speak. Frequently, Françoise was the reason why they had been kicked out of their living arrangement with their boyfriends and lovers. He put these lovers and ex-lovers up in one of the apartments in his apartment house until they could find other living arrangements. Never on any occasion did he allow them to live with him, nor he with them.

Now that he was a member of the landed gentry, Françoise decided it was time to acquire his first servants. He hired a cook and a valet. They were all he needed to make his transition to Parisian gentleman complete. Whoever said money can't buy happiness obviously had never met Françoise Goldman. He was one of the happiest bachelors in all of Paris. He had it all – good looks, money, a house of his own, servants, and some of the most beautiful women in all of Paris clamoring to be seen on his arm.

After Françoise's father passed away, his sister and her husband moved in with his ailing mother to care for her. Two years later his mother also passed, Françoise thought, from a broken heart. Françoise did not want any parts of the house in Pletzl. He sold his interest to his sister Jokima and her husband. That severed all ties he had with his old neighborhood. And with that, except for the occasional dinner at the home of his sister, he severed all ties with the Jewish community he had grown up in, as well.

Françoise had been bitten by the show business bug at the age of seventeen when he had attended a musical performance and was lucky enough to get a seat literally front row center. He was mesmerized and hooked. When his father encouraged him to get an after-school job, his father meant for Françoise to ask one of the neighborhood merchants for a job delivering groceries or performing some other menial task for small wages.

Françoise went to the theater manager and asked for a job at the theater. He somehow juggled his school schedule and managed to work at the theater part time while attending his last year of lycée and two years at the Sorbonne. Finally, the theater called to him full time and he left the Sorbonne to take a job as an assistant stage manager in a cabaret production. During that production, Françoise worked nearly every position in the theater, including that of ticket taker. Money could not have bought the kind of experience he gained.

By the time Françoise met Laura and was hiring for La Petite Cozettes de Couleur, he was a theatrical agent and producer and he was practically engaged to Michelle Mineaux. At least that is what Michelle told everyone, although Françoise had never asked her to marry him or given her a ring of any sort. Michelle was a beautiful showgirl who Françoise had plucked from the back row of the chorus and made into a household name. She was just the way he liked them – tall, leggy, and blonde. She was also best friends with Mistinguett, one of the most famous women in all of Parisian show business.

One long look at Laura and Françoise's love for Michelle ended then and there. Laura became the woman he thought about, dreamed about, and wanted to be with. All he thought about was taking her to bed and making wild passionate love to her. He literally wanted to kiss her all over. His only question was how would he get her to let him kiss her where he wanted to kiss her the most? American girls were prudes about such things.

Françoise knew this because he had had his share of American girls, rich ones, poor ones and everything in between. In fact, he preferred American girls to French girls, and he preferred all girls to nice Jewish girls. Nice Jewish girls, he wanted no parts of. Perhaps that is one of the reasons why he seldom made arranged visits with his sister. Each time he did so, there was always a dinner party, and there was always an unattached girl in the dinner party who they tried to pair him with. For some reason they could never find him a pretty one. No, she was always described as someone with a "great personality". His bachelor radar knew that was an euphemism for "she's not quite attractive even if she does have an advanced intelligence level and hold double PhD's". Couldn't they just once find him a tall, leggy, blond with knock-out looks?

As much as Françoise was smitten by Laura, he did not let that get in the way of his good business sense. He insisted on solid performances from her and everyone else he represented and also those in theatrical productions that he hired for or produced himself. If they could not or would not deliver the goods, they had to find themselves another position. Laura was a solid performer. She came to rehearsals prepared and on time. She was also gracious, allowing others in the show to display their talents even if it meant her giving up a minute here and there of her own stage time.

Françoise wanted Laura more than he had ever wanted any woman. And he waited for her longer than he had waited for any woman. He was determined to have her. Even though they began to spend all of their free time together, she held him at bay. One day, after the show had been running for about six months and it was a definite hit, Françoise surprised Laura with the car of her dreams – a Mason

Marvel. He had made a boatload of money from the profits from the show and he wanted to show his gratitude. Or so he said.

The story went that in 1905 the Duesenberg brothers, former bicycle makers, now into race car manufacturing, designed and built the prototype for the Miracle. It was seen by Edward Mason who capitalized and founded the Mason Motor Car Company just to produce the car. The plant was located in Des Moines, Iowa and only produced a handful of cars before the company was taken over by Fred Maytag. Mason regained the company but it later folded. The Duesenberg brothers went on to found their own company for the express purpose of producing high end luxury motorcars and racecars.

The marvel was how, in 1906, Laura was even aware that the car existed. It was not yet on the market, still only being built as test models. There were French cars to be sure, but all Laura talked about was owning a car designed and executed by the Duesenberg brothers. To her, their cars were the ultimate luxury cars. The fact of the matter was that she had become acquainted with the car when she had been squired about in one owned by the son of an Arabian prince of the Saudi Royal House. Al-Jabal bin Saud, or Al, as Laura called him, was the third son of Abdul-Aziz bin Saud. Abdul had begun the conquest of Arabian cities until he finally was able to recapture his family's ancestral home in Riyadh. Wealthy beyond belief, Abdul had sent each of his sons to the west to be educated. Al had come to Paris to study international economics. What he studied most was fast living and faster girls. He had met Laura after coming backstage after one of her performances. At one point it was thought that he would displace Françoise as her steady beau, but before that could happen, his father sent for him to return home. Although in his 30's he obeyed his father without question and left Paris, bidding a fond farewell to Laura, taking his car with him. Odd how his father happened to send for him and take him out of the picture, leaving the path clear for Françoise.

Laura did not miss Al as much as she missed that car. She was determined to have one. Not just any car, but one just like that one. She talked about it constantly.

The Duesenberg brothers, Frederick and August had produced only ten models in 1906. Françoise managed to get them to sell him one and had it him retooled to his specifications. Totally hand-made, it came from the factory a hideous putrid green. Françoise had it painted a gleaming red for Laura. Outfitted with white leather interior, white-walled tires, a side mounted spare, and sporting gleaming chrome exhaust pipes, after the modifications were completed, it was shipped to France just for her. The total cost was $20,000 US. In comparison, a Cadillac cost around $2,000. Françoise then had the unenviable job of teaching Laura to drive the car. He was not sure his love for her would last through that ordeal. Driving a car in 1906 was not an easy task. But thankfully, this car did not have to be manually cranked to start. It had an electric starter in it that started with the push of a button. Although all-electric starting systems were not introduced into general use until the 1912 Cadillac, Charles Kettering, the inventor of the electric starter, made it available to a select few who were building custom automobiles earlier than that. The Duesenbergs were among that select few. They had dropped the electric starter in the Marvel. Within a few short weeks Laura was driving herself and her friends all over Paris. They motored out to the countryside for picnics on their days off. Then in August, when all of Paris goes on holiday, she and one of her friends drove to the part of the country where champagne was produced, about 200 km north-east of Paris. There they spent three lovely days before returning to the sweltering city. Laura returned with a case of Moët et Chandon, which became her lifelong favorite drink.

Françoise was a notorious womanizer and except for Michelle had never been faithful to any woman for very long. That is, until he met Laura. From the time he met her, he had gradually let more and more of these girlfriends go. They would call him on the telephone and ask him when he was coming to see them. To all he would say, "bientôt, bientôt" but he never made good on his word. All of them, except for Michelle eventually stopped calling. Finally it was just Laura.

Françoise had tried in every way he could to get Laura in bed with him. He wined her. He dined her. He bought her presents. He sent her flowers. He gave her jewelry, clothes, and furs. And of course the Mason Marvel. Still she would not have any part of him. Françoise knew that Laura had children. She had not tried to make a secret of it. What he did not know was that Laura was afraid to have sex with him or anyone else for fear of getting pregnant yet another time. She was content to just be his friend, if he could handle such an arrangement. He could not.

Chapter 6. Dancing

Laura, along with all of Paris, loved to dance. There were nightclubs all over Paris where Parisians and tourists indulged this craze. In addition, there were many balls given by military regiments, clubs, organizations, and of course private parties – from the wealthy to the poorest of the poor. All of Paris danced, including the very old and the very young. If people could get a couple of bottles of wine and a few eggs together for an omelet, they threw together a party, and they all danced the night away. Laura was right in there with everyone else, only she got paid to do it. Next to singing and Françoise, for by now she did love him, there was nothing she loved more. Laura and Françoise routinely went out dancing together after her shows.

Dancing as a craze swept through nearly all major large cities and Paris was no exception. This craze was led by young women eager to express their sexuality. There were ballrooms and saloons that specialized in dancing, some serving alcohol and some not. For those that served alcohol, the dances were three to four minutes in length with 10 to 15 minute intervals – the more time to buy alcohol. For those that did not serve alcohol the reverse was true. This put young women in a precarious position of being seen as fun-loving and seeking a good time or, heaven forbid, being seen as prostitutes. Since both decent girls and prostitutes frequented the same dance halls, it was often difficult to tell the difference between the two.

The only girls whose reputations were protected were those who had steady beaus who stood between the girls and unattached young men who would roam the dance hall asking total strangers to dance. If a girl accepted such invitations, was unattached, and frequented the same establishments on a regular basis, her reputation became tarnished.

Laura was an entertainer. In that day and time female entertainers were seen as one step above being prostitutes as it was. Not that they were, that is just how they were perceived by the general public. Laura did not have to worry about this tarnishment. Françoise stood between her and this lack of respectability. He would give his assent or dissent when a total stranger asked her to dance.

The favorite dances of the day were the One-Step, the Turkey Trot, and the Grizzly Bear. Laura knew all of these and more. When they went to balls they did more sedate waltzes and grand marches, but elsewhere, Françoise would lead her out onto the dance floor and let her strut her stuff. More often than not, the other dancers would fall back and let her have the dance floor. After the dance number was over, she could hear the whispering, "That's Laura Boult. She's a professional. She's currently at the . . ." and they would fill in whatever theater she was currently playing at. And they came to see her in droves. It did not matter that she had a semi-burlesque show. No matter where she played, they flocked in. She and Françoise knew she was the draw because when they would move on to another theater, Françoise would get calls, letters, and telegrams asking for a return engagement. She was booked for a year in advance.

Because theatrical performers loved to dance, not just on stage, but on dance floors, as well, they often went out to dance after their performances. Laura and Françoise were among those who frequently "partied" into the wee hours of the morning at cabarets and other dance halls. Laura saw these ragtime dances being performed and quickly learned how to do them. Françoise loved to dance but knew he was outmatched by Laura on the dance floor, so he would allow other men whose talent was equal to hers to dance with her.

This was to his benefit because Laura took these dance floor dances and modified them into stage dances and worked them into her act. The results of which was that she literally taught Parisians how to do the latest dances, just by showing them how to do them. Thus they were saved the expense of having to go to dance studios to learn them, much to the chagrin of dance school owners and operators.

The dances they danced all seemed to have crazy names. The Turkey Trot was a face to face dance where each partner took a step on each beat of the music. The male held the female tightly around the waist and they swayed while going in a straight line around the dance floor, occasionally flapping their arms, hence the name the Turkey Trot.

The Grizzly Bear was even more bizarre. Dancers imitated the movements of a dancing bear, hugging each other and lumbering sideways and backwards, occasionally yelling out "It's a bear."

Another dance involving animals was the Bunny Hug. It was another face to face dance, this time done to very slow music and involved a lot of shaking, wiggling, and grinding.

And then there were the ragtime dances. These included the tango, the one-step, the Castle Walk, the hesitation waltz, and the Maxixe. These dances were best performed to what was described as ragtime music. Created in the Negro communities of St. Louis and New Orleans, ragtime music's main trait was its' syncopated or "ragged" rhythm. These ragtime dances were popularized by the dancing duo, sophisticated Vernon and Irene Castle. On their return from Europe they opened a dance studio in New York and taught all the popular dances. From there, the dances crossed the oceans on ocean liners and wound up on the dance floors of Paris.

Another dance made popular by Vernon and Irene Castle was a dance invented by Harry Fox called the Fox Trot. The dance was composed of long, continuously flowing movements across the dance floor. Done properly it was smooth with the slow movements blending seamlessly with quick movements. Usually danced in ballrooms to big bands and done to 4/4 time instead of 3/4 time, it replaced the waltz as the most popular dance of the day. This was Laura's favorite dance rhythm. When she and Françoise took to the floor in a Fox Trot, people often gave way to them and would stop dancing themselves just to watch the couple. Because it needed a lot of room to perform, it was difficult to work this dance into her performance routine.

On stage, Laura refused to do the gyrations that were so popular with burlesque dancers. She was a theatrically trained dancer. "Surely I can put together something more tasteful than bumps and grinds", she told herself when she decided that she was going to be a burlesque queen. She did everything but what people expected. She strutted her stuff, she pranced around the stage, and she had a male dancer who she danced with doing the popular dances of the day. But always at the end of her act, she dropped her strap as Françoise had taught her, and from there, as he had promised, how much she took off in any given show was entirely up to her.

Laura was interviewed by a newspaperman after one of her spectacular performances. She had ended her show with a strip tease after a wonderful pax de deux with her dance partner, Jerome Hendricks. From the smoothness of their moves together, many people thought they were a couple. Oddly enough, they were not even good friends, they were just dance partners who enjoyed dancing together.

The noted newspaper reporter Pierre LaCosta once asked her who her favorite dance partner was.

"Jerome Hendricks," she answered without hesitation.

"Is he French?" asked Pierre.

"No. He's from Jamestown, New York," she replied.

"Where did the two of you meet?"

"We came over on the same boat together but we weren't in the same troupe. There weren't enough Negro men to go around on the dance floor on the boat coming over, so he, like a gentleman, tried to make sure that all of us unattached ladies, and most of us were unattached, got a chance to dance. All of the younger, pretty girls set their caps for him but he's ten years younger than me and extremely handsome, so I didn't get to dance with him much. In those days Jerome wore his hair slicked back in the manner of all the other hip young skates of the day." She chuckled. "Nowadays, what hair he has left, he wears it au natural."

She went on, "I liked the way he moved on the dance floor even then. At that time, I was with a troupe and worked the same hours he did but did get to see him perform several times. Then when I was looking for a dance partner, he came in and auditioned. I actually did not select him, my manager did. He liked the way we moved together. Jerome has a little move he makes when he's about to lead me into an unpracticed dance maneuver. He squeezes my waist just the tiniest bit. It's his hidden signal to say 'Hold on. Here comes one you may not be expecting.' I use him in my act whenever I can."

When the newspaperman interviewed Jerome on Laura as a dance partner, Jerome said, "I enjoy dancing with Laura both on stage and off. Sometimes after a show, we go dancing together just for the heck of it, usually when Laura's boyfriend can't take her. When he's around, well, Laura doesn't have time for anyone. She and my wife are great friends. My wife isn't much for dancing with me. She says I show off too much on the dance floor. When I show off with Laura she shows off right back. She seems to sense my every move even before I make it. She's the best dance partner I've ever had."

LaCosta concluded his review of Laura and her dance partner by saying, "They seldom take a misstep when they dance together. Their act is not to be missed."

Chapter 7. The Apartment

One day, after rehearsals, Françoise called for Laura in the Marvel. He took her for a long, relaxing ride. It was a chilly day in November and he made sure she brought along the full length white mink coat with the fox collar he had bought for her the winter before to keep warm because he wanted to drive with the top down.

They rode out to Meudon, one of Laura's favorite spots, a municipality in the southwestern suburb of Paris. The northwest part of the town, built on the hills and valleys of the Seine, was known as Bellevue. The hill where the Paris Observatory sits 150ft above Paris is there in Bellevue and commands an imposing view of the city. Françoise knew Laura liked to come and look down upon the city and contemplate her life. This is where Françoise took her on that day. He wanted her to contemplate her life with him in it.

As they were leaving the Observatoire, it began to snow lightly. Françoise wrapped Laura up in her coat, placed her in the passenger seat, and pulled her hat closer about her head. She rode the entire way snuggled up next to him with her arm through his as he drove. They came to the end of their ride on a side street off the Avenue des Champs-Élysées. He stopped the car, got out and came around to her side, and opened the door for her.

"Why, Françoise, what are we doing here?" she asked. She knew this was his house although she had never been inside of it. He parked her on the sidewalk while he covered the car with a tarp to keep the snow off the upholstery.

"You will see, mon petit. And you will be glad you have seen," he said to her as he worked. When he finished he said, "Come. Come with me."

It was beginning to snow heavier now. He wrapped her tighter into her coat. He walked her up the steps that led to the entrance of the house in front of them. He opened the door with a key he took from his pocket. Not saying a word, he led her up the wide stair case to a door on the second floor. There he dropped her hand, and again with a key from his pocket, opened the door in front of them. He put the key back into his pocket, took both hands and threw open wide both of the double doors. "Your palace awaits you, mon cheri," he said.

Laura sucked in her breath sharply. She could scarcely believe her eyes and ears. He was bringing her to live in his house. She knew that he had other women live in the house with him over the years. However, she also knew they did not live *with* him. He maintained an apartment on the lower floor. He installed his girlfriend of the moment in a separate apartment in the house. Several months previously Laura had heard a rumor that Michelle had taken laudanum and that she had been hospitalized while she recovered. Françoise had been absent during that time and Laura thought for sure she had lost him. After two weeks he started appearing backstage to wish her luck before her performances once again. Then Laura heard another rumor that Michelle had moved out of his house and was living with a skate she had met at one of her shows.

Françoise had arranged for all of Laura's things to be transported from the furnished apartment she rented to the gorgeous apartment that she now stood in. Laura wondered if this was the apartment that Michelle had lived in or had Françoise done all of this just for her? The furnishings and wall papers looked new enough. She was in a quandary. She did not know if she should accept this largess from Françoise or not.

She saw two women bustling about within an inner door, taking clothing from a packing trunk and readying them for hanging. She walked into the room which she soon found was a bedroom as large as her old apartment. The two ladies were ladies' maids hired for the occasion to get her settled in.

"Françoise, can I afford this? How much does it cost? When did you arrange all this?"

"Yes. Nothing. I've been thinking about it for some time. Are there any other questions?"

"No. But how?"

"This is my house, mon petite. I own it," Françoise told her. "This is one of several apartments in it. I have other show people living here. It's more convenient to have my clients close to me. This apartment just became vacant and I thought you might like to have it. I added the clothes closet for you. You don't have to stuff your clothes into an armoire any longer. Or rather, not stuff them, because you have too many clothes to fit into any contrivance such as that."

He proudly showed her the closet. "There are shelves for your purses and hats, and a place for your shoes. Your coat goes here," and with that, he removed her mink coat and placed it on a hanger in the closet.

In awe, she turned to Françoise. "Oh, Françoise! It's a girl's dream come true," she said reaching for him. She kissed him full on the lips.

"Are you sure that is where you want to kiss me?" he asked her with a twinkle in his eye.

"No," she replied. By this time, they were familiar enough with each other that each knew what the other wanted. Today would be the day that she gave herself to him. If she would. Twice before she had rejected his advances. Today she sensed that he was determined. But she knew he would not try to force himself on her. He was a man who wanted it to come naturally or he would not want it to happen at all.

Françoise dismissed the two maids, telling them to return in an hour. The giant bed covered with a white satin coverlet. He stripped Laura to her bare skin and led her over to the bed. He knelt on the bed and pulled her to him. Her pubic hair was right in front of his lips. He kissed her there, once, then twice, then a third time. She shivered down to her toes. He pulled her down to him and kissed her on the lips. Then, very gently, he eased her onto the bed. Her breath went slowly out of her body.

He was finally where she wanted him to be the most – between her legs. She reached down to guide him into her. His firmness did not disappoint her. She thought she would pass out from the sheer ecstasy of it all. He came repeatedly, first turning her this way and then that. He turned her face down upon the bed and entered her from the rear. Again she shivered. He put his hand underneath her and rubbed her clitoris between his fingertips. She started moving faster and faster, harder and harder against his hand with him inside of her. He brought her to climax, once and then once again. Her climax excited him so that he raised a hard and came inside of her all in one swift motion.

Then he sucked her and kissed her and licked her, tasting their mingled come with her murmuring, "Oh, Françoise," over and over again into his hair and his mouth, that is, when he stopped sucking on her long enough to put his mouth to hers. Finally, he stopped moving within her. "Je t'aime, Laura," he said, as he looked deeply into her eyes. He gathered her to him and kissed her deeply.

With them both tired and exhausted, Françoise came inside her one last time. Then he wrapped his arms about her and together they slept the sleep of lovers, until the maids, not hearing noises coming from the room anymore, knocked on the door.

"D'une heure plus, s'il vous plait," Françoise called out. They feel asleep in each other's arms again and slept for yet another hour. There was a knock on the door again.

"Allez-vous-en," he called out to the one knocking on the door. "Nous dormons. Revenir plus tard."

Laura stirred. She got up and meant to go into the bathroom. Françoise pulled her back down onto the bed. He reached over to the night table beside the bed and took from the drawer a long thin box. He opened it and removed from it a diamond bracelet. He gently placed it on her wrist and closed the clasp. He kissed the palm of her hand and sent her on her way. He leaned on his elbow and watched her as she went to her new closet. He looked around him. He could be proud of himself. The rooms had turned out nicely.

Hanging on the outside of the closet door, Laura found a white robe with thick ostrich feathers about the neck opening. She had seen it at Le Bon Marche and had admired it but did not buy it because she decided it was too expensive. Now it was hers. She took it down and wrapped it around her naked body. Inside the closet, she also found matching slippers with marabou feathers on the toes. She slipped her feet into the gorgeous shoes. She felt like the most glamorous rich woman in the most glamorous palace ever to live in Paris.

Never in her imagination had she put herself into such a luxurious suite of rooms surrounded by so many beautiful things. Laura had dreamed many big dreams as a child but she had never thought that her dreams would take her first to New York and then to Paris. She had always thought of New Orleans and St. Louis as the big cities and if she really dreamed big, Chicago. But not New York, and certainly not Paris. She did not go so far as to dream what she would do when she got to these big cities of her dreams. She had just assumed that she would meet a wonderful man who would take her away from the red clay dirt of North Louisiana and give everything to her. Never had she dreamed that she would be the one to earn these things for herself. And in doing so, that she would meet such a wonderful man as Françoise who would help her make it all happen. The little girl from Louisiana was now, although not a big named headliner, was a definite success in the career she had chosen for herself. She stood there in the midst of all the beauty and her good fortune, and fingering the bracelet on her wrist, she cried.

Chapter 8. A Trip Back Home

In May of 1906 Laura received a cablegram that her mother was desperately ill and if she ever had hopes of seeing her alive again, to return home right away. Isabella had suffered a heart attack.

Laura took the first steamer back to America. She arrived in Louisiana two weeks from the time she had received the cablegram. Her mother, although bedridden, seemed to be strong enough. Confined to her bed since the attack, by morning she was gone. It was as though she had waited for Laura to come home.

There were many visitors who came to the house after Isabella passed away. It seemed as if Laura saw everyone she knew from her past. They all came except for those who had moved up north, mostly to Chicago and New York, and out west to California.

There was something about the house that left a creepy feeling in Laura. First, it had no indoor plumbing. If she had to name the one thing she loved about living in a big city, it was indoor plumbing. That was her hands down favorite. She dreaded each time she had to head out to the outhouse.

The other thing about the house was that it was smaller than she remembered, and much shabbier. Her parents did not have the luxury of having a parlor.

Instead the front room, as they called it, was the room where her parents had their bed. The room was sparsely furnished with just a bedstead, a chest of drawers and a dresser. In this room was the only fireplace in the house.

Laura recalled that in the winter time, every member of the household would sit around the fire trying to keep warm. They had no sofa or lounge chairs. The only chairs they had were plain wooden chairs that had been hand made by her father in his workshop. Not counting this makeshift bedroom there were four other bedrooms in the house. It took a lot of beds to sleep eleven children.

One of these bedrooms did double duty with the dining room table, which no one ever sat at to eat. This bedroom was shared by two of her brothers. It was in this room that the family used to set up the tree at Christmas time. Not that they ever had that much to go under the tree. They were poor. Very poor.

Because they lived on a farm, having a turkey and a ham at Christmas was not a problem for them at all. Nor was it difficult for them to laden the table with vegetables of all manner and kinds. And the women of the family were geniuses at whipping up cakes and pies out of practically nothing. The dining table groaned under the weight of all of the food stuffs at Christmas each year. And now it groaned with the gift offerings from friends and neighbors to ease the load of family members having to cook during their time of grief. Other than days such as these, the table seldom held a morsel of food. Instead it served as a general catch-all table for just about everything else.

One of the bedrooms that was only used as a bedroom was the bedroom that Laura had shared with one of her five sisters. Four of Laura's five sisters and Laura were very close in age - Cora, Josephine, Elizabeth, Jeroline, and Laura were like little stair-steps, all having been born between 1868 and 1877, one child approximately every two years.

It was her eldest sister Cora who Laura turned to when she needed advice or help in any way. It was Cora who had introduced Laura to performing in front of audiences. It was Cora who Laura poured out her heartbreak at having to leave her sons when she left Louisiana. It was Cora who had taken Laura's two youngest boys when Laura's mother had become too ill to care for them any longer. Laura never let it show, but she felt guilty because of this all of her life. No matter what she did for her sons in later years she never forgave herself for leaving them behind.

Isabella's funeral was held in Natchitoches at the Episcopal Church, but she was buried in the cemetery at the Evergreen Baptist Church. That cemetery had been the final resting place for two generations of Boults. The cemetery began at the top of a slight hill at the edge of the church yard and extended into the valley below. After the burial, there was a large gathering in the front yard of the church under a huge oak tree that was draped with moss. After saying her last goodbye to her mother, Laura climbed the hill from the cemetery to where the wagons were parked. There the rest of the family waited for her. Laura sat down on the back of a wagon after the long trek up the hill. The ladies of the church served dinner on the ground. Someone handed Laura a plate with fried chicken, turnip greens, and corn bread on it. She had not eaten such fare since she went to Paris so she barely touched it. She chewed as if she enjoyed it but it tasted like cardboard in her mouth. Mercifully, someone eventually took the plate from her hand. She hoped they chalked up her lack of appetite to her grief over her mother's death.

Finally it was time for them to go home. She got in the wagon and was driven back to her parent's house. There was a general air of festivity. It was always this way after a funeral in a southern Negro family. More like a reunion than a funeral. It lasted until two of her brothers, Charlie and Henry, got drunk and began cursing each other in the front yard. Someone had to separate them to keep them from fighting. Charlie and Henry were close in age. It did not take much to set the two of them at each other. Henry had always tagged along after Charlie and Charlie had always resented it and it angered him. Her older brother Hewitt went into the yard and told them to cut it out or he was going to knock them both out. For emphasis he had a piece of two by four in his hand. For some reason they listened to him. Charlie got on a horse and left. They did not see him again, drunker than a skunk, until very late that night.

Laura remained in Louisiana for a month. When she returned to France she took Randolph and Hamp to live with her in Paris. They were then ten and twelve and of course they did not speak a word of French. From the very beginning they was miserable. Hamp was sullen and withdrawn and Randolph cried at the drop of a hat.

Laura enrolled them at a prestigious school run by an American, Professor Alexander Land, for American children whose parents were living in France. Their classes were entirely in English but the children were encouraged to speak French at every opportunity so they could learn the language. Laura knew that her boys were behind in the Louisiana school they had attended, but testing showed they were two years or more behind. It was no wonder that they made very poor marks and could barely read.

She hired a tutor for them. After weeks of tutoring they were finally learning how to read properly but they were behind in so many other areas it would have been impossible for them to catch up. The school put them both back by two years. This did not affect Randolph much, indeed nothing much seemed to bother him at all. He was always withdrawn and unresponsive. When Laura asked him how he was doing in school, he would shrug his shoulders and reply, "I dunno." Always the same shrug and always the same answer.

However, being put back two grades made Hamp angry. He especially took out his anger on his school papers. He did not just cross out words in his tablet, he would literally obliterate the words and destroy the paper. Instead of being a twelve year old in sixth grade with learning difficulties, he was a twelve year old in fourth grade, with learning difficulties, and an attitude. He was bigger than all of the rest of the boys which lead to his being picked on and that in turn lead to him fighting. He fought with anyone and everyone about anything whatsoever. If you told him his hair looked nice, he would want to start a fight.

Laura did not know what to do. She had not been a mother for a long time. Having to take over the entire care of the boys, even with household help, and still work at nights, was very draining on her. She talked to the teachers at the school and the tutors she hired for the boys. They could only give advice but they could not solve the problem for her.

And the apartment. While it was fine for Laura, it was too crowded for her and the two boys. The boys were sleeping in a bed she had put into the parlor. None of them had any privacy. While this did not bother Laura overly much, the boys were at an age where they did not want to expose themselves to any female at all. Life was very difficult for all of them. She had begun to look for a larger apartment so the boys could have their own bedroom.

One day Laura received a letter from Professor Land. He wanted to meet with her concerning the boys. As soon as Laura sat down in front of the head master, her troubles came pouring out. "Professor, what am I to do? I'm at my wits' end. I don't know what to do with my boys. The youngest, Randolph, will not talk to me or anyone. The oldest, Hampton, fights with everyone about everything. He constantly picks fights with his younger brother. I've punished him by making him stand in the corner, I've taken away his treats, I've whipped him with a belt, and still he's like this. And I think he hates me."

The head master answered, "Mademoiselle Boult, I have watched your boys with great anxiety since they started school here. I have assigned them special work and have them working with their teachers to learn the things they need to learn. On that front we're making headway. However, is a lot to be desired. As you say, Randolph is withdrawn. He will not respond to his teachers. We have tried bribery, cajoling, offering incentives of all sorts, and we still cannot reach him. I'm afraid for his future, if we're not able to affect a change in him. I see him taking his inner anger out on the world. I don't know what lies in store for young men who behave like this."

Laura gasped.

The professor went on, "Young Hampton's a different matter entirely. If we can't reach him, his level of anger will only grow. Already he takes his anger out on things around him. It will just be a matter of time until he begins to take this anger out on people. From there it's just a short step to hurting people. This type of anger can lead to his killing someone in a rage."

Laura was sobbing. "I know you don't want to hear what I am saying to you, Mademoiselle," said the head master. "But it's better you hear it from me now than to hear it from the constabulary later. You much act soon - before it's too late. If the boys didn't act like this r before you took them away from their aunt, was it you said? Then you must send them back to her. Maybe with a lot of discipline and right living she can convince the boys to change their ways before it's too late."

"But you don't understand, Professor," said Laura through her tears. "There isn't anywhere for them to go to school there. The school's open only six months of the year. That's why they came to you in such bad shape in the first place."

"Yes, Mademoiselle, I understand. We have the same problem here in the provinces. It's only in the cities that children are allowed, no required, to attend school for so many months a year. In some other places there're no schools for children at all. The parents must provide tutors for them. Most parents cannot afford that expense, so many don't go to school at all. Children all over, those who are fortunate enough to have schools to attend, are behind as well. We educators are proud when we're able just to get them to read, write, and do simple arithmetic. But here's what we can do. Is there anyone in your family who can read and write?"

"Yes, I have several uncles who were sent away to boarding school when they were young, and they read and write beautifully," she answered.

"Excellent. Perhaps they'll agree to be tutors for the boys. All that's necessary is that they spend about four hours a week, if they can spare that much time, in going over the lessons with them. It can all be done at one time – say on Saturday mornings. Then we'll set up a correspondence program with the boys. Their teachers here will send them their lessons and the boys will send them back to be graded. It's not an ideal plan but it's working for children who're living now in Africa and China who were once students with us, and it can work for your boys as well. There will be a cost to you, to be sure, but as you haven't objected to the tuition so far, it's probably an amount you can bear."

"Oh, what an excellent idea! I'll write a letter to one of my uncles right away. I'm his favorite niece. He'll surely do it for me, especially if I offer to pay him."

Finally, someone had the courage to tell Laura that the boys were unhappy at being taken away from the only home and family they had ever known. They were rebelling against her and she needed to return them to the place they were familiar with. Laura stuck it out two more months, but she knew the professor was right. She made the decision to send them back to Louisiana and set her plans into motion.

She was under contract at the time and could not go herself. They were too young to travel alone so she sent for the only person who she could call on to come and get them – her brother Charlie. He came across the ocean and got them and took them back to her sister Cora. This traveling adventure bonded Charlie and the boys together for the rest of their lives.

Laura cried the day she put the boys on the train to LeHarve where they would then board a ship for the crossing to America. And she cried each day for a month. She would miss them terribly, but she knew that to keep them with her would have do irreparable harm to them.

Laura's career was beginning to take off and she did not return home again for more than ten years although, she sent money home to be used for the boys on a regular basis. She followed through on her commitment to have her uncle tutor them. He was delighted to do so. At least he said he was. More than likely he was delighted to have the $20 gold piece she included with her letters to him asking about the boys' progress.

She did not see Randolph again until he was twenty-one. He came to visit her when he was in Europe during the Great War. It was longer still before she saw Hamp again. Laura felt guilty that she had gone so long without seeing the only two sons who she had contact with. After Randolph visited her, because travel was easier, and because she had the money to do so, she started to return home on a more regular basis – about once every two years or so.

Laura did not see her two eldest boys again until she was in her sixties and had returned to Louisiana for an extended visit. Their father had told them about their Negro heritage only after they were adults. They continued to pass for white until the day they died. It was left to their grandchildren, who learned about their ancestry from genealogy research, to tell the truth about their heritage.

Chapter 9. The Baby

Laura and Françoise had been living under the same roof, although in different apartments, for over a year. Françoise wanted to have sex with her every day. There was no way she could escape her fate. One month, Laura did not get her period. She groaned. She knew exactly what that meant. She was pregnant. There is no way she would have another baby. Not now. Not at her age. Not when life was going so good for her. It only remained for her to tell Françoise and seek an abortion. When Françoise came to call on her that evening after she returned from the theater, she dove right in. Françoise was sitting on the sofa in the parlor with a snifter of brandy that he had poured for himself when he came in. He was reading a newspaper.

"Françoise, I have something to tell you," Laura began.

"What is it, mon cherie?" Françoise asked absent-mindedly as he turned the page of the paper.

"I'm going to have a baby," she said matter-of-factly. "Rather, I'm pregnant and I'm not going to have a baby."

He laid the paper aside. She now had his full attention. "What nonsense you talk. Are you going to have a baby or not?"

"I'm pregnant. But I'm not going to have the baby."

"Oh, I see," was all he said. "Why not, may I ask?"

"Because I'm 36 years old and I'm not going to have another baby out of wedlock."

"Then let's get married."

Just like that. He said it. She could not believe her ears. The man who claimed he would never marry anyone, just said to her "let's get married".

"Mind you," he went on, "let's make it a grand marriage for we shan't ever get married again."

"No," she replied. "I don't want to get married. I don't want to have a baby. I don't want my life to change."

"You talk non-sense," he said. "Of course you want to get married. You can do it up like royalty and invite everyone you've ever known. I won't object. We have to get married for the baby's sake. The baby can't have his or her mother and father not married to each other. That would not be right."

She stamped her foot. "I tell you, I don't want to have a baby."

"Of course you do. You don't want just any baby. You want my baby." He tried to take her in his arms but she refused to be held. "Let's talk about it when you've calmed down," he suggested.

"There's nothing to talk about," she pouted. "And I am calm. I've thought about this since I found out. I want an abortion and I'm going to have one. I know where to go. And if I can't have an abortion I'll take laudanum and kill myself."

"Well," he shrugged. "If that is what you want, I can't stop you, but let me put this to you. If you don't have an abortion, and if you decide not to kill yourself, then give the baby to me. I want it. But mind you, I don't want just any baby. I want your baby. And mind you further, it has to look exactly like you. It has to have your beautiful blond hair and your hazel eyes with flecks in them and it has to be able to sing like a bird just as you do. Otherwise, I'll send it packing. What do you say? Have the baby and give it to me. Huum?"

She was silent for a few moments. Finally, she spoke. "Now you're talking nonsense. I can't guarantee any of those things. We'll have to take whatever we get."

"What?" he asked with mock incredulity. "Did I just hear you agree to have the baby? Tell me that again."

She had her head down but she was smiling. "Do you really want my baby?" she asked softly.

"Oui, mon chérie. Why do you think I make love to you every day? It's such a chore but it's the only way I can guarantee there'll be a baby. Now my job's done and I can do as other men and only make love to my woman once a month."

"Oh, no you don't" she said threatenly. "You'll keep right on doing what you're doing or I won't marry you. Do you hear me?"

He took her in his arms and this time she did not resist him. "Oui, my pet, I hear you," he said softly. I'll continue to make love to you every day. I'll keep my promise if you'll keep yours."

"Then it's settled then? You'lll marry me?" she asked wanting to make sure he wasn't just telling her that to get her to promise not to kill herself.

"It's not settled yet. We have to seal it with a kiss," he said.

He kissed her deeply, his tongue darting in and out of her mouth like a serpent. She started to pull away. "What's the matter?" he asked.

"Don't do that. If you do, you'll make me want to have sex with you now, and the way you make love, we might hurt the baby."

"I promise I won't hurt you or my baby. Come, I will show you."

He took her to the bed and ever so gently, removed all of her clothing, tasted the sweetness between her legs, then very gently mounted her and more gently still, entered her very slowly. He then proceeded to make love to her more gently than she had ever known in her life. When he had come, he very gently, withdrew from her and just as gently, he went down on her and brought her to the most stupendous climax she had ever experienced.

"Oh, Françoise," was all that she could manage to say.

The next day she spent the afternoon looking over patterns at the dressmakers' for a wedding dress she liked. Since Françoise had said with fervor that this would be the only wedding she would ever have, she wanted to make it the wedding of her dreams.

They were married six weeks later. Over five hundred people attended the wedding. The reception they limited to two hundred and fifty – mostly notables and show people. The bride wore white. The gown, like all of Laura's clothing, was unique and very elaborate. It was made of fabric roses, hundreds of them, sewn all over the skirt and bodice one adjacent to the other. Françoise gave her a beautiful diamond encrusted watch from Cartier for her wedding present. She gave him gold cufflinks with her initials on one and his on the other.

Françoise had the second floor of the house made into one large apartment. Luxury living arrangements at affordable prices were at a premium and he had no trouble keeping the rest of the units filled, including his own bachelor flat, that truth be told, he hated giving up. He took to the upstairs apartment, all of his clothes, his valet, Georges, and his cook Madame Prusette. Laura wondered how they would all get along together but it needn't have troubled her The two household staffs blended together beautifully.

Everyone pretended not to notice the baby was a few weeks early. It was a boy. Laura named him Adrien Françoise – Adrien after no one in particular, just because she liked the name and Françoise so the father would have cause to stick out his chest when anyone asked him the baby's name.

The baby did not look like Laura but instead looked like his father. Françoise insisted on keeping him anyway. They spoiled him rotten. His favorite thing to do from the time he was old enough to run and frolic was to go to the marionette show at the Luxembourg Gardens. He would sit and stare at the puppets and when Judy socked Punch, the baby would laugh with glee.

The gardens were what was left of the elaborate gardens that Marie de Médici had planted at her palace when she was the queen mother. The palace now housed the French Senate. There was also a pond for sailing toy sailboats. Adrien would clap his pudgy little hands together at the sight of the boats on the water.

It was decidedly his second favorite afternoon outing. And of course there was the carousel. What kid doesn't love the carousel? Adrien was no exception.

Laura got pregnant again two years later. This time she was more than willing to have the baby. She gave birth to a little girl and much to Françoise's delight, she looked like her mother with pale blond ringlets and hazel eyes which sparkled when she laughed or became very angry. They named her Marcella Celestina.

As Marcella grew, much to Adrien's consternation, the little girl delighted in following her older brother around and pestering him. He in turn would push her down, but under no circumstances was anyone else ever allowed to hit her. That would bring about the biggest fight on the playground.

Françoise had wanted Laura to stop stripping when she became pregnant with Adrien. He assured her repeatedly that her performance skills were such that her singing and dancing could stand on their own. He was right, but she wasn't so sure. Yes, she put on a great show, but so did hundreds of others in Paris she reasoned, and most of them were barely eking out a living. She, however, was making a grand living doing what she was doing and she did not see any reason to change the formula. She did not want to kill the goose that laid the golden egg, so to speak. After the baby was born, she resumed doing her song and dance act with a little strip tease thrown in. She played all the minor theaters and burlesque houses in Paris and other points in Europe. After Marcella was born, she went right back to stripping.

They hired a nanny for the children and another maid to do general housecleaning. Madame Prusette did the cooking for them all. And Georges. He took care of all of Françoise's needs and tended to the marketing as well, but he refused to be called a butler. Occasionally he would answer the door, but mostly he just sat around in the kitchen and waited for his employer to return home so he could attend to his needs. Altogether they had a household of eight Laura was supporting off what she earned as a singer, dancer, and strip tease artist. Françoise was still a booking agent and still produced an occasional show himself. He had a good income from those endeavors so he paid Georges' wages himself. The rest, Laura covered.

In recent years, Françoise had become an agent representing not only the producers of shows, but theatrical talent as well. He had several other clients besides Laura, however, she was his primary client and he acted not only as an agent for her but also as her manager. He was kept very busy keeping her and her bookings straight, interceding on her behalf when she was unhappy with a theater or its staff, accompanying her out of town when she had to travel, and in general being her all around gofer. And he loved every minute of being her agent and manager, yet having his own income from his other clients. It was this atmosphere of having their lives just where they wanted them to be, that the events of 1914 intruded upon their perfect world.

Chapter 10. It's War

The causes of the Great War and the trigger that began the fighting were two separate disparate events. Long-term causes of the war included the imperialistic foreign policies of the great powers of Europe – the German Empire, the Austro-Hungarian Empire, the Ottoman Empire, the Russian Empire, the British Empire, the French Republic, and Italy. But it was a Yugoslav nationalist, Gavrilo Princip, in Sarajevo, Bosnia, who fired the shot heard round the world. On June 28, 1914, he assassinated Archduke Franz Ferdinand of Austria, the heir to the throne of Austria-Hungary and his wife, Sophie, Duchess of Hohenberg. The incident resulted in a Habsburg ultimatum against the Kingdom of Serbia.

The tiny Kingdom of Serbia, which had been established when Mila IV Obrenovic was crowned King of Serbia in 1882, had already endured two Balkan wars. But it was the invasion by Austria-Hungary after the assassination of Archduke Ferdinand, that put Serbia's continued existence at stake. Several alliances formed over previous decades were invoked. Within weeks, the major powers were at war with each other, as were their colonies. Conflict soon spread around the world. It was The Entente Powers, or Allies, - the major nations being

Britain, France, Russia, and later Italy, against the Central Powers – Germany, Austria-Hungary, the Ottoman Empire, and Bulgaria.

Within a month, the Germans were just 15 miles from Paris. The city was full of refugees from the northern part of the country that had already been overrun by the Germans. The government evacuated to Bordeaux and Parisians fled to points east and south. Laura, Françoise, and the children were among those who decamped to Marseille by train.

It was expected that Paris would fall to German forces within hours or at least within a few days. However, the Germans did not have enough tanks or motorized artillery and were unable to consolidate their gains. This situation was not helped by the fact that their supply lines were stretched as a result of the rapid advance and the Germans were hard-pressed to supply their troops.

With a desperate French effort to reinforce their lines, in what became known as the "miracle on the Marne", the government commandeered thousands of Parisian taxis to carry soldiers to the front lines. The Germans failed to press home the attack and the city was saved from German invasion. In fact, the French pushed the Germans back to Oise, 75 miles from Paris. The French government was so confidant they could contain the Germans, they gave the all clear to return to the city.

Other than that, the war seldom touched Paris. Oh, there was an occasional bombardment from enemy aircraft and giant long distance artillery guns sent almost 200 shells toward the capital. Although over 800 died in these attacks, there was no wholesale attack on the city. Eventually however, the impact of the rationing began to wear the city residents down. There were meatless Mondays and wheatless Wednesdays in the United States but in France, there was a shortage of everything every day.

The Goldmans, because of their position in show business, and knowing so many influential people, hardly suffered from the shortages. They still had eggs for breakfast, there was plenty of strong, hot real coffee, not the chicory blend most of Franch had to endure, and there was butter for their bread. For meat, they knew people who maintained farms in the south of France who supplied them with beef, pork, and chickens on a regular basis. And there was never any shortage of wine.

Russia, France and Britain's ally, was embroiled in its own internal turmoil. The country was in the midst of a revolution. This prompted Russia to withdraw from the war and sign a peace treaty with Germany. If France was defeated, that would have left Great Britain alone to fight the Germans. The United States had loaned and/or provided almost $3 billion in aid to the Allies. If the Allies lost the war, there would be no possibility of the United States ever getting that money back.

On April 6, 1917, the United States declared war on Germany after Germany sank seven US merchant ships in the North Atlantic. This declaration of war was immediately preceded by the revelation of an encoded telegram from German Foreign Secretary Arthur Zimmerman to the German ambassador in Mexico. The telegram instructed the ambassador to approach the Mexican government to gain Mexico as an ally in case the United States entered the war on the side of their allies. The inducement to Mexico would be the restoration of territories lost to the United States in the Mexican-American War, namely the states of Arizona, New Mexico, Texas, and southern California. When this encoded message was deciphered by Great Britain and revealed in the press, President Woodrow Wilson asked Congress to declare war on Germany, which it did.

The United States was never formally a member of the Allies but became a self-styled "Associated Power". When the United States entered the war, it had a small army, but after the passage of the Selective Service Act on May 18, 1917, 2.8 million men were drafted. By the summer of 1918, the US was sending 10,000 fresh soldiers to France every day. Two of these soldiers who were drafted and sent to France were Hampton and Randolph Jones of St. Maurice, Louisiana.

The American Expeditionary Forces Commander, General John J. "Black Jack" Pershing insisted on two things. 1) He refused to allow ill-trained American troops to enter the campaign. This resulted in only 14,000 American troops being deployed in Europe in 1917. 2) He refused the British and French requests that American troops be used as reinforcements for their armies. He would not allow his army units to be broken up for this purpose. By May, 1918, over one million U.S. troops were deployed to France, half of them being sent to the front lines.

As an exception to his second rule, Pershing allowed Negro combat regiments to be used in French divisions. An all-Negro New York Army National Guard unit, created as the 15th New York National Guard Infantry Regiment, had been constituted in 1916 in New York City. It was mustered into Federal service in 1917 at Camp Whitman, New York. The entire unit was drafted into the federal army in August of that year. They were sent to Camp Wadsworth in Spartanburg, South Carolina for battlefield training.

Because many Negro units of the Louisiana National Guard did not have enough soldiers to fill out their units, Negro soldiers from those guards were often reassigned to National Guard units from other areas. Both Hamp and Randolph were assigned to the 15th New York National Guard Infantry Regiment. This regiment was renamed the 369th Infantry. They were later nicknamed the "Harlem Hellfighters" by their German adversaries. In France, the entire 369th Infantry was assigned to the 16th Division of the French Army. In this capacity they were used to help repel the German offensive and to launch a counteroffensive.

The 16th was assigned the task of retaking Belleau Wood, which they did, and lost, and regained and re-lost for a total of six times before the Germans finally retreated. With the French, the Harlem Hellfighters also fought during the Aisne Offensive at Chateau-Thierry and Sechault. All members of the 16th received French Croix de Guerres for their actions at these three battlesites. Hamp was in the action at Sechault and Randolph at Château-Thierry so they both received the prestigious medal.

It was the flu epidemic that began in 1916 as much as the armed assaults that brought about the end of the war. More soldiers died in the trenches from the flu and dysentery than from enemy gunfire. The European armies were decimated by the disease, allowing the fresh troops of America to completely overpower them. There was hard fighting to be sure, but the war would have been more protracted had there been healthy troops in the German trenches. This seemingly endless stream of fresh healthy American troops began to destroy the morale of the German soldiers.

It was at the Battle of Château-Thierry during the offensive on the 3rd and 4th of June in 1918 where Randolph performed the actions that earned him an individual medal. The Germans had advanced thirteen hard fought miles on the first day of the offensive. They eventually reached the Marne at Château-Thierry where the French Army and General Pershing had deployed parts of their armies to defend the bridges.

Randolph and seven other men were parked in a trench by their lieutenant and told to defend it at all costs – including their lives. Randolph and the other soldiers hunkered down in the trench, including an older soldier who had befriended Randolph. This older soldier's name was Bill Robinson. After four hours with no enemy engagement, the squad decided to cook themselves some dinner before they lost the evening light. They had finished eating the meals from their field packs – boeuf bouilli, a dry powdered soup, and two biscuits from their store of twelve that they always carried into battle with them.

Randolph left the trench to relieve himself, when either driven by the voices coming from the trenches or the smell of the cooking food, a German soldier appeared out of nowhere. The soldier, scrawny and extremely pale, was literally no more than a boy. He looked as though he could barely stand. He held a rifle on Randolph and spoke in German. Randolph did not know what he was being told to do. His eyes were fixated on the gleam of the bayonet attached to the German soldier's rifle.

Suddenly, the young soldier lunged at Randolph. Randolph side-stepped him and grabbing the barrel of the rifle with his right hand and pointing it upward, he used his left elbow to sock the German in the jaw. Stunned, the young man stumbled backwards grabbing for non-existent air. Randolph, never having killed a man, was content to let it go at that and to allow the German to escape back to his own troops. However, the soldier got up from the ground, and lunged at Randolph bare handed. Randolph hit him an upper-cut, again sending the German sprawling. This time, the young soldier pulled a knife from his boot, and again he tried to rise. Seeing the knife in the soldier's hand, with his adrenalin pumping, Randolph stepped into the young man, placed a choke hold on his throat and squeezed with one hand while grappling for the knife with the other. Finally he felt the young soldier struggle no longer. Randolph then released his grip and the man fell to his knees and then onto his face.

By this time, Randolph's squad had begun to wonder what was taking him so long and had come looking for him. They rushed to the soldier just as Randolph let him go. Bill stepped over to the German, placed two fingers on his neck, and pronounced, "He's dead. Deader'n a door nail. Come on let's get out of here." All this time, from the beginning of the attack to its end, Randolph had not made a sound.

Bill led Randolph, in shock, back to their trench. When the Lieutenant returned later that evening, they had all prepared their written reports of the events. The following day a detail was sent to recover the body.

A short time later, after the fighting had stopped but before the war was officially declared over, while he was waiting to be deployed back to the states, Randolph was summoned to the commander's office and told to dress in his official dress uniform. When he arrived there he found over fifty other soldiers and officers already settled into chairs in the war room. The commander began speaking. Randolph listened as the commander read off a list of actions, after each one calling a soldier or officer by name. That individual would stand and go forward and receive his medal. When Randolph heard his name read off, he stood in disbelief. He was then signaled to come forward. His action was read off, "With great personal risk to his own safety, Corporal Jones single-handedly engaged and subdued an enemy solider ." It was signed, "by command of General John J Pershing". Randolph's commander pinned the medal to his full-dress blouse. To date, that was the proudest day in his life. Receiving the Croix de Guerre along with his division, was the second.

At the 11th hour of the 11th day of the 11th month of 1918, the guns fell silent and the lights went on again all over Europe. The war ended with the signing of the Armistice at Compiegne to the northeast of Paris. American soldiers were given a ten day leave in the area where they were deployed if they requested it and were in good standing regarding work ethics and obedience to military rules and regulations. Hamp was given his leave in Germany. Randolph in France. Randolph decided to go to Paris to see his mother who he had not seen for ten years.

Chapter 11. Randolph Visits

While Laura had worried about Randolph and Hamp's safety during the fighting, their being in Europe did give her an opportunity to see at least one of her sons on her own turf. Randolph wrote that he had a ten day pass and if she could put him up, he would like to spend it with her in Paris.

She wrote back, "Come, along. I can't wait to see you!"

Laura went alone to meet Randolph at the Gare de l'est. He was tall, at least six feet, and to her amazement, except for his green eyes, did not look like his father at all. Andrew was pale. Randolph had her coloration –a hint of yellow to his skin. His nose was pointed but not sharp or angular, and definitely not wide like her brother Charlie's, and he had thin lips – like Laura. The light blond hair he had as a boy had darkened to dark blond, bordering on brunette. It was thick and wavy like Laura's. In fact, he did not look like he had Negro blood in him at all. And he was downright handsome in his army uniform.

Their meeting was awkward. Laura did not know if she should hug him or shake hands with him. Finally, her emotions got the best of her. She threw her arms around him, took his face in her hands, and kissed him on both cheeks. He responded by putting his arms around her and burying his face in her hair. "Mama," was all he said, but she could feel him sobbing.

They talked for ten days straight. In between Laura took him to every major tourist attraction, monument, palace, and museum they could squeeze out time for. There was so much to show him. The first thing he wanted to see was the Tour Eiffel, where they climbed the stairs to the second level. Randolph went up to the upper level, but Laura, afraid of heights, declined, citing her age.

On Sunday they attended mass at Notre Dame. Laura had been baptized as an Episcopalian as a baby but had joined a Baptist church as a child just so she could sing in the choir on Sundays. She preferred the more soul stirring Negro spirituals sung in the Baptist Church than the staid ones sung in the Episcopalian Church. Now here in Paris, she attended Catholic services but never converted to Catholicism. She just liked being inside of Notre Dame with all of its rich history. And when the organ played, she felt it way down deep in her bones.

Laura was a decided history buff. She reveled in reading all she could about different eras in French history and was probably as knowledgeable about things French as any French citizen who had studied French history in school. So each monument and each museum they visited, each street she walked down with Randolph, she gave him a history lesson.

Whereas most tourists were most impressed with the Tour Eiffel, Randolph was fascinated by the Arc de Triomphe de l'Étoile. Laura lived within blocks of the Place de l'Étoile and they passed the arc nearly every day. The arc, designed in 1806 by Jean Chalgrin, depicts nude French fighters against armored German fighters. Of course, it shows the French fighters winning the imaginary war. This monument set the tone for all monuments erected after its inception.

One day Randolph went out for a walk and was gone for over two hours. Laura assumed he was shopping on the Champs-Élysées. When he returned he told her that he had been at the arc reading the names of all the French victories and generals inscribed on its inner and outer surfaces.

On Randolph's third day of leave, Laura and Françoise took him to a show at the Moulin Rouge. At first Randolph's eyes devoured the bare-breasted showgirls.

Then he sat back in his seat and just drunk it all in, the room, the stage, and the acts. He laughed aloud at the talking dog act. But then again, who didn't? Laura was between engagements during that time period so he did not get a chance to see her perform.

The next day they went to see the Chateau at Versailles. When they got to the Hall of Mirrors, Randolph just sat down on a chair. Coming from his poverty stricken background, he could not comprehend the lavishness of the French monarchy. As they moved from room to room, it became more and more evident that Randolph was overwhelmed by all that he saw. They ended up in the gift shop where Randolph bought post cards that depicted the opulence he had seen.

He did not say much on the train ride back to the city. When he finally did speak he said, "And the people were starving in the streets." His voice sounded bewildered.

"Yes, they were," said Laura. "But don't judge too harshly. That's always been the case. Those with power have lived lavishly while the peasantry barely scraped out a living. That's the way it is now. If you don't believe me, when you get back home, look around you. You might not be able to see it in St. Maurice but I'll bet you can in Shreveport. In fact, I'd be willing to bet the high and mighty live so high that you can't even get near their houses. Chances are they've got fences up to keep people like us out."

"Maybe you're right," he agreed reluctantly.

"I know I'm right," said his mother. "You'll understand this better as you get older. Just keep your eyes and ears open. The rich live a life that's impossible for the poor to understand. I know. I've seen how they live."

Randolph was quiet all of the way back into Paris. When they got to the apartment he sat down on the sofa and appeared to stare into space. Finally he said, "You're probably right. It takes some getting used to, that's all."

They also visited the Louvre. At that time the Louvre was not the museum it became in later years. It was close in with very little natural light, dank, and at times, in some parts of it, smelly. The display that impressed Randolph the most were the Egyptian artifacts – especially the mummies and the artifacts that had been recovered from the pyramids thus far.

The other exhibit in the Louvre that impressed Randolph was the Winged Victory of Samothrace, also called the Nike of Samothrace, Nike being Greek for Victory. Nike was sculpted of a fine-grained semi-translucent pure-white marble called Parian. Many pieces sculpted during the classical period were made from this marble quarried from the Greek island of Paros because it was without flaws.

Nike originally formed part of the Samothrace temple statuary dedicated to the Great gods, commonly called Megaloi Theoi during the era during which they were displayed in Greece. The statue, once resting on a block of marble intended to represent the prow of a ship, was displayed in the Louvre on a stand that reminded you of a piece of rock or something similar. The detailing on the statue was so lifelike, with its draped garments reminiscent of a figure caught in a strong breeze, it seemed as if Nike was alighting from the heavens after a great sea victory, proclaiming the news for all to hear. It really stirred something deep within Randolph. So much so that he made a trip to the museum the day before he left Paris, just to see the Nike one last time. He liked the paintings and sculpture of military life, but not nearly so much as the mummies and Nike.

One day as they were visiting the postcard stands on the banks of the Seine, Randolph suddenly said, "Why did you send me away?"

Laura stopped walking and faced him. She took a deep breath. "I didn't think it was right to keep you unless you wanted to be with me," she began. "You and Hamp were miserable. Don't you remember? Hamp was angry all the time. And you used to cry in your sleep and call for your Big Mama nearly every night."

"I was a child. I would've gotten over it," said Randolph in a quiet voice.

"Maybe you would've. But after six months Hamp was still angry and you were still crying. I didn't know what to do with you. We were all cramped up in my one bedroom apartment. I was looking for something bigger but other things came up before I could find a place. The head master asked me to come and see him about the two of you. He said I was being selfish by keeping you here; that I should send you back home. That if I didn't there could be some serious consequences when you got older. He thought that Hamp might wind up hurting someone and end up in prison and he didn't know what would become of a boy who was as quiet as you were. None of that was a future I wanted for either one of you. I tried to pretend he was wrong but I knew in my heart he was right. It was wrong of me to try to keep you when you didn't want to be here. I should never have left you in the first place. I failed you. But hindsight is perfect. I had to make the decision as to what to do from that point forward. I decided it was time to send you back to where you belonged; where you would be happy. My sister wrote constantly about how much she missed you and how she wanted you to come home. When you got back, she wrote to me many times that you were happy, so I knew I'd done the right thing. Cora wrote to me that eventually Hamp stopped fighting with everybody and started smiling and talking again, especially when he was riding the horses. And you stopped crying. But why do you bring it up now? What's done, is done."

Randolph hung his head and said quietly, "I thought it was because of Françoise. I thought he didn't want us around."

"No, it wasn't because of Françoise. He only wanted what made me happy. I wasn't happy because you weren't happy, so he agreed that I should send you back home. You didn't know this, perhaps you don't know it now, but Françoise owns the house we live in. He has for some time. Now we have the entire second floor but when I first moved in there, it was all cut up into four apartments. Françoise lived in an apartment on the first floor that he had put together with another apartment, to give himself a really large place and he was going to do the same thing with the one I had." She chuckled. So you see, he was about to do something really wonderful so that I could keep you with me, but before he could do that, I sent you back. It was me who made the decision and had Charlie come and get you."

"Oh, I see," said Randolph. "I thought he made you send us back. I guess I was wrong in hating him all these years."

"Oui, mon chérie. You were wrong. But that's okay. You were a child then. You didn't know any better. You're a man now so you should put away your hatred and forgive both me and Françoise. We did what we thought was best for you."

Laura noticed a decided difference in Randolph's attitude toward Françoise for the rest of the trip. When it was time for him to leave, they all went with him to the train station. He picked up his younger brother and sister and kissed them both on the cheeks. There were hugs, kisses, handshakes, and backslaps all the way round.

When they arrived at the train station, there were several other Negro American infantry men standing around, also waiting for the train north back to their army units. Among them was Randolph's friend Bill. Randolph called his friend over and introduced him to his family. Something about the tall slim dark man made Laura look at him intently for several minutes. Then she blurted out, "Why you're Bojangles!"

"Yes, ma'am. Have we had the pleasure?"

"No, but I've seen you perform in New York. I had no idea you were in my son's unit."

"Yes, ma'am. I'm proud to say that we've served together. A fine brave young man you have, ma'am."

She turned to Randolph. "Why didn't you tell me you were serving with Bojangles?!" she chided him.

He shrugged. He had no idea she would even know who Bill Robinson was.

The train blew its whistle indicating it was about to pull out. Randolph and Bill grabbed their grips and hopped aboard the train. Laura was left with her mouth hanging open as the train pulled out of the station.

Randolph wrote of their triumphant return to New York, "Bill was our drum major and led the regimental band up Fifth Avenue. Such strutting and prancing and high-stepping you have never seen in your life. He even marched backwards for half a block. You should have seen it. It was something else."

Randolph sent his mother pictures of the triumphant march into New York on the troops' return to the states. Although pictures had been around for some time, they were still a novelty, and Laura had each one from Randolph framed and hung in her "Rogues Gallery". That is what Françoise called the hallway on either side of the stairway in their apartment. The Gallery was already full of pictures of Laura and other show people who she knew, as well as dignitaries, local and national, who had graced her shows with their presence over the years. For Randolph's pictures, she rearranged everything and gave him a special place of honor, grouping his pictures, including one of them together that she had taken when he was in Paris, all in a special collage at the end of the hallway.

During their many talks together, Randolph had confided in Laura that there was a special girl back home in St. Maurice, Lida Beguine, who he was especially fond of. Laura remembered Lida's mother, another girl in the Evergreen Baptist Church, named Laura also. Laura Nash. Slow walking and slow talking, the other Laura was tall, slender, and very stately in nature. She had married another member of the church who Laura remembered also - Thomas Beguine. Laura Nash had a child the year after she married Thomas and contracted tuberculosis soon afterwards. She died when the child was two. That child was Lida. Laura had already moved away by then but her mother had written to her about Laura Beguine's untimely death.

According to Randolph, Thomas had soon married again and Lida was raised by her stepmother Ada. Also, according to Randolph, the stepmother had been mean to Lida, favoring her own children by Thomas over the stepchild. "She's got a sadness in her," Randolph had confided in Laura. "I know I can make her happy deep down inside."

The day before Randolph was to leave, Laura had slipped him 2500 francs, about $100 US - "for a gift for your special girl", she told him. He went out by himself and was gone for over an hour. When he returned, he showed his mother a beautiful ruby and diamond ring, although he swore he was not thinking of marriage. He said he saw the ring and he thought Lida might like having it as a souvenir from Paris.

Although Randolph had denied that he did not have any intention of marrying any time soon, he and Lida were married within months of his getting out of the army. A baby, a little girl, was born seven months later. They named her Ladine. Laura was very surprised when Randolph sent her a picture of the happy family. It is said that men often marry women like their mothers. Lida could not have looked more unlike Laura. She had expected Lida to be tall and thin like her mother Laura Nash, but much to Laura's surprise, Lida was short and already leaning toward the dumpy side. Laura, knowing how hard it was to loose baby weight, empathized with the new bride.

Chapter 12. Her Career

A storm of change was sweeping the western cultural centers. Art forms of all kinds were being radically, and irrevocably changed – the visual arts, music, theater, dance, the written word, and more. Paris was at the forefront of this change. The city on the Seine was a major melting pot for artists in every discipline.

Artists and writers alike were instrumental in this change, most notably of which were Americans Aaron Copland, Gertrude Stein, and Ernest Hemingway, French Henri Matisse and Jean Cocteau, Spanish Pablo Picasso, and Russians Marc Chagall and Igor Stravinsky, just to name a few. Relations were formed that would last a lifetime.

Laura's career thrived in this enlightened, integrated Parisian society. Originally, except for a few notable exceptions, to date she had starred or been a featured act only in small shows in burlesque houses and small inconsequential theaters. When those runs ended, Françoise immediately booked her into a another local venue, usually a variety or vaudeville show in a theater or burlesque house, perhaps in a play, or sent her on tour. Although very lucrative, these gigs did not lead to stardom.

Françoise was careful that Laura did not overwork herself. There were tragic stories of actors, actresses, and other performers who, because of their contracts, literally worked themselves to the point where their health declined. Françoise did not allow this to happen. On many occasions when Laura had been rehearsing all day, he would step onto the stage and call a halt – usually to the loud objections of the producer or director. Françoise's retort would be "Read her contract. Eight hours a day. Period. She's now been her eight hours and ten minutes. She'll be back tomorrow." He would then take Laura by the arm and usher her out of the theater. They put up with it, not only because it was in her contract, but because they knew he was right.

As time went along, Laura's billings and the venues she played in improved. She played a six week run at the Olympia, a cabaret show at the Paradis, headlined an act at the Cabaret des Arts, was in a play at the Théâtre des Variétés, and had a part in a musical at the Théâtre du Châtelet. They were all big name theaters, but she only had small parts or small variety acts, never star billing. In the bigger venues that was all that came her way.

Because she could tap dance and chew gum at the same time, and do both pretty well, she was never between engagements for long periods of time. She worked steadily this way for years and made a lot of money for a lot of people, including Françoise and herself, but she wanted more. She wanted a really big show in a major theater. She wanted to be a star. There is an old saying, "Some people want to be a big fish in a little pond and some people want to be a little fish in a big pond." Laura wanted to be a big fish in a really big pond. She felt the time to accomplish this monumental feat slipping away. Before you knew it she would be 40 years old.

One day as they were walking through the streets going nowhere in particular, Laura linked her arm through Françoise's. He could tell she was about to broach a subject to him.

"Françoise, I've been thinking," she began cautiously.

"Yes, my pet, what is it you've been thinking about?" he replied, even more cautiously still.

"Well, you know that I'm very grateful for all you've done for me and my career. Because of you I've not only been able to send money home to my family, but also thanks to you, I've managed to save quite a bit and also invested a lot. Before I met you, I had no prospects, and now, well, I have more money that I had ever dreamed of having."

"Yes, come out with it. There is a 'but'. Let's have it."

"Well, I want to get on the bill in a big theater. I want to be a headliner and I don't see it can happen the way I'm going."

"What would you like for me to do?" he asked her.

"I would like to play the Moulin Rouge. Can you get me a booking there?"

"No, I don't think so, my pet." He knew he had to tread cautiously here. "Well, there are problems with your act that would prevent that."

"What is that?" she asked, knowing the answer before he even spoke it.

He hesitated.

"Go on, tell me. What is it?" she prodded.

"Well. Truthfully, they're looking for younger dancers." There. He had said it.

"Yes," she said. "I'm aware of that, but surely experience must count for something."

"Huuum," he said musingly. After some time he said, "I can't promise you anything but I'll see what I can do. Up until now I only sought to place you in venues where I knew you would excel. Where you would get top billing. At the Moulin Rouge you'll only get middle of the bill at best. Are you willing to give up star billing? That would mean giving up star treatment, star dressing room and all. You won't be allowed to have your theater maid."

"Yes, I'm willing to give all that up. I'll be just a regular showgirl if only I could get into the Moulin Rouge. Oh, Françoise, do you think you can make it happen?"

"Well, I definitely can't get you in as a showgirl. I can tell you that up front. Why the Moulin Rouge anyway?" he wanted to know. "Why not one of the other top-drawer venues? How about the Le boeuf sur le toit? I had an inquiry from them just last week. I didn't tell you about it because they didn't offer enough."

Laura thought for a few minutes. "No," she said. "I want to play the Moulin Rouge. Their cabaret acts are style and class. If I could just get on the bill there, it would be the pinnacle of my career."

He sighed resignedly. "Okay," he said. "I might be able to do it. I can't promise you anything," he warned. "But I'll see what I can do. If I pull out all stops and pull in a few favors, I might be able to get you an audition. We'll see. After that, it's up to you."

Just then something caught her eye in a shop window. She dragged Françoise to look at a charming tea set. Not that she had any real use for it. It was something that she had always wanted and now that she was older she had begun to drink more tea than coffee and have more guests who did likewise. Now was the time to acquire a silver service.

As they were looking in the window, Françoise said very quietly to Laura, "You do know that I'll have to talk to Mistinguett, don't you? And she will probably talk it over with her lover Maurice (you do know that she's been seen all over town with Chevalier) and her best friend Michelle. Do you know what you're asking?"

"Yes, I know," she said in a very quiet voice. "I know it's a lot to ask from you." They walked on arm in arm, neither of them speaking to the other for a very long time.

The next day Françoise began to set in motion the plans they had discussed. Françoise purchased a completely staged production from a writer/lyricist team who had worked in New York theater. They created an act for Laura which featured 10 dancing and singing young women and men. This was going to cost a pretty franc.

That night in bed Françoise told Laura he wanted her to sketch him out some ideas for costumes. The next day she did as he asked. Françoise took her ideas and added a few of his own. Then he hired a costumer to design and execute their sketches.

The costume they came up with was a two piece affair that looked like a typical one piece dance leotard. It was made in two pieces in order for it to give during her high kicks. Laura had tried a one piece leotard and had trouble with it pulling and even splitting at crucial moments. She preferred this two piece design of hers. The new leotard was highly boned in white with gold trim over the boning. Françoise suggested that the costumes be made of a tightly woven satin, of a fabric that had a high shine to it so that when the spot lights hit it, it would seem to glimmer. Laura saw herself with two large white ostrich fans.

The male singers/dancers were to be costumed in white tails with white shoes. The female singers/dancers were to wear white corsets with gold trimming on the boning and short white tutus. The female dancers had to make a quick change into a second outfit that consisted of bras with gold trimming with a beaded swag adorning the midriff. This top was paired with a beaded swag draped over the most strategic area of a brief dance panty. That along with white high-heeled tap shoes was all that was needed.

The costumes, when executed, were just as Laura had envisioned them. She did not consider any part of her act to be successful unless it got a mention in the press. With over a dozen newspapers reporting on the theater, there was always room for theatrical productions. That was a lot newspaper space that had to be filled each week and her shows, though up to this point, small and inconsequential, got its share of notices. This helped to guarantee that people would continue to pack the audiences. Advertising in the local papers and on billboards and handbooks was effective but a mention in the papers was advertising that was more valuable than that which could be purchased. A good review could mean the difference between a highly successful run with the house packed for each performance and a lukewarm run with lots of vacant seats. Lots of vacant seats could translate into not being asked back or even, heaven forbid, a short run. These costumes were sure to get more than a mention.

The show that Françoise staged was spectacular. It's bevy of show girls were some of the most beautiful in Paris; the music was bright and lively. Laura had at first decided to perform four songs. Then she decided, no, three would be better and she would increase her dance time.

When all was in readiness and Françoise was satisfied with the dance routines, he made an appointment with Mistinguett, the best friend of his former girl friend, Michelle. Mistinguett was now a headliner at the Moulin Rouge and reported to be the mistress of the manager Francis Salabert. No one knew for certain but what was well known throughout the Paris theatre world was whatever Mistinguett wanted at the Moulin Rouge, Mistinguett got. That included who would play the cabaret and who would not. Mistinguett had blamed Françoise for Michelle's turning to alcohol and drugs after they broke up. For many years she would not even speak to him. Over time, she had learned that Michelle was a troubled woman who had already started using long before she had ever met Françoise.

Mistinguett listened to Françoise's request for her to intercede on Laura's behalf. Much to his surprise, Mistinguett agreed to bring the matter to Salabert. Salabert did not want the high yellow Negro singer and dancer who often performed in burlesque houses. When he put Negroes into his shows he wanted the whole world to know they were Negroes. Laura looked white – just like so many other European girls. True she could tap dance like crazy and she was very shapely, more so than European girls, and she was a little bustier. Still he hesitated. That is until Mistinguett went to work on him. One day, out of the blue, Françoise got a call from Salabert who asked him to bring in Laura and the troupe for an audition.

They were hired!!! Salabert gave Laura and the troupe a twenty minute slot in the middle of the show. In one night, Laura was able to do what she had been trying to do for ten years, get back into legitimate theater. Her contract was for six months. Laura's songs were executed to perfection with her clear alto voice giving the audience first a fast number, then a slow number, a dance routine with a male partner, and then ending with an upbeat number. She got plenty of press, being reviewed by reporters in five papers on her opening night. They all declared the act to be a hit.

After her contact with the Moulin Rouge was up, with nothing else in sight, Françoise booked her into another burlesque hall for six months, then miracle of miracles, he got a call from Salabert again. He wanted Laura and the troupe back! They played the Moulin Rouge for another six months. Seeing that they were beginning to get stale performing the same routine night after night, when the Moulin Rouge contract was up, Françoise had Laura and the backup dancers rest for two weeks while he restaged the show. He brought her back by sending her on a Northern European tour through six cities over a four month period. Based on her recent success at the Moulin Rouge he was able to get her star billing in top notch venues.

After returning the troupe to Paris from their European tour, Françoise then booked them into Le Boeuf sur le Toit, where they stayed for another six months. In between each engagement he gave them two weeks off. They always came back fresh and refreshed, ready to dance their hearts out for their audiences.

Then Françoise sent them on tour again, this time to Italian cities Torino, Milan, Rome, Naples, Palermo, Catania, playing each city for two weeks, and ending her Italian tour back in Rome. In four months they was back in Paris for a stint at the Follies-Bergère, also for six months.

From then on, the most Françoise would ever let her and her troupe work anywhere was six months. After that, he would let them rest while he sought a booking somewhere else while he restaged the show. This kept Laura's act fresh and her audiences clamoring for more of her unique talent. She had arrived. She and Françoise were then able to write their own tickets to whatever theater she wanted to play in.

Between Paris and her European appearances, she became known throughout Europe as "L'artiste avec moistest" – the entertainer with the mostest.

Chapter 13. The Dance Craze of '20's

The dance styles of the '20's were full of energy. The perennial dance favorite, simply because even the most clumsy-footed men could learn it, was the one-step which had been renamed "the Fox Trot". Much to the dismay of dancing instructors, it was a simple dance that was easy to learn and could be mastered by almost anyone without the assistance of a dance instructor.

Post-war social mores were different from those of the pre-war era and women were not thought of as being loose or prostitutes just because they danced with total strangers. Whenever Laura went out cabareting, she was barely allowed to sit out a dance and she danced with all polite gentlemen who asked her.

Laura's stage dance partner during the 20's was Lawrence Philbig. Lawrence was a New Yorker by birth and training. He and Laura were masters of the Fox Trot. He guided her through the intricacies, swinging her to and fro, and twirling her around, all while she danced backwards, and as another famous dancer once put it "and in high heels". It was a beautiful dance on the dance floor and on stage when the stage was large enough to accommodate it. When they were not, Laura and Lawrence danced an abbreviated version, with the couple close in together, moving as one to the music. It was always a crowd pleaser, but because of its low-key energy, she never used it as the finale of her act, instead using it to open the show with.

Other popular dances Laura incorporated into her show were the West Coast Swing and the Collegiate Shag. The West Coast Swing was a swing dance done to a very slow tempo – much slower and smoother than its earlier forms. It was done in a "slotted space" namely an area approximately 6' x 9' wide, with other dancers giving way and staying within their own space. It was not particularly good for dancing on a crowded dance floor. It was perfect for older Parisians, because it did not tax the body so. When Laura and Lawrence did it on stage they always had a little step that can best be described, as a hop and a kick. Few others incorporated these little hops and kicks into their performance so theirs got notice in the press.

The Collegiate Shag, so named because it was made popular on college campuses, was a favorite of young people because it was lively and full of energy with hops and kicks performed to fast tempo music. Not many older Parisians tried it. Laura and Lawrence used this dance style to close out their dance routine together. It was always near the end of the show as it was lively and often brought the audience to its feet with roaring and clapping. When she and Lawrence shagged, they shagged. During the time the Shag was a part of their act, it was guaranteed to get them a press notice at least once a week. When the Shag began to get stale and Laura had to abandon it in favor of more modern dance steps, she regretted doing so because she thought that nothing would replace the Shag's energy. She was wrong.

The last two dance styles of note that Laura and her dance partner routinely performed were the Balboa and the Jive, also called the American Jive and the Jitterbug Jive, both derived from the Lindy Hop. The Balboa evolved from packed ballrooms somewhere in Southern California. It was thought that its form derived from not having enough room to move around to readily show off fancy footwork. Laura loved this dance because it could really show off a couple to advantage when they moved in sync to each other. It all had to be performed within a couple of square feet of space. The Balboa could be danced to either fast (300 beats per minutes) or slow music (100 beats per minute) or anything in-between. When dancing to slow beats it required great finesse and intricate footwork using short, swift graceful movements. It was more of a dancer's dance rather that a spectator's dance in that the male partner guided the female partner through the intricate steps more through body language and intimate contact rather than choreographed steps. For this reason, Laura seldom used it in her act but she loved dancing it on the dance floor.

The Jive was just the opposite. No one knows where it came from. It just sprang up spontaneously throughout America and Europe. It required a lot of room to perform. Thought to be a variation of the Lindy Hop, it featured a swing out style with the boy and girl both performing a sort of twist step as they danced far apart holding onto each other by one hand only. Extremely beautiful when executed properly, it was not done by many older people as it, too, required a lot of energy to perform. If you were out of shape, one round of the Jive and you were sitting out the next few dances. The Jive was what Laura and Lawrence replaced the Shag with. It had the Shag's high energy and was a definite crowd pleaser often bringing the crowd to its collective feet to show its appreciation for the finesse which she and Lawrence performed it. It really left the crowds rollicking and wanting more.

And enough cannot be said about the shimmy in all its forms. No one knows where it originated from, having been performed by Polish dancers, gypsy dancers, and Negro dancers all about the same time. What Laura did know was when she threw in a shoulder shimmy into an already hot dance number she got yells and hoot calls you would not believe from the male members of the audience. It was especially effective when she wore a red chemise with fringe costume that she adored. The shimmy set the entire dress moving and seemed to electrify the entire room.

Laura mastered all of the modern dances like few others. She did not however, like one of the new dances, the Charleston. She thought that all of the gyrations with the knees, which in turned put the hips into motion, looked vulgar. So she refused to do it – both on the dance floor and on stage.

Now mind you, when Laura danced with Lawrence, the entire act was not about them dancing together. Hers was not a dancing act per se. It was a variety show unto itself. They shared the stage for about three minutes of a twenty minute routine and about ten minutes for an hour long one, with varying times for the dancing duo based on the amount of overall time Laura was allotted for her act. Her act had dancing and singing with a little strip tease thrown in. It was a lady's afternoon or evening pleasure and a gentleman's delight. Both sexes came away satisfied with her performance and vowing to return to see her perform again.

Chapter 14. Marcelle de St Martin

After the war, Laura began to use a rather unknown costume designer who was introduced to her by Laura's stage manager, Jules Etienne. The French-born costume maker Marcelle de St Martin lived and worked in England. Marcelle was born in Paris in December of 1898. Like so many other fashion designers before her, she had been a lover of dolls, and spent many hours designing and constructing clothes for her play things. She began studying at the Sorbonne at the age of 17 and had a thorough study of drawing and painting, modeling, the human anatomy, and an overall study of the history of art. She studied dress styles throughout the ages by studying the clothing depicted on subjects in the artwork left behind. Marcelle developed her skills as an artist and costume designer literally by copying the great masters. During the Great War when it appeared as if Germany was going to take Paris, Marcelle and her mother left and went to London to live with an older sister who had married and immigrated there.

Marcelle, while still in her teens, became attracted to actress Doris Keane who was working on a show called *Romance* in London. Marcelle started drawing sketches of Miss Keane in elaborate performance gowns. One such sketch became passed around among the members of the *Romance* cast and crew and Miss Keane saw it. She then commissioned several pieces from Marcelle. Several prominent actresses of the day also saw the sketches, among them Violet Loraine and Kyrle Bellew, who also commissioned Marcelle to produce performance gowns for them as well. Then Marcelle was commissioned to design for the performance *Valentine*. Immediately following *Valentine* she did costumes for *Jack and Beanstalk*. She was on her way as a theatrical costume designer.

Laura's stage manager, Jules Etienne, was first cousin to Marcelle and introduced the two of them when Marcelle came home for a visit one summer. Laura was readying a new show for the fall and was unhappy with sketches of costume ideas being presented to her by her then costume designer.

Marcelle, who was there in the theater waiting to go to cocktails with her cousin, dashed off sketches for about a half dozen costumes while waiting for rehearsals to end. Jules showed these to Laura. Laura was amazed and contracted with Marcelle to develop full drawings. Liking what she saw, Laura executed a further contract with Marcelle for Marcelle to construct and deliver the costumes to Laura in six weeks. Marcelle did not disappoint.

The reviews of that show specifically mentioned the costumes and Marcelle by name. Laura went so far as to give Marcelle a mention in the show's printed program and advertisement. This was almost unprecedented, but the costumes Marcelle designed and constructed were that fabulous. They were literally eye-poppers.

The gown Marcelle designed for the finale was especially spectacular. It was Laura's favorite color – gold. It was cut to cling to the body from throat to hips. At the hips, there were yards and yards of the filmy fabric that the gown was made of, causing it to move like a whisper - whipping about the ankles like liquid gold. Multiple layers of gold beads completed the ensemble. Laura had fallen in love with the sketches but when she donned the dress for the first time, she let out an "Ahhhh," that expressed her deep satisfaction with what she saw in the mirror. The dress was stunning and she was stunning in the dress. She decided then and there that whenever she wore that dress, she would wear her hair piled high upon her head. Laura had extremely long hair, and it curled into ringlets all on its own so that Laura did not need to use extensions or hair pieces in order to augment her own hair. Nor did she need to use a marcel iron to produce the curls. They just happened naturally. Normally, she would do everything she could to get rid of them, but for this dress they were perfect all on their own.

The gown was designed so that Laura could get into it and out of it by herself during a quick costume change during her act using a relatively new invention called a zipper. That one costume alone got more press for Laura than some performers get for their entire acts.

Another costume Marcelle designed was one in three pieces. It consisted of a bra, a corset, and a panty. This was one of Laura's strip costumes. When it started coming off, the men were not only out of their seats they were generally in the aisles yelling for her to "Take it off. Take it all off" which she never did of course. For what would be the fun in that?

When Marcelle designed the costumes for Laura she was freelancing, looking for someone who would employ her fulltime. Her talents came to the notice of Hockley of Bond Street and she went under contract to them. While with them she designed costumes for *Kissing Time, Tilly of Bloomsbury, Eastward Ho!* and numerous others. Laura was proud to say, "I knew her when," meaning that she had known that the young artist had a special talent that would someday lead to her fame.

Marcelle had a unique, for that time, viewpoint of designing. She dressed actors and actresses for the parts in the time period in which they were written, and not to mimic fashions of the day, as was the trend during that time. Because films could be played for years hence, Marcelle wanted the costumes to always be relevant, and they could not be if they were committed to a particular fashion trend. This method of dressing actors and actresses was novel for its time but soon became the norm.

Marcelle so impressed theater executives, when American backers decided to open a film studio in London, her name came up. Having already hired a costume design department, they took her on as a dresser. It was not long before they had her designing costumes. This studio was The Famous Players-Lasky Corporation of America which later became Paramount Studios. Marcelle designed most of the costumes for films made at their London studio until its close.

In 1922, Marcelle was approached by Cecil B. DeMille to come to Hollywood with him and design the costumes for his epic *The Ten Commandments*. Marcelle did not take him up on his offer, a decision she regretted for the rest of her life.

Laura and Marcelle were wonderful friends. Marcelle came to Paris frequently for fashion shows to gather design ideas, always returning to London with several sketchbooks full of sketches, some complete, others just mere doodles on paper. While in Paris she also visited with family and friends. She was to be seen nearly every night backstage at Laura's performances being entertained by Laura and Jules. In addition, Laura made at least two trips across the channel each year to confer with the costume designer where she conferred with Marcelle in here workroom. By this time Marcelle had a staff of ten and they were always working on costumes for one show or another. Laura loved going there because Marcelle had all manner of fashionable gowns under construction and she allowed Laura to play "dress up" in them.

Marcelle married a Jewish reporter from the United States and first she, and then Laura fled to the states, to evade the Nazis. Marcelle moved to Kansas City, Missouri where her husband had family. Marcelle never returned to Europe after moving to the states, later finally accepting an offer to design for a Hollywood studio. Although Laura was happy for her friend's good fortune, each time it was time to have costumes designed, she complained that she never found another designer to rival Marcelle's talents.

The two friends wrote to each other frequently. Marcelle's letters were peppered with sketches of costumes that she had designed or was thinking of designing for Laura. Save for once, sadly, they never saw each other again.

Chapter 15. The Roaring Twenties in Paris

To understand the impact that music in the states had on the world after The Great War, we have to look at Paris and the flowing of American music to this post war city during les Années Folles, the Crazy Years.

George Antheil lived in Paris and performed his Symphony Mechanic there. Aaron Copeland studied under Nadia Boulanger, the noted French composer, conductor, and teacher who taught many of the leading composers and musicians of the 20th century. In 1924 Copeland wrote his Organ Symphony under her tutelage. And everyone knew of Americans George Gershwin and Cole Porter, and Frenchman Maurice Ravel. They all lived and worked for a time in Paris during the '20's. Local composers like Darius Milhaud and Eric Satie's music was provocative and had what was called an American "new wave" sound.

However, even though there were American composers in all areas of music, it was the influence of American soldiers and their jazz music during and after The Great War that changed attitudes about music where Parisians were concerned. Now the French listened and danced to the jazz greats. It was jazz music that enlivened the socio-economic structure during the recovery after the war.

It was American entertainers like Ada "Bricktop" Smith, the great Josephine Baker, and Laura who performed nightly to enthusiastic Parisian audiences, and whose songs were on everyone's lips. In addition, many other Negro entertainers were a household name in Paris during the '20's. People flocked to any show they were in. And the music they performed was jazz.

During this time, the United States was in the middle of prohibition. Rich Americans vacationed in European cities, especially Paris. They went there to take in the shows, listen to the music, and drink. Nightclubs like Bricktops's was the place to see and be seen, listen to hard-driving jazz, dance the night away in near-vulgar hip-gyrating movements, and get pie-faced drunk.

When Laura had first come to Paris, Montmartre had been the center of art, cafes, and bars. In the '20's this center shifted to the more sophisticated area of Montparnasse. The way its' inhabitants dressed, acted, and even did their hair came to influence the styles and looks throughout the world. And Laura was right there in the forefront of that change.

And all the while whites were elbow to elbow with Negroes, living with Negroes, eating with Negroes, and dancing with Negroes. Yet as soon as they returned to the states they insisted on being segregated from Negroes. Negro musicians arrived in Paris and were overwhelmingly accepted by the Parisians. Occasionally there was a racial incident in Paris, but Parisians made it known to visitors that racism was strictly frowned upon in their country and if one did not like it, they were more than welcome to take their racist attitudes back to their home countries. Paris experienced one of the most decadent eras in French history. Men were sleeping with men. Women were sleeping with women. And everyone wanted to sleep with Negroes. It was this phenomenon created by early Negro entertainers that allowed people like Laura Boult to become a star. She did in France what she could never do in the U.S.

Laura and Françoise were regular guests at the homes of people like Nathalie Barney, Gertrude Stein, her brother Michael, and Gertrude's lover, Alice B. Toklas. They hobnobbed with, entertained, and was entertained by "everybody who was anybody, " including Ezra Pound, F. Scott Fitzgerald, James Joyce, and Ernest Hemingway, just to name a few.

Politicos and the military were also represented in Laura and Françoise's friends and acquaintances. A regular visitor to Laura's shows was Charles de Gaulle, a young commandant who had been wounded and taken prisoner in The Great War. He was always a welcome visitor backstage as Laura's guest.

Also present at her shows were staff members of the government led by Alexandre Millerand. The French had a different view of the human body and saw nothing wrong with entertaining the staff of visiting foreign dignitaries by taking them to, what would best be described in America, as a peep show.

These regular visitors to Laura's shows were invited to her apartment for lively discussions and she, in turn, were invited to their homes and country estates for the same. They discussed the arts, fashion, theater, music, politics, and socio-economic affairs.

Fueled by wide-eyed Americans fresh off the boats – five thousand a week to be exact – this society of artists, fashion designers, entertainers, writers, the military, and government leaders was called the New Generation. They brought their wit, wisdom, naiveté, and their money, and they all hobnobbed together. If anyone had listened to them they could have saved the world. But no one listened to the New Generation. And so Europe set itself up for another world war.

Through all of this, Laura was living high. She indulged herself in clothes, jewelry, and lavish spending. She had no idea that life could be like this - when you only had to imagine yourself with some magnificent bauble and the next thing you knew, it would be yours.

Her favorite restaurant was Maxim's located at No. 3 on the Rue Royale. Originally a bistro, it was opened in 1893 by former waiter Maxime Gaillard. It took on its Art Nouveau look, the look that everyone associated it with, under the ownership of Eugene Cornuché. It was he who began packing the house with beautiful, well-dressed women. Laura was one of those regulars who Eugene always had a table for, preferably by the window where the women could see and be seen by all who passed by, whether on foot, by carriage, or by automobile.

This was the good life there was no doubt about it. Laura was present at every major opening in Paris. Laura and Françoise were present when the newly renovated Café des Amabassadeurs reopened with the hit show "Black Bird Revue" on Friday May 28, 1926. They were present when Florence Mills made her first appearance in Paris by emerging out of a birthday cake singing her first song in Paris, "Silver Rose". They were there to see the pink-themed room decorated in roses, hydrangeas, and wisterias. They rubbed elbows with the smart set of Paris society - the most fashionable people in the western world, including some of the most famous American and French celebrities.

Florence Mills was inarguably one of the greatest performers ever. She had started performing as a small child and had performed continuously since then. She was a singer foremost, dancer, and comedienne all rolled into one performer. She was praised by black and white alike. One of her greatest songs was "I'm a Little Blackbird."

Before leaving for Paris on May 15 with the Black Bird Revue, there were all kinds of run-up farewell performances, tributes, and toasts made to and for Florence. She had a three-week run at the Alhambra Theater. It went over so well that it was extended primarily so that, at Florence's requests, more dollar theater seats could be offered so more Negros could attend. She invited all her friends and supporters to come. She promised autographed pictures to the ladies in the audience. The performance was extended once again – this time billed as "one last time" through the week of May 3. Billed as a "colored Charlie Chaplin", Johnny Hudgins, a dancing miming clown was added to the bill the final week before they sailed for France.

One of the farewell parties thrown for Florence was a dinner hosted by Bill "Bojangles" Robinson and his wife Fannie at the Exclusive Club. Performers from the Club Alhambra, the Cotton Club, and other venues were invited for dinner and refreshments. Florence was presented with a gold and silver cup. A week later there was another farewell party for her at Small's Paradise. Entertainment was provided by dancers from the Cotton Club. The applause for Florence was so thunderous that her voice could not be heard above the roar of the crowd and she had to pantomime her thanks. One of the oddest tributes to Florence was the bringing in of a prize-winning mare that had been named after her, to the Plantation one Sunday night. A special stall was built for the horse. Florence sang songs picked especially for the occasion.

Florence sailed for Paris on the *France*. Another notable on the crossing was writer Anita Loos and her husband. Florence so impressed Anita that Anita mentioned her in one of her plays that she wrote years later called "Gentlemen Prefer Blonds". The crossing, by all accounts, was uneventful.

There was a special late night opening that first night especially so that theater people could attend. That night was a magical one. Everyone who was anyone attended. It was later rumored that the first show brought in 450,000 francs – roughly $18,000 US. While Laura's shows never brought in that much, Laura was the first to admit that her talent was not on the level of Florence's or Josephine Baker's. Hers was a unique, solid, pack the house every night, type of talent that never seemed to grow stale – as long as she and Françoise restaged the show every six months, that is. She had year after year of solid bookings to her credit. She did not envy others their talents. In fact, she was happy for their successes. All she ever wanted was to make a living in order to be able to provide for her children. She used what talents she had been given and crafted a career around them.

Maurice Chevalier was there that night for the opening of "Black Birds" with Mistinguett on his arm. He made a special point of parading her in Laura's face. Laura had lately been seen out cabareting with Maurice, thirteen years her junior, oddly enough the same age difference as he and Mistinguett. It was rumored by one of the columnists that he and Laura were secret lovers. They were. Laura did not consider it to be cheating on Françoise. Each time she returned to Françoise after being with Maurice, she was more passionate in her love making. Lately, she and Maurice had been growing stale together. Laura was not sure if she was tiring of him, or he of her. What she did know, is that he did not adore her as Françoise did. He did not put himself above her. Maurice was all about Maurice and his career, whereas Françoise was all about helping Laura be a success in her chosen profession. After they broke up, it was rumored that Maurice went into a deep depression and attempted suicide. What is known is that later that year he met Yvonne Vallée, a young dancer. She helped him through his depression and they married in 1927.

Josephine Baker came to the show unfashionably late dragging a full length ermine coat on the floor behind her. She was surrounded by ten white men in white tails – obviously dancers hired for the occasion. She was always trying to upstage someone, thought Laura to herself.

Laura did not hold Josephine's antics against her. After all, she had gone to Josephine's first performance where Josephine danced her famous Danse Sauvage, an erotic pas-de-deux, wearing only a string of feathers around her neck and waist. When Josephine moved her act, *La Folie du Jour*, to the Folies Bergère, Laura and Françoise had been given advance notice by Josephine and Françoise had arranged for Laura to have the evening off so she could attend. When Josephine appeared on stage in the banana skirt dance the show had every bit the wow-factor that Josephine had promised. The costume and the dance were an eye-popper all right.

Françoise had to pull a lot of strings and call in several favors in order to get someone to substitute on the bill for her the night of Josephine's Folies opening but he finally got management to approve Laura being off to attend. Josephine welcomed Laura and Françoise enthusiastically when they went backstage to congratulate her after her performance. In turn, Josephine invited them to a party at her house. They partied until 5 o'clock that morning when Laura finally begged off, citing a rehearsal that afternoon. They could still hear Josephine's peals of laughter echoing out the front door and down the doorsteps as they found their way to their car.

Although Laura was much older than Josephine, they became great friends. The Goldman family was invited to the Baker estate in the country many times. Josephine recognized that much of her success was owed to the ground that Laura and others like her had plowed, leaving the audiences clamoring for more and more colored acts.

Another famous person who attended the premier of Black Birds was Bill Robinson. That in itself was not remarkable. Nor was his presence at Josephine's show at the Folies Bergère show. What was remarkable that while in Paris he also attended Laura's show.

Laura was backstage after her performance with a crowd in her dressing room, when a note was delivered to her. It read "Miss Boult, I would love the opportunity to come and pay a tribute call on you backstage." It was signed Bill "Bojangles" Robinson. Laura squealed and dropped the note. Françoise picked it up from the floor. He read it then turned to the usher who had brought it. He took a coin from his pocket and gave it to the boy. "Please tell the gentleman to come backstage; that Miss Boult would be proud indeed to receive him."

A few moments later, Bill's all too familiar smile entered the door. Laura stood up to greet him. "Mr. Robinson," she began. On Bill's arm was an elegant lady who he introduced as his wife Fannie.

Bill held up his hand. "No, it's Bill. Please call me Bill. May I just give you a hug? I think your show was fabulous, Miss Boult."

"It's Laura. Just Laura. And thank you so much. Coming from you, that is praise indeed. Please sit down," she invited them.

Before doing so, he gave a little tap step. Much to his amazement, Laura followed his lead. He gave another little tap step, and again she followed his lead. Then he took her hand and guided her in a combination step. They danced together for about a minute then Laura sat down in embarrassment. "Bill, I'm no tap dancer any longer. I can't keep up with you."

"That's okay. Few people can," he said as he grinned broadly. He then proceeded to give them a little show of his own.

When he finished, he took a seat. He was grinning. Laura was grinning. Françoise was grinning. And it seemed that everyone in the dressing room was too. Then Bill said, "How's your son? I think his name was Randolph? I haven't heard from him since we mustered out. We all promised to write to each other and keep in touch, but you know how it is."

"Yes," Laura said. "We all get pretty busy." She proceeded to tell him all about Randolph and his family. Bill and his wife stayed for an hour. She invited them to an afterhours café where she and Françoise often went for pork chops (for her) and a steak (for Françoise) after her performances. The two couples sat and talked show business until late into the morning.

Then one night Laura's theater maid came to Laura with her eyes as big as saucers. The girl was French and she was babbling in her native language so fast that Laura could barely understand her. Finally she got the girl to calm down and tell her what was happening. Just as the girl got the words out of her mouth "Florence Mills is backstage looking for you," the door opened and the stage manager ushered Florence through the door. In a sweep of flowing gown, Florence came in and walked over to Laura with her hand outstretched.

"Oh, Miss Boult, may I say what an honor it is to meet you. You have been one of my show business idols for some time."

Laura was flabbergasted. Florence Mills was back stage to see her! She could not believe it. She finally recovered herself and offered her guest a seat. Florence went on and on about Laura's performance. When Laura was able to get a word in edgewise she told Florence that she had been in the audience on Florence's opening night and she, Laura, was very proud of the young entertainer. Although there was almost twenty years difference between their ages, there was an immediate bond between the two. Their careers had not paralleled each other and were not even similar but they each keenly knew what it was like to be Negro in a racist world and had lived with that and had still managed to overcome that obstacle that was placed before them. They were both successes in their own right. That night was one of the best nights in Laura's career – the night Florence Mills came backstage at her performance.

Florence went on to Belgium and London with her performances and then back to the United States. Then on November 1, 1927 after contracting tuberculosis and undergoing what was released to the press as minor surgery, Florence died. She was 32 years old. The whole world was stunned and saddened by the news – Laura among them. She received the word in a telegram from Bill

Robinson who had been notified on a train traveling across the states from New York to California. Like millions of others, Laura wept at the news. Florence, "the Queen of Happiness" was gone from their midst, never to entertain and delight them again. When Florence was in Paris, Laura had made it a point to see her performance more than once. In fact, she saw it six or seven times. She wanted to learn from the talented artist – her footwork, her timing, her craftsmanship. And she did. After each performance she felt that she was taking away a little more knowledge about how to put over a song, a skit, an act. Laura was gratified that the world gave Florence her flowers while she was alive but they honored her also in death.

The night after they learned of Florence's death, Laura received a phone call from Josephine Baker. Josephine wanted to know if Laura would like to meet the next morning and talk about Florence. Laura welcomed the opportunity to share her grief with someone she instinctively knew understood how she was feeling. Josephine came to Laura's for breakfast at 10. Laura met her at the front door personally. They walked arm in arm up the stairs to Laura and Françoise's apartment. Josephine sank onto the sofa. Laura had never seen Josephine when she was not upbeat and gay. This was a side of Josephine that few people ever saw. Laura felt honored to be one who was allowed to see inside the "the Black Venus".

Laura poured Josephine a cup of tea from her magnificent tea service. The cup full of the dark liquid sat untouched. Finally Josephine said, "I just can't believe she's gone. She was so vibrant and full of energy. When she was here we spent many evenings together after our performances. I tell you that woman could make me laugh. It wasn't that she told jokes or anything. It was just the way she said things that made them funny."

Laura agreed. "I liked the way she delivered a line," she said. "I could watch her for a year and still not get a hook on her timing. I tried. Lord knows I tried."

The two women sat and shared their memories. Josephine had known Florence in New York, and therefore had more memories to share. Laura was just glad to be considered a friend who Josephine could lean on.

At two, Josephine got up to go. Both of the ladies had shows to put on that evening. Each had to be at her appointed theater in just a few hours. They had to get themselves into the right mood to perform. Doing comedy was hard enough. Trying to do it when you were down was murder. Although they went on with their lives, Florence's gaiety and her melodious voice haunted Laura for months.

Françoise could not help her through her grief. No one could because no one understood the sisterhood of colored women except another colored woman. That is when she and Josephine became not just acquaintances, but real true friends. From then on, they knew that they could lean on each other in a time of real need. Eventually the hurt they felt from Florence's passing began to heal.

Laura had much to keep herself busy. For one thing, many Broadway shows and individual entertainers came to Paris during the 20's and there was a constant stream backstage to see her after her performances. After Josephine's show, the next show on their "must see" list was Laura Boult's show.

But theatrical performers were not the only ones who honored Laura. During the '20's, Laura had numerous pictures drawn of herself by famous and not so famous artists. Pablo Picasso, Monet, Marc Chagall, Salvador Dalí, and Amedeo Modigliana were among the many who had their studios in Montparnasse. Among these famous artists were many more who were not famous, who were one step from starvation. They would draw a picture of you in exchange for a few francs or even a meal. Laura considered herself to be fortunate indeed that she had a roof over her head, and so elegant a roof, mind you, that she felt obligated to feed the starving artists around her. Before her death she had collected about twenty drawings and paintings by these unknown artists. She had each one framed in an elaborate frame and hung them in what Françoise called her "Rogue's Gallery".

Famous artists would also draw you just because they liked what you did for others less fortunate. These portraits she hung in her parlor. Among these works were drawings by Picasso, and no, he did not draw her with two heads or three breasts; a Modiglani, dashed off one night just because he felt like it; a Dalí, well, because everyone else was doing it; and a Chagall. On her death, these portraits collectively were worth over a million dollars US. Twenty years later, they were worth over ten million.

And through it all, from obscurity to fame, Laura loved to shop. One of her all-time favorite stores was Le Bon Marche. Located where Rue de Sevres crosses boul Raspail, bordering on the Rue du Bac, it was a feast for the eyes. It's architecture, designed by Gustav Eiffel, was Art Deco. Completed in 1887, Louis-Aristide Boucicaud's grand magasin had something for every taste – upscale and mid-priced clothes and lingerie, exquisite and basic household furnishings, French and imported specialty foods, and unique items of all descriptions, from dirt cheap to downright ridiculously over-priced. It was where Laura did most of her shopping for the two youngest ones for school uniforms and play wear, and the two older ones for gifts from their mother. Although Laura was not able to visit Hamp and Randolph on a regular basis, she kept up a regular correspondence with them and sent many packages to her sons and her grandchildren containing clothes, candy, cookies, small household goods, and anything else she thought they might enjoy. Everything except shoes. Laura considered shoes to be a personal thing – something everyone should pick for themselves so all of her packages and letters contained money for items such as those, and for their personal upkeep.

Chapter 16. The Movies

Of the 100+ French films that were released during the '20's, Laura was in at least a dozen of them. None of her performances were noteworthy enough to be credited or even get a mention in the press.

Laura learned of her role in her very first film just after she and Françoise had just finished making love. She had padded into the bathroom wrapped in her white dressing-gown with the ostrich feathers, to tidy up.

Françoise called to her. "You wearing that robe, looking like a movie star, reminded me of something I meant to tell you when I came in. Mon chérie, I have a surprise for you," he said to her in French.

"What is it, Françoise?" she asked in English.

Again in French, he said, "I have gotten you a little part in a movie. I hope you will not mind."

She came back to the bed. "A part in a movie! Oh, Françoise, you goose. Of course I don't mind. It's what I've been wanting. Tell me about the part." She settled down onto the bed beside him.

"Well, it won't stretch your talents very much I'm afraid. They want you to perform your act for them and there're about a dozen lines for you to say. That is, if you want the part."

"Why, of course, I want the part. When is it? Will it interfere with the show?" Oh, she had a thousand and one questions. He could tell that the love-making was over. Oh, well. He knew before he began this, that performing was her first love. He would always come second in that regard. After he had told her all about the movie role, she gathered her clothing and walked back into the bathroom to get dressed.

The movie was *Napoléon,* a silent film directed by Abel Gance. *Napoléon* tells the story of Napoleon's early years. The producer had planned on making several sequels to the original movie with Laura to have a recurring role in all of them, but the remainder were never made.

That was the first of over a dozen films Laura was in. Thereafter, Laura was in two or three movies a year, all un-credited minor roles. Sometimes, she had spoken lines but mostly she was in a background scene doing all or part of her act.

For one day's work in the movies Laura got paid the equivalent of what she earned in a week of cabaret work. In some movies, they wanted her entire act on camera with her, in others, just her. She was never going to be a movie star but it was fun being treated like one on the sets of the movies. And she never got over the thrill of seeing herself on the big silver screen in the movie theater.

Laura's biggest role was in *Liliom*. It was a 1932 film directed by Fritz Lang. Released in 1934, tt starred Charles Boyer and Madeleine Ozeray. The beginning of the film was set in a carnival. The main character, Liliom, worked at a carousel at the carnival. Laura was onscreen in three separate scenes, all set at the carnival. In all three scenes she did different portions of her 20 minute act. Laura had over five minutes on-screen, all in the background of the main action, except for one small interchange she had with the main character.

Laura's favorite film that she was in was the 1938 *Hôtel du Nord* by director Marcel Carne. It was about the comings and goings of simple people residing at a rather seedy rundown hotel on the banks of the Canal St. Martin in Paris. Laura's scene was an un-credited performance on the hotel's stage as a backdrop for a scene that takes place in the bar area of the hotel. Laura is seen in a gray (which gives the illusion of red on-screen) velvet leotard and giant white burlesque fans. Laura is shot flourishing the fans in a seductive manner which says "I'm about to take off all my clothes now," as nothing else can say.

One memorable role that Laura had that involved more than just stripping was that of an aging prostitute in a Maurice Chevalier film noir. He played the part of a detective searching for a killer. In the process of tracking down a lead, he came across a clue that lead him to Laura's character. He had to interview her and later find her dead body, having been murdered by the antagonist for talking to the detective.

Laura had not seen Maurice for some time. He had enjoyed a highly successful career in Hollywood, returning to Paris in '37. On his return, he had headlined the revue "Paris en Joie" at the Casino de Paris. Laura had heard that he had separated from Yvonne after meeting and falling in love with another lovely, the dancer, Nita Raya. Before their scene together he came to Laura's dressing room to speak to her.

"Mon chérie," Maurice said to Laura, kissing her on both cheeks. "It is so good to see you after all these years. I have followed your career. You have done well. How has life treated you otherwise?"

"Wonderful, Maurice," answered Laura. "Françoise is so good to me. There are no other women in his life, no girlfriends, no mistresses. As you know, I have two adorable children by him. My eldest sons came through the war unharmed, in fact, both of my sons who were in the war were given medals by our government. I have money, clothes, and a place to lay my head at night. God has been good to me. And you? I know your career has skyrocketed, but how is your personal life treating you?"

"It is wonderful," replied Maurice. "I am in love, but then again, I am always in love with someone. I was in love with you, once. But, alas, but you left me for your husband. You broke my heart." How Maurice did exaggerate. The truth of the matter was that they had grown tired of each other after the novelty of the affair wore off. At least that was the way it was for her.

"Oh, Maurice, don't be ridiculous," she chided. "You didn't love me. You were in love with the idea of being in love. I was just a fling to you."

"No, Laura, you were not just a fling. You were my passion but I knew that I could never have your heart. You were a married lady and I was an interloper. After you ended our affair I was a completely broken man. But of course you read about it. It was in all of the papers. They did not know the real reason why I was so depressed. It was you. Had it not been for Yvonne I don't know if I could have gone on. That is why I went to the states when the opportunity presented itself; to find a place where my heart could heal without being reminded of you. But here, let's not talk of unpleasant things. Today we are both happy and in wonderful relationships, and here you are on the set of my movie. What are the chances of it happening in this lifetime that we have an opportunity to return to the friendships of our youth? Tell me, can I help you run your lines?"

"No," Laura replied, all business now. "Françoise has helped me with them and I had a rehearsal with the third director this morning. I'm prepared. We shoot my first scene with you this afternoon I'm told. We shoot the second scene tomorrow morning and the remaining scene and any retakes the day afterwards. That last scene, the one with me being dead, may be difficult for us to get in the can, I'm afraid. I don't know if I can hold perfectly still for a lot of retakes but I'll give it my best effort."

He took both her hands in his. "Wonderful. Then you're all set. If there is anything you require, anything at all, please remember to call on me." He kissed her on both cheeks and left.

Much to everyone's amazement, they got her final scene in one take and because all of Laura's scenes were accepted at the rushes each night, she did not have to do any retakes.

Maurice did not have many flops in his career, but that movie, which shall remain nameless, was one of the few. The reason this movie was not Laura's favorite is because of the role she played – an aging prostitute, without makeup, and with tousled hair. She was used to appearing onscreen in full make-up with impeccably coiffed locks. She said this role made her feel old. However, Laura got some great stills out of it for her scrapbook and it gave her something to talk about in her old age - the movie she was in with Maurice Chevalier.

Chapter 17. The Great Depression

The roaring '20's went skidding headlong into the 1930's and came to a crashing halt up against the great depression. The great depression that so devastated the United States with its collapse of financial institutions, high unemployment, coupled with crop failure, affected every country that did business with, or was any way connected to it. That included its ally and trading partner, France.

Although France was not as hard hit as the United States and Britain, the depression affected France almost the entire decade – from 1932 to 1939. In the middle of it all, tired of the same old approaches to social and economic ills, the French, on February 6, 1934 rioted at the Place de la Concorde near the French National Assembly. Since long before the fall of the monarchy and the establishment of the First Republic, Parisians were notorious for taking to the streets when government was not going their way.

This time, these protests from the street led to the fall of the fifth government of the Third Republic. Thirteen demonstrations had already taken place since January 9th. The right wing was trying to use the protest to cause the downfall of the government led by the left-wing majority elected during the 1932 elections.

The underlying themes of the protest were anti-Semitism (fear of or dislike of Jews and anything associated with Jews), xenophobia (dislike of all things foreign), what can be described as Freemason phobia (fear of having anyone in the higher echelons of Freemasonry associated with government), and a desire to end the parliamentarian form of government. In other words they were against everything that made France unique – a place for everyone.

While out for a walk that night, Laura and Françoise had completely forgotten about the recent protests. They turned onto the Place de la Concorde and ran headlong into the protestors. Their intent had been to walk to the fountains and back home with their dog Sophie, stopping for chocolat chaud on their way back.

They heard the shouting but were discussing an upcoming booking and were not paying attention. It was when Sophie started barking that they stopped talking and looked around them. They were between one of the two fountains located in the square. Françoise steered Laura towards the Fontaine des Mers, the south fountain, the one dedicated to the seas. This fountain, closer to the Seine, represented the seas with figures representing the Atlantic and the Mediterranean oceans; harvesting of coral and fish; collecting shellfish and pearls; and the sciences of astronomy, navigation and commerce. Many times they had walked to there and back, looking at its beauty yet never really seeing it. And now, here tonight, it might be the last thing they would ever see. Maybe it was fitting, seeing the square was the site where the infamous guillotine once stood that took the lives of so many, including a king, his queen, his sister, and a head of state. They probably could not believe it was happening also.

Above the noise that was the riot, Laura heard someone shout out, "He's a Jew. Kill the Jew bastard."

Françoise, yelled, "Run for the bridge." Laura dropped the dog's lease and ran toward the Pont de la Concorde, losing her shoes along the way. The police had set up barricades on the other side of the bridge to try to contain the rioting to public areas and away from the residential sector. Several police officers raced from the bridge to meet her. Several more ran past her to Françoise. Three men were kicking and stomping him. The policemen dragged them away from him. They helped Françoise to his feet and half-dragged, half-carried him over the bridge. Once at the safety of the bridge, behind the barricades, Laura and Françoise were safe. They were put into an ambulance together.

Françoise's face was beaten and already beginning to swell. His eyes were nearly swollen shut. He was breathing laboriously. Laura was shaking and crying, "Why did they do this? Why?" she sobbed.

One officer, one of the ones who had helped her to the bridge said to her, "That's the way of rioters, Madame. There is no rhyme or reason to their actions. An angry crowd will do collectively what each individual would never dream of doing alone. You and Monsieur are lucky. There are already reports of deaths from the riots. Monsieur is broken but he will heal. Tell me, what was it the man called out before your husband told you to run?"

She repeated what the man had said. How ironic, a non-practicing Jew who never attended synagogue and only donated to Jewish relief charities when someone remembered to put the bite on him, had been chosen to be attacked. Françoise did not live as a Jew. He did not act as a Jew. He did not worship as a Jew. But still he was hated and singled out because of his Jewish heritage. Laura thought to herself, "just like in the good old USofA".

Once the crowds were disbursed at about 2:30 in the morning, it was discovered that 16 people had been killed and over 2,000 had been injured – Françoise and Laura among that number. At the hospital, Françoise was thoroughly examined. Bruised and battered he had a broken nose, a broken collar bone, and two broken ribs. Laura only suffered cuts, scratches, and bruises. They never saw their dog Sophie again.

What this riot did to Françoise and Laura was to open their eyes to something they had not noticed before – the growing anti-Semitic and anti-American forces at work in France. That is when they both decided to get involved in the happenings of the day. They both had something very much at stake. From that night forward, both Françoise and Laura kept up with what was going on in the world around them and while they still enjoyed the fruits of their labors, they also began to give back to the world.

Françoise joined a group of Jewish men who had ties to the Eastern European countries. One night a man named Varian Fry came to speak to their group. He came and brought news of the plight of all Jews in Nazi-occupied territories. He explained that the same things would happen in France, and yes, even in Paris, when, not if, the Germans invaded and conquered the country, one town at a time. He was there to educate but also to collect funds to help those who had escaped with only the shirts on their backs, to reach countries where they could live and be free without worry of reprisals because of their religion or ethnicity.

The New Generation, mostly right-wing extremists, offered impractical solutions to very severe problems – free love and sex for all. That had been the prevailing attitude of Parisians through the '20's and now into the '30's. There was this lust for living, as if life were going to end soon and all of these acts had to be accomplished now and could not be postponed. Laura had been one of their number. Now with the prevailing attitudes in most European countries, Laura realized that they might have been right after all. As improbable as it may have seemed in the '20's, their way of living might soon be coming to an end.

But for now, life went on as it had in the '20's – carefree, gay, and with a lust for living that could not be understood unless you were there in the midst of it. Art, theater, and music exemplified this lust for life and Laura's burlesque act capitalized on that same lust. Her act never missed a scheduled performance and the house was always packed. They came to see others on the bill but mostly they came to see Laura. Even Josephine Baker and her show-stopping performances could not cut into Laura's loyal fan-base.

Laura was 50 years old and still going strong. She was still dropping her strap and stepping out of her tap pants behind a giant fan. Still completely disrobing hidden by the edge of the giant stage curtains. And the audiences loved it and loved her.

She had maintained her slim figure even after having six children. And even though she now used a blonde rinse to hide the gray strands that were beginning to creep into her hair, everyone who saw her remarked that if you did not know she was 50, then you would never know she was 50.

But there was sadness in Laura's life as well. For one thing, it was constantly on her mind that she had abandoned her boys, especially the two oldest ones. She returned to the states every two years or so to visit and saw the younger ones but she never saw her two oldest boys again until she was in her sixties when remarkably, they had finally looked up their family. Laura silently grieved over this misstep of hers all of her life. And now she was beginning to question her own reasons for her actions. More and more she thought about her career and the twists it had taken to wind up where it was. Had it been selfish to want more out of life that what she had in Louisiana? And was it more selfish still to put this desire above her children? Would it have been better if she had remained even though there had been no future and no hope in that place? Other people had done worse than what she had done. She wondered if they were plagued by these same guilty feelings.

Laura, never one to overthink anything very much, thought about what was happening in all of Europe and especially in France and in Paris. She saw things begin to change before her eyes. There was less tolerance for those foreign born and for those who were non-white. It barely affected her because of her fame, but she saw it happening to others around her – those not so famous.

Suddenly, they were let go of jobs they had held for years, with little pretense at hiding the racism.

They were denied apartments they had been hoping to move into. Apartments that had been advertised for rent were suddenly let. They were told "I let it this morning" or some similar such thinly veiled lie.

They were refused service at restaurants. It was not uncommon to see signs in restaurants that said "We don't serve Jews here."

At department stores they were "overlooked" and the clerks would wait on someone else.

Finally, with her head bursting with all the rumors and secrecy that was swirling around Paris, Laura lost one of her biggest supporters on July 3, 1935.

Andre-Gustave Citroën, known as the "King of Paris", had been her financial rock during the years when she and Françoise were producing their own shows and needed capital investments in order to stage these shows. Citroën died after undergoing surgery for a bleeding ulcer, developed after his financial empire collapsed earlier in the year. His death greatly affected Laura and that summer she decided that she needed a real vacation.

She asked Françoise to take her to the south of France. She wanted to get away; to think about things without the hurly-burly of everyday life. He agreed but business matters would not allow him to leave until August. Laura wanted to go before then – before the crowds descended upon the beaches. She invited Adrien and Marcella to join her on the road trip. They both agreed to go with her so she packed up her latest Duesenberg, a red 1932 SJ LA Phaeton, and headed to Nice. When a Ford could be had for less than $800, Françoise had $35,000 for the Duesie and to have it retooled to his specifications for Laura. She had loved all of her Duesenbergs but she particularly loved that one. Andre had chided her many times because she preferred the American over-blown automobile to his own French Citroën. He pretended to be mortally wounded by her passing over his auto but in reality it was his way of teasing her. He too, loved that car, and because it would have been unseemly to own one, he often invited Laura and Françoise to his country estate where he could be seen tooling around in the car at every opportunity he could invent.

The car, never called an "SJ" by the manufactures, was nearly eighteen feet long, sported a 420-cubic-inch inline-8 engine and was said to pull like a train. "Too much horsepower for a woman to drive", said one of her male friends who had driven the car. Able to garner an easy 112 miles per hour, its enormous steering wheel guided the wheels straight and true. However, it was thought that the car's vacuum-assisted drum brakes lacked sufficient braking power to stop the car from a high speed in an emergency. Laura was not a risk-taker so she was not a fast driver. Even though the car could have easily gotten to 80 with little effort, she had Adrien keep it under 60 the entire way.

Truth be told, the steering was more than a little stiff. After Laura complained about it on more than one occasion, Françoise had it looked at by the mechanic who took care of their cars. The mechanic said he could find nothing wrong. "That's just the way it drives. Maybe it's too much car for a woman," was his comment when he returned the car to Françoise. Françoise did not pass on the comment to Laura. He did not want to see the gentleman get beat up by a lady.

They were traveling from Monte Carlo to Nice on the Moyenne Corniche (Middle Coast Road - Highway 7) with Laura driving. She had just spelled Adrien who had driven all the way from Paris. He was planning on taking a quick nap in the back seat. Marcella, also in the back, had been reading quietly for most of the trip. The children's old nanny, Emily Gautier, who now served as a personal maid to Laura, was in the passenger seat in the front. The top was down and they were enjoying the warm sun on their bare skins. It was there on the winding road between Monaco and Nice that the big Duesie failed her. They had just gone through Eze-Village when the car left the road.

Georges Pellier, driving in a car behind the Duesenberg gave a statement to the police. "It seemed as if the car had a mind of its own. The driver tried to navigate a particularly sharp hairpin turn. It looked as if the car did not respond and it overshot the turn."

The big car plunged down an embankment and overturned. The two young people were thrown from the car. The driver was pinned behind the wheel. The passenger was killed instantly.

Laura was taken off to hospital with a broken leg and a head injury. Adrien and Marcella, although shaken and bruised, were otherwise uninjured. Françoise was summoned. When he was shown into the room with an unconscious Laura, tears streamed down his face. Bandages completely covered her head. In his heart Françoise thought that Laura would not pull through. She lay in a coma for four days. Gradually she began to stir. He had been standing by the window looking out when he heard a rustling sound.

Laura at long last opened her eyes and began to talk. She whispered his name, "Françoise."

He turned to see Laura trying to sit up in bed. "No, Chérie! Don't move. Lie still. Let me get the nurse."

"No, Françoise. I have to tell you something," her hoarse voice was barely a whisper.

He rushed to her side, "Oui, mon petite. What is it?"

"I'm hungry. Tell my mother. I want some pancakes." With that, she sank back onto the pillows and went back to sleep.

Françoise, frantically rang for the nurse. Two nurses hurried into the room. He relayed to them what had happened.

"Pancakes? What is this 'pancakes'?" asked the head nurse in French.

"They're like crepes only thicker," replied Françoise. "Her mother died many years ago. Pancakes was a favorite Sunday morning breakfast when she was a child."

The two nurses smiled. "That is a good sign," said the tall, thin one. That means she is starting to process her inner needs. She knows she is hungry. The next time she wakes up, she'll be awake for a longer period of time. We will feed her then. I will notify her doctor at once in case he wants to adjust her medicines."

And indeed, Laura did wake again, about two hours later. This time, Françoise was ready for her. He watched as her eyes fluttered open.

"Oh mon chéri," he said choking back his emotions. He took her hands in his.

"Françoise, where am I? What happened? Where are the children?"

"You were in an accident, my darling. The children are fine but Emily did not survive."

"Oh, my God. I remember," she moaned. She grasped the sheets. Emily was more than a servant to her, she was her friend. She could tell Emily anything and never have to worry about its being leaked to the press or in any way become part of society gossip.

"My leg!" She suddenly realized she was in traction.

"Oui, mon chérie. It is broken. They had to operate on it but luckily they did not have to remove it. It will heal eventually."

"Did I say something about pancakes?" she inquired.

Françoise laughed aloud. "Oui, my pet. You did. Do you want some? I can have some brought to you."

"Why, yes, I guess so. Is that allowed?"

"I don't know, but I'll get you some pancakes. Shall I go now?"

"No, first, tell me where the children are."

"They're at the hotel resting comfortably. They're worried about you, of course. I'll bring them to see you when the doctor says you can have visitors. I didn't see any need for them to wait around the hospital hallways when they themselves need to rest to recover from their own injuries."

By this time, the nurse, who Françoise had summoned as soon as Laura had stirred, was coming into the room with a cart. On it were towels and other grooming aids.

"Let me freshen Madame Goldman now, monsieur."

"She says she wants pancakes," his voice trailed off.

"Pancakes?" asked the nurse in a puzzled tone.

"Crêpes," replied Françoise. The nurse still appeared puzzled. "Fritella," he said in Italian.

"Oh, oui, monsieur. I remember now. She is American. They have such strange foods there I am told." Getting back to the subject at hand she said, "Your wife is not on any dietary restrictions, monsieur. There's a restaurant in the next block. They might cook some for her if you want to walk down there."

"Oui. Oui. I shall return shortly." He gathered his hat and left the room on a fool's errand.

When he returned, the doctor was with Laura. After his examination, he spoke to Françoise outside in the hallway.

"It looks as if she's turned the corner, Monsieur. Now, it is just a matter of time until she regains her strength and her leg heals. I don't think there will be any problem with her walking. But I understand that she is a dancer. She might never dance professionally again. For that we'll have to wait and see."

"Merci, Monsieur Doctor. Merci. She asked for pancakes. Crêpes. Is that okay?"

The doctor chuckled. "Oui. She can have whatever she likes. She asked to see her children. You may bring them in for a few minutes this evening. She'll rest quietly once she knows they're all right. The police will want to talk with her of course about the accident – what caused it. I'll notify them that they can talk with her tomorrow."

Françoise entered the patient's room. "I have your pancakes, my dear. I'm afraid they might be cold but here they are."

Along with three pancakes, he had brought an omelet and bacon. She ate the whole thing, then settled down in the bed and fell asleep.

The next day when the police interviewed her about the accident, Laura told them about the stiff handling of the car. Françoise verified her account that they had the car looked at and the mechanic had confirmed the car handled stiffly but had assured them it was safe for driving.

The police fined her for reckless driving anyway, but they did not charge her with manslaughter as they could have done. Her license to drive was suspended for one year. She had to pay restitution of 100,000 francs to the family of Emily Gautier. Laura sent them that and more each year. She could never make up to them the loss of their loved one but she could ease the financial burden that being without her income produced for them.

Laura was a rapid healer. She was in the hospital in Nice for six weeks. At the end of that time she was released to go home. Her broken leg had healed but as the doctor predicted, her dancing days were over.

Laura and Françoise met with their financial advisor. With frugal living, they would be able to survive for a year or more without Laura having to return to work and without them dipping into their savings or having to sell any stocks or bonds. They also had some real estate holdings and those were safe as well.

Françoise sent letters of apologies to all of the theater owners and booking agents who were responsible for the various venues she was booked into for the upcoming months and rescheduled all of Laura's upcoming tours. Most were reasonable and agreed to reschedule. Two threatened to sue her. One vowed at the top of his lungs that she would never work again.

Although they needed the income from the apartments on the lower floor of their house, Françoise converted one of the apartments into a rehearsal hall. To Laura's amazement when she finally got into the rehearsal hall, her voice was clear and steady. She would be able to continue with her career, slightly altered, but it would survive. She began readying a new show with all new songs.

Françoise hired a dance master and miraculously he was able to teach Laura some "fake" steps that she would be able to use to hide her inability to perform even the simplest shuffle-ball-change anymore. It was all he could do to get her to prance without limping. On the day she was finally able to do this, they all celebrated by opening a bottle of Moet & Chandon, her favorite champagne. The dance master maintained that with enough beautiful young people cavorting around the stage in various stages of undress, no one would be looking at her footwork anyway.

Laura gave herself a year to recover. What this year did for her was two-fold. First, it gave her body a chance to recover from the physical damage caused by the accident. Second, and most importantly, it let her come to realize that she could survive in show business without stripping. At the end of her yearlong "rest", Laura came back stronger than ever. Françoise got her booked for one year straight with no gaps in her schedule, except for the two weeks that he always gave her between engagements, and not one of the theaters was a burlesque house.

Laura opened to rave revues close to home – at le Théâtre des Champs-Élysées. Her act lasted 45 minutes with one costume change. Laura had made a trunk call to Marcelle who was now out in Hollywood and implored her to design just one more complete set of costumes for her. Marcelle was under contract to one of the movie studios. She went all the way to the head of the studio to get permission to design the costumes. Because she was required to turn over her fee for the design project, she deliberately undercharged Laura.

Marcelle more than out-did herself with the costumes. At Laura's request, Marcelle reprieved a previous gown of Laura's that she had designed. It was the gold one with the high neck with the slinky body that flared at the hips to yards of swirly filmy fabric. Laura had worn that dress until it had begun to shred in her hands. Now she had a new one just like it.

The only fans anywhere near Laura's body was on her hairpiece, a real show stopper. Marcelle called it a "fascinator" and it was just that - fascinating. Fitted close to the head with a gold comb trimmed in rhinestones holding it in place, it ended in a fan flourish. No other hat during the century was so talked about than that fascinator of Laura's.

Laura was ready to take to the stage again. On her opening night at le Théâtre des Champs-Élysées, Laura sang, she strutted her stuff, she did a few fake dance steps. She pranced, both with a dance partner, and without. She talked to her audience, telling them how much she loved them, and they in turn showed her how much they loved her by giving her standing ovation after standing ovation.

She sang "Smoke Gets in Your Eyes", a show tune written by American composer Jerome Kern and lyricist Otto Harbach for the 1933 musical, *Roberta*. She also sang "Cocktails for Two" written by Arthur Johnston and Sam Coslow and made popular in the states by Duke Ellington, only she sang it very slowly, with much emotion. Her repertoire included a French song, "Parlez-Moi D'amour" (Speak to Me of Love) by Jean Lenoir. She sang it in both French and English. That one brought the audience to its feet. She rounded out the show with "I Only Have Eyes For You" by composer Harry Warren and lyricist Al Dubin, from the movie *Dames*.

All in all, it was a show to remember. Her dressing room was full of flowers before the performance and full of congratulatory telegrams and friends afterwards. The press were in the hallway outside clamoring to get in for an interview. The ruckus was so loud backstage that the stage manager had to come back and threaten to put everyone out if they did not tone it down.

Françoise proposed a toast, "To my dear, wonderful, sweet Laura who has just made a fabulous successful comeback from a horrific accident. To you." He raised his glass high.

"To Emily," was her reply.

"Santé" he said as he touched his glass to hers.

Everyone drank to their combined toast.

They waited up for the morning papers to get the first press notices. The papers were full of rave reviews. There was not a negative comment in any of them. One reporter did say that he kept expecting her to drop her strap or break out a fan at any minute but the overall tone of his article was complimentary and talked about her choice of music and the strength of her voice – her range and the solidity of her notes.

Laura was too excited to sleep. "Come", she said to Françoise. "End my wonderful day on a perfect note. Put me to sleep. Make love to me." He obliged her.

Chapter 18. The Winds of War

In September of 1939 Germany invaded Poland and annexed the Free City of Danzig. The British demanded an immediate withdrawal. On the 3rd of September, British Prime Minister Neville Chamberlain announced on BBC Radio that the deadline for the British ultimatum for the withdrawal of German troops from Poland had expired and "consequently this nation is at war with Germany". The same day the French Government also declared war on Germany. Within hours of the British declaration, the Germans torpedoed a British cruise ship, the *SS Athenia*. The Battle of the Atlantic had begun.

When war was declared, General Maurice Gamelin was commander-in-chief of France's military. France saw little action during the "Phoney War", so dubbed because although both Britain and France had declared war, neither had committed to launching a significant offensive save for a few French divisions crossing the German border. These forces only travelled about five to eight miles into the German interior. They did not even penetrate Germany's unfinished Siegfried Line, a defensive line stretching for more than 390 miles into the interior of Germany along its French border. The Siegfried Line had more than 18,000 bunkers, tunnels, and tank traps. It was built opposite to and to counter the

French's Maginot Line which was a line of fortifications facing Germany from the Swiss to the Belgian borders.

The French were hampered by outdated methods from World War I. These methods relied heavily on stationary artillery which took time to transport and deploy. In addition, the French were further hampered by older ordnance, some retrieved from storage after having been put there after the Great War. However, at this point in the war, France had more and better tanks than the Germans but chose to disperse them rather than to concentrate them on the areas where they could have been most effective. Because the Germans were occupied with their offensive against Poland, if France had attacked in September, the German forces could not have held out for more than one or two weeks.

Instead General Gamelin wanted to wait until France's military strength was fully built up, even if it meant waiting until the following year to attack. The General ordered a halt to the French advance into Germany and would not allow French aircraft to bomb the industrial areas of the Ruhr in order to not provoke the Germans into retaliating. The French retreated back to France behind the Maginot line and awaited the German invasion. Germany invaded the Netherlands, Belgium, and Luxembourg, all countries that had declared themselves to be neutral. Then Germany attacked France using a three-prong approach they called "Blitzkrieg", utilizing air, tanks, and the infantry.

Laura's youngest son Adrien had tried teaching when he had graduated university but soon found that he did not like children, not enough to teach them, that is. He had been a history major, focusing on French history, especially the military and its part in shaping the country into what it was in the late '30's, and that is what he loved to read about. He turned his hand to writing and he proved to be an extraordinarily gifted writer, earning his living writing for an historical publication and freelancing while working on what he called a "great historical work on French history". Françoise called it loafing. Adrien earned enough to keep body and soul together, having enough left over to be seen frequently squiring around some of the loveliest girls in Paris. He shied away from showgirls, saying their free time did not mesh with his but in reality he had seen first hand what a chaotic, up and down life show business could be and he wanted no parts of it.

When war broke out, like many loyal French citizens, Adrien enlisted. He was sent to officer training camp and came out a commissioned Lieutenant. It was because of his writing and teaching skills that he was selected to be on his commanding general's staff. As the fighting became more fierce and it looked as if France was going to be overrun, all able-bodied men were assigned to the front lines. Adrien was no exception.

More than half of France's 800,000 troops, including Adrien, manned the Maginot Line. But the Germans totally bypassed the Maginot Line, and attacked the French flanks by advancing against France through the Ardennes Forest, a marginally protected portion of the border. The French had considered this route to be impassable to tanks and by doing so underestimated the Germans' ability to breach the wall of armed enforcements there. This breach in the lines widened rapidly, allowing German tanks through. The Germans crossed the River Oise on May 17, 1940 and reached Abbeville near the coast on the 20th.

The British, French, and Belgium troops were cut off by the German army during the battle of Dunkirk, and were trapped between the enemy and the sea. Inexplicably there was a pause in the fighting by the Germans, which gave the Allies enough time to plan an evacuation of around 340,000 troops from Dunkirk and another 220,000 from other French ports. Amid heavy enemy aircraft fire the dramatic rescue of these troops took place between May 27 and June 4, 1940. The evacuation across the channel was code-named Operation Dynamo. It was commonly known as the Miracle of Dunkirk.

In all, over one half million soldiers, British, French, and other allied forces, were rescued by a hastily assembled fleet of 850 boats which included 42 British destroyers and other large ships, and more than 800 merchant marine boats, private yachts, fishing boats, pleasure crafts, and plain ole lifeboats. Some of the evacuees waited for hours in chest deep waters waiting to be picked up by the rescuers.

The initial evacuation estimate was 30,000 British troops, to be carried out over two days' time. Only about 7,000 were evacuated that first day, May 26, with an additional 18,000 the following day. On the 29th, under heavy aerial attack by the German air force, 47,000 additional British troops were rescued. The following day another 54,000 men were picked up from the beaches and offshore, including the first of the French troops. On May 31st the commander of the British troops, Lord Gort, was among the last of the British to go. An additional 64,000 soldiers of other Allied nations were picked up on June 1st with the British rearguard leaving the night of June 2nd along with 60,000 French troops. The operation ended when the last of the French troops to be rescued, 26,000, left on June 3rd.

Holding off seven divisions of the German army, 40,000 French soldiers remained behind in a delaying tactic to give the larger force an opportunity to escape. These men were either killed in action, taken prisoner, or deliberately machined gunned by the Germans as being too numerous to guard, house, and feed during the remainder of the war.

Beginning on May 9th, the Germans bombed several major French cities. Paris was bombed by the Germans for almost two weeks in June of 1940. However, as the Germans advanced, Paris was declared an open city by the French. That meant that the French Army would not occupy or defend the city. The city was thus spared the destruction that many other French cities suffered.

Chapter 19. The Flight from Paris

Before Paris was declared an open city, five hundred German planes bombed Paris in three waves. Air force bases, train stations, and factories, particularly in the 15th arrondissement, were targeted. Over 850 people were killed and injured.

These bombing raids panicked the population and there was a wholesale exodus out of the city, clogging the railroads and the roads and hampering the military from moving troops into position. In all between eight and ten million people fled before the Germans toward the south of France.

Marcella, who had been living in an apartment on the left bank, moved back home into her old room. Except for going to work, she kept close to home. Laura, believing that "the show must go on," went to the theater each evening and put on her show to almost empty houses. Looting and stickups were commonplace and there was little the police could do to stop it. Françoise accompanied Laura to the theater each night with a pistol in each pocket. They always took his Alfa Romero which was less conspicuous than the Duesenberg.

Like so many others, the Goldman family had procrastinated about leaving France. They were in disbelief that Paris would fall into the hands of the

Germans. It wasn't until the bombing started that reality sat in. They were unprepared financially to flee the country.

While at one time Laura and Françoise made a lot of money, their lifestyle used up their funds almost as fast as they could earn them. It wasn't that they were broke, they just weren't liquid. What they had was tied up in stocks and bonds which were now worthless as stocks were no longer being traded in France. They also owned choice pieces of commercial real estate, including several apartment buildings, which although not worthless, was a drag on the pocketbook with so many Parisians off in the war or in the provinces hoping to escape the Germans. To make matters worse, the French banks had frozen all foreign transfers and the government limited the amount of funds that could be withdrawn from an account at any one time. French francs were almost worthless except in France.

Laura went to her good friend Josephine Baker and asked for assistance. Laura knew that Josephine did not trust banks, any of them, and kept large sums of US dollars hidden in her apartment and her estate house in the country. Josephine knew that Françoise was Jewish and that put him and Marcella at risk should they be captured by the Germans. Josephine went into her giant walk-in closet and came back and handed Laura $10,000 in US currency. This would have to buy transportation for the three refugees back to the states and tide them over until they could find work. The two women kissed each other on the cheeks and parted company, maybe for the last time.

After talking with friends in the resistance, Françoise concluded that the safest route was to travel overland to Lisbon. They could leave the car in the port city, to be called for later by friends. From there they would take the clipper to America. Laura and Françoise debated about taking the Duesenberg, it being large enough to convey the three of them and all of their luggage. Also, it would have afforded them transportation around Lisbon while they arranged for their transport out of the country. Françoise decided that the car was too conspicuous and would only draw attention to them.

The owner of the house previous to Françoise did not keep horses, choosing instead to hire a coach when he needed one. The stable became used as a shed where all manner of household castoffs from tenants were stored. When Françoise acquired his first automobile he had the stable cleaned out and he parked his car there. After Laura came to live with him she objected to having to go into the tumbledown stable to put her car away. Françoise had the stable pulled down and erected a modern up-to-date garage instead. It was there that he parked Laura's latest Duesenberg, put it up on blocks, took off its tires, and covered it with a tarp.

The Alfa Romero that he drove was too small to hold all three of them and their luggage, so he sold it and with the proceeds bought an inconspicuous three year old black Renault Celtaquatre four door sedan. In it he piled his wife and daughter and their luggage. They packed all of the clothes they were not taking with them and Laura's costumes into trunks and stored them in the basement of their house. They packed up the entire household furnishings and with the help of their tenants and servants, moved them to the basement, also. Their tenants and servants then decamped by train to Lyon .

The Germans were 75 miles from Paris, approximately four days away. The Goldmans packed only what they truly needed to take with them. Françoise and Marcella had two suitcases each. Laura had five. Early on the morning of June 9th, joining other terrified Parisians, only days ahead of the Germans, the Goldmans locked up their house and left for the Portuguese coastal city. They drove away not knowing if they would ever see Paris, their house, or any of their possessions ever again.

Lisbon was three days away if they could make good time. Françoise was very concerned that there would be a shortage of petrol along the way. He was planning on driving straight through without stopping for the night if he could get Laura and Marcella to spell him at the wheel. The roads were severely crowded with every type of conveyance imaginable – cars, trucks, carts, bicycles, and of course people on foot. The trio was ever vigilant whenever they stopped for food or fuel to keep their eyes and ears open lest they be robbed for their money or transportation. There were many attempts to flag them down, but driving with a pistol on the seat between him and Laura, Françoise kept the car moving.

They were stopped three times by the French police. First, near Bordeaux, and again just a short distance away at Pessac, and once more as they were nearing the Spanish border, near Bayonne. This last time they were ordered out of the car and their papers were examined closely, checking to see if they could possibly be forged. They weren't, having been signed by the mayor of Paris who Laura and Françoise knew personally. They were ordered to completely unload the car. All of their luggage was searched. Laura had most of their money pinned to the inside of her undergarments. It would never do to be caught with American currency on them. All they had was a few thousand francs in Françoise's wallet, and the ladies had about the same amount each - just enough to prove that they could buy food and petrol and book passage out of Portugal. After being detained on the side of the road for about two hours, they were finally told they could go.

They crossed into Spain at Irun in the dead of night. There they stopped for the night at a small inn. They had a cold dinner of roast chicken, bread, cheese, and wine. The innkeeper would not take their francs but did accept their US dollars. The next morning, Françoise went to an exchange outlet and exchanged some of their dollars for pesetas and escudos.

After filling up their tank with petrol, they resumed their journey. On the one hand, crossing Spain was much easier than they had anticipated since they had valid passports and transit papers. Françoise and Marcella both spoke flawless Castillan so they had no trouble communicating their needs to merchants along the way. There was less traffic on the road, a great number of people having been turned back at the Spanish border. On the other hand, it was harder because there were fewer petrol stations and inns where they could purchase a meal.

They crossed into Portugal between Fuentes de Oñoro, Spain and Vilar Formosa, Portugal. Fuentes de Oñoro is a small village in the province of Salamanca in Western Spain while Vilar Formosa is one of the most important border crossing towns in Portugal.

They stopped for the night right across the Portuguese border. The town was so small that they found no inns - only small private residences. Françoise had been given the name of a man in the town by associates of Varian Fry who Françoise had meet in his activism work. He was told he could call on this contact if need be for a meal or lodging for the night. Not allowed to write down the name or address of the contact, he had to memorize it. Easing the Renault slowly through the narrow streets, they finally came to the house of this person, who after only a few exchanged words, agreed to put them up for the night. He had them park their car in the barn, facing outward. Laura later learned the man and his family were resistance fighters from one of the Low Countries who had fled before the Germans.

Françoise woke Laura and Marcella before daybreak the following morning. The good Samaritan's wife had prepared an egg apiece for them for breakfast. As they were leaving, the woman handed Laura a sack with bread and cheese in it. Françoise tried to give the man some money but he refused it. The egg, bread and cheese was all they had to eat until they finally found a small roadside restaurant about ten o'clock that morning.

After what seemed like a week, but was only three days, they finally arrived in Lisbon, tired, disheveled, and each of them very much feeling as if they needed a long soak in a hot tub.

Lisbon, nicknamed A Cidade das Sete Colinas (The City of Seven Hills), was the only city in Europe where the allies and axis powers operated openly. It had refugees, people with letters of transit, and people desperately trying to get letters of transit to get to cities that were not in the hands of the Nazis – preferably cities in the United States, Canada, or neutral countries. It was the last chance to get out for those who would surely go to the death camps or ovens if the Germans captured them. The Goldmans was one such family. Thankfully their letters of transit were already arranged for by a friend of a friend of a friend – for a price of course.

Lisbon was divided into six districts - Baixa (downtown); Bairro Alto and Chiado (the cultural and bohemian centers with night clubs, shopping and restaurants); Belém (with its museums and monuments); Parque das Nações; Uptown; and Alfama. They headed to the Baixa where they had been told they could get a room until they could fly out.

Parks and gardens, shimmering white buildings, and red-tiled roofs greeted the refugees from Paris. They passed a gothic cathedral, a magnificent monastery, an imposing castle, a palace or maybe two, museums, and monuments. As they drove down tree-lined elegant boulevards through the city to where they were going to spend the next few days, their minds were on the city they had left behind.

Laura, Françoise, and Marcella, coming from a blacked-out Paris, were fascinated by the lights that were left on in the city at night. Except for issuing letters of transit to refugees, who were not allowed to linger in the city, Lisbon lived as if the war did not exist at all. There wasn't even food rationing. The travelers had been told that you could have all the butter you wanted on your morning croissant.

There were other stories, as well, whether true or not, of the Nazis kidnapping people of interest, especially Jews. For the first forty-eight hours the Goldmans were there, except for meals and going to the airline office to purchase their tickets, they stayed in their rooms. On the third afternoon, the day before they were supposed to leave, there was a commanding knock on the door.

Françoise opened the door to find four men standing there. Two of the men entered the room without being invited in. The other two stood in the doorway.

"Who are you and what do you want?" Françoise demanded to know.

The one who seemed to be in charge was ugly with a pugged nose. He said, "We ask the questions. We are the official police." He showed Françoise a badge. "Show us your papers," he demanded.

Françoise went to the dresser and picked up a portfolio, fingered in it, and produced some papers. He also extracted the three passports. He handed them all to the man who had spoken. To get to Portugal, they had to have exit visas from France, transit visas for Spain, and a Portuguese entry visa. They had them all. In addition, they had to have proof of booked passage on a plane or boat. They had that also. Françoise showed them Laura and Marcella's ticket but he did not show them his ticket.

As the ugly man with the pugged nose looked through the papers he said to Françoise in French, "Goldman. That is Jewish, no?"

This is where Françoise told his first lie of the trip. He answered the man in French also. "No. We are not Jewish. My wife and daughter are of the Episcopalian faith. I do not attend any church or congregation."

"Who are you and what are you doing in Lisbon?"

"My wife is an American entertainer and I am her manager. I brought her and my daughter to catch the Pan Am Clipper."

"Why is it necessary for her to return to America?"

"My wife's mother is dying and wants to see her one last time."

"Where does her mother live?"

"In a state called Louisiana."

"I have heard of it," said the pug-nosed man. After some time he continued his interrogation of Françoise. "How did you pay for your tickets?" he asked.

"Knowing that my wife's mother was ill, and fearing she might take a turn for the worse, I thought she might have to leave France in a hurry to be by her side. So weeks ago, I exchanged some francs for other currencies, some of it escudos. It was this money that I used to buy tickets."

The man with the pugged nose looked Françoise dead in the eye. Françoise could not tell if he was believed or not. Suddenly the man changed the subject.

"Does your wife hold French citizenship?"

"No. She has never renounced her American citizenship."

"I see," the man said as if he were rolling that fact around in his brain. "Does your daughter hold dual citizenship?"

"Yes. She has never renounced either her French or American citizenship." The man was silent for a few moments as he continued to look over their papers, examining each carefully.

Finally he spoke, "You and your daughter are forbidden to leave. You must come to the office of the Policia de Desgurança Pública tomorrow morning. We must investigate your reasons for going. If you do not remain where you are voluntarily, you will be imprisoned while the investigation takes place."

"How long will this investigation take?" asked Françoise.

The pugged nosed man shrugged his shoulders as he turned his palms upward. "This could take months, perhaps years. Because your wife is an American citizen, she is free to go as she pleases."

"But my wife and daughter leave together tomorrow on the 11AM plane to New York," protested Françoise.

"No, senhor. Your daughter will remain. She is a French citizen. She must obtain the proper permit to leave." The pug-nosed man was adamant.

Françoise knew it would be disastrous to argue with them. "As you wish. What time shall we be there?" was all that he replied.

"By 9 o'clock."

"Very well. We will be there."

Much to Françoise's surprise, the ugly man returned the letters of transit, the passports, and the tickets.

As soon as they left, Françoise's hand started shaking and would not stop. Laura stepped over to the dresser, opened the top drawer, and took out a bottle of Courvoisier. She poured two fingers into a water glass and handed it to Françoise. He downed the drink in several gulps, miraculously not spilling any of it.

As soon as he had calmed down sufficiently, Françoise slipped out of the door and down the backstairs of the hotel. When he returned two hours later he had three new letters of transit, properly signed and stamped. They had cost him $100 US each.

At 7:00 AM the next morning, after showing their letters of transit and their passports, they exchanged their tickets to New York for tickets to Havana, Cuba. They would fly from there to New York City. None of them breathed a sigh of relief until they were out over the ocean.

Chapter 20. The War Rages

When they landed, Françoise was detained because he did not have a visa to enter the United States. Laura and Marcella, because they were American citizens with valid passports, were allowed to go on their way. They went to Françoise's relatives. Through his activist work Françoise had heard about the US's non-involvement in saving the Jews from their fate at the hand of the Nazis. He knew not to make it known that he was Jewish. Instead he applied for a visa based on his wife's natural citizenship status. Ten days later he was released with a temporary work permit. Laura and his relatives greeted him as he came out of the detention center.

June, 1940 was a particularly devastating month for the French and anyone who were Francophiles:

On June 3, the Germans bombed Paris.

On June 11, the government officials left in Paris moved to Tours.

On June 13, the Germans entered Paris. What was left of the French government moved to Bordeaux.

On June 16, after increased pressure to come to a separate peace with Germany, and believing that his ministers no longer supported him, Paul Reynaud and his government resigned. Philippe Pétain was appointed Premier of France by President Lebrun, thus ending the Third Republic. Pétain was 84 years old.

On June 18, in Great Britain, General de Gaulle formed the Comité Français de la Liberation Nationale.

On June 21, the tattered French government began negotiations with the Germans at Compiègne.

On June 22, the Franco-German armistice was signed.

On June 25, France officially surrendered to Germany at 1:35 PM French time and a collaborationist government, the French State, was established.

Laura and Françoise, at Françoise's relatives in New York, wept in each other's arms at the news. They knew then they would never be able to return to their beloved Paris. New York was now their new home.

A month went by without a word from Adrien. His family, knowing that he had been at Dunkirk, did not know if he had been killed or captured. They wrote letters to his military unit, but not knowing what had happened to his unit, they were not sure that anyone had received their pleas for information about their son and brother. Finally, they got a letter from him. Much to their relief he wrote that he had been part of the forces evacuated across the channel from Dunkirk to Britain.

Adrien had written to his family to tell them of his safe rescue by the British immediately after he landed in Britain but because the family had fled first to Lisbon and then to New York, they did not get his letters. When his letters to them went unanswered, he had written to Randolph. Randolph had written back to Adrien and had given him the address where their parents were staying in New York. It had taken Adrien a month to track his parents down and send them word that he was safe. For the time being. More than that he was prohibited from saying.

The day Laura and Françoise received Adrien's letter was the first good night's sleep Laura had gotten since her youngest son went off to war. Four years later when word broke in the papers and on the radio of the invasion of France by the Allied forces, her sleeplessness returned. Had she known that he had been assigned to the staff of General de Gaulle, she might have rested more easily.

In Britain, after France fell to the Germans, the general had set about putting together a staff to support the new Free French Coalition. Adrien had been recommended because of his superior understanding of French military history and his ability to explain it so that it made sense to even the least educated reader. The Free French High Command set him to writing propaganda literature. He was the author of leaflets that were dropped by Allied troops over the French countryside in the dead of night, encouraging the French people to hold on and be strong, that not all hope was lost.

Laura did not know until the year following the end of the war how close she came to loosing Adrien. His unit was first ordered to remain behind as part of the French rearguard, then at the last minute they were ordered to march to the beaches. When they were ordered into the water there was not a ship in sight. They thought their high command had gone berserk. Soon on the horizon they saw the flotilla coming to rescue them. If Adrien had been left behind, because of his Jewish ancestry, if he had not been machine gunned immediately, he would surely have been sent to the ovens as part of "The Final Solution."

After joining de Gaulle's staff, Adrien never faced combat again. But his mother who worried about him, as did the mothers of all soldiers, did not know this.

Chapter 21. New York

Françoise had been assured by relatives of his in New York that he could come to work for them in their theaters. However, he would no longer be a showman. He would be a mere stage hand. This wounded his pride but he was willing to sacrifice anything to provide for his wife and daughter.

Françoise went to work for a cousin who was a backer of several shows on Broadway, not off-off-Broadway mind you, or even off-Broadway, but Broadway itself. This cousin got him a job as a stage hand for a variety show. Françoise worked twelve hour days and was thankful for them.

After Josephine Baker's disastrous engagement in New York a few years previously, Laura did not hold out any hopes of success in the theater on that front. The popularity of Vaudeville in particular, and variety acts in general had waned. Her prospects of getting onstage in New York were bleak indeed. *Cabin in the Sky*, a musical about Negros was set to open in October of that year, but their cast was set and they were already in rehearsals. There were quite a few revues in production but none that needed an aging Negro diva from France. Oh, why wasn't there another Florenz Ziegfeld or a George M. Cohen with a hit musical that needed a singing Negro maid, much as the movies did in *Saratoga*? Who could forget Hattie McDaniel singing "The Horse with the Dreamy Eyes"? That was what was needed. A role for a Negro singing maid character with spunk. But there was only one Hattie McDaniels in show business. Any Negro character actor who got out of line, whether onscreen or off, soon found themselves out of work and so out of show business.

Laura was sixty years old. She was in the autumn of her years. She did not have the body or stamina to recapture her fame, plus the climate of the states would not allow her that opportunity. The only roles offered to her were one liner maids' roles and one theater manager had the nerve to suggest that she would also have to assist in the upkeep of the star's wardrobe. She reasoned that since she had to help with wardrobe she might as well be a wardrobe mistress. To be fair, she was offered dates in jazz joints around New York City working for tips only and a tour of what Negro entertainers referred to as "The Chittlin' Circuit." Françoise declined on her behalf without even telling her about these offers. He got her a job as a wardrobe mistress at the theater where he worked. At least they were together.

Everyone knew Françoise was Jewish. These days he was proud to proclaim it to anyone who cared to ask. The cast and crew knew he and Laura were married. But very few knew she was Negro. She remembered the day distinctly when the word spread that she was not one of them. How they found out she would never know. What she did know was that a certain distance came between her and the other backstage workers. It was so thick you could cut it with a knife. "Oh. They've finally figured out I'm colored," she thought to herself. Except, for the distance, since Laura kept mostly to herself anyway, nothing much changed. Laura kept waiting for the other shoe to fall, when they would fire her, but it never did. She was one of the family now.

Finding an apartment that would accept mixed race couples was not easy but they finally found one within walking distance of the theater district. Fairly new, it was owned by a Jewish friend of one of Françoise's relatives. After moving in, it occurred to Laura that she had not seen any Negroes, except for maids, in the apartment building. It looked like she was the first to integrate it. She was so light-skinned and looked so white that it was a hollow victory. They had no problem with letting someone who looked like them move in.

Racism still abounded in the United States but strangely enough no one paid Françoise and Laura any attention. They came and went in their apartment building unaccosted. Maybe it was because of their age. Maybe it was the fact the he was Jewish, and she was high yellow. Maybe it was because people had bigger things to worry about, like whether or not their sons, brothers, and husbands were going to be drafted into the army to fight what most Americans thought of as a European war. Whatever it was, Laura and Françoise were never harassed on the street and racial slurs were not hurled at them the way they would have been just a few years earlier.

Dealing with the hair issue was a little harder, believe it or not, than the employment and living issues in a racist society. It was impossible for Laura to find someone south of Harlem to do her hair for her. She had been seeing professional hairdressers for forty years. Oh, sure she could wash her hair herself but styling it was a different matter. She was not adept at doing that. Her hair was long and thick and doing it was an all-day affair that she was tired of having to having to contend with on a weekly basis. It required lotions, rollers, and a hair dryer with hot air that she did not possess, so she had to let it air dry. Most of the time that meant that anytime she washed her hair she went to bed with a wet head. She set about finding someone who would do her hair for her who was not north of 110th Street.

Again Françoise's relatives came to the rescue. Sadie, the wife of one of his cousins, told Laura about what was probably the only beauty shop in midtown that catered to black women. Sadie said most of the maids in midtown probably went there. The place was called the Midtown House of Style.

Laura had mixed feelings. Her hair was not kinky in texture but it was not like white hair either. She had had several bad experiences in Paris until she had finally found a salon that could work with it without using caustic lyes, hot combs, or marcel irons. Le Salon de Coiffure et Ongles, or as all the patrons called it just

Le Salon, had always kept her looking bandbox fresh. But she had no choice unless she wanted to keep trekking up to Harlem, so she took a chance.

The beautician who she had the appointment with was named Eloise. Laura was greeted warmly enough on her first visit.

"Hello, ma'am. My name is Eloise, and I'm going to be your beautician today. Mr. Rick, our salon owner says that we wuz recommended to you by Polly who works for Miz. Feinstein. She's a very good customer of ours. Do you work for Miz. Feinstein too?"

"No. My husband is her cousin," replied Laura. She was beginning to regret her decision to come here.

"Why, you don't say!" said Eloise. "Imagine that. You speak with a slight accent. You not from here are you? Polly says Miz. Feinstein has relatives from France. Is that where you from?"

"Yes. I'm from Paris. But I'm originally from the states. I've been living in Paris for some time."

"Oh, you're one of the ones who escaped! Polly told us about you. She said the Nazis were hot on your heels."

"Yes, we were just days ahead of them." Laura was quiet. She hoped this woman was not going to talk her to death.

"Oh, that's just lovely, ma'am. Well I sure am glad to make your 'quaintance. I'm from the here myself - Harlem. I've never been nowhere outside of New York except for Jersey. Is your husband in show business like Miz. Feinstein's? Some people those show people."

"Why yes, my husband is working on a show right now. We've both been in show business for many years."

"Why, you don't say. Say, ma'am, you sure do have a different grade of hair. Do you want me to trim the edges for you today? There aint any real need, you don't have nary a split end, if I do say."

"No, I don't think you need to trim it. I like to keep it long."

"Yes, ma'am. Do you go to the beauty shop much?" asked the girl, fingering in Laura's hair.

"Well, I did in Paris, but not since I've been here. I've been having to do it myself a lot. And not a very good job of it probably."

Eloise shampooed Laura's hair and with expert fingers massaged Laura's scalp. By the time she had finished with rolling Laura's hair and getting her ready for the dryer, she had stopped chattering.

Quietly Eloise said, "Ma'am, have I heard of you before? Are you famous or some'en?" she asked.

"In Europe, yes, but not here in the United States." Now she's going to ask me all about show business said Laura to herself.

"I thought so," said the beautician. Your hair's been looked after in a way I don't see of'en. I'll take good care of you tho'. You can count on me." Eloise grew quiet again.

Later, after she had taken Laura from under the dryer, when she was taking the rollers out, again very quietly Eloise said. "I think I've heard of you. You're Laura Boult. My finance said he saw your burlesque show in Paris a couple of years ago. He said you're real famous over there. Why ain't you performing here?"

"Things are different here, Eloise," explained Laura. "I'm working on a show but not performing."

"Imagine that. Me working on the head of a famous person." Laura did not say anything else and thankfully the beautician let it drop.

Once a week Laura had a standing appointment with Eloise of Midtown House of Style. The salon had a manicurist on staff so Laura's two main beauty concerns were handled at one location. And true to her word, Eloise took good care of Laura's hair.

Between Laura's salary and Françoise's they earned enough to pay their rent, keep body and soul together, while allowing Laura her little luxuries. They also managed to save a little something in the process.

Françoise did not remain a stage hand for long. Within a few months he became the stage manager, then shortly thereafter when the producer booked in a series of lousy acts, thanks again to his cousin, he was asked to take over as producer by the show's backers.

With this raise in pay, they continued to live as they had before, but now Françoise started investing again as he had in Paris. His relatives gave his shrewd investment advice and before long he had built up a small portfolio again. He did not invest in theatrical productions. He bought stocks in International Business Machines, General Motors, DuPont, Ford, Edison, GE, RCA, American Telephone and Telegraph, and other companies that were contributing to the war effort even though they were not currently paying dividends. He bought government and municipal bonds that would mature in ten years. He invested small amounts on a regular basis and watched his portfolio rise slowly but surely.

New York was an enigma. On the one hand it was a very sophisticated, cosmopolitan city. On the other, because of its large immigrant population, it was very provincial in tastes, flavors, and superstitions. There wasn't a single New Yorker who did not have an opinion about whether or not the United States should enter the war. Based on their ethnic roots, they were for it or against it. When Japan attacked Pearl Harbor on December 7, 1941, "the date which will live in infamy", all the squabbling about whether the US should or not enter the war became a moot point. The United States declared war on Japan on December 8, and Japan's allies, Germany and Italy, declared war on the United States three days later. The United States reciprocated. It was no longer a European war. It was now truly a world war.

New York City became the major debarkation point for troops headed to the European Theater. Because the city was so vital to shipping, commerce, the procurement of wartime supplies, finance of the war effort, and just about every other aspect involving the war, there were immediate efforts to beef up security. Military presence in the city increased dramatically. Practically overnight the city became a high security zone.

During the war, New York City was transformed in other ways as well. Companies large and small converted to wartime production.

IBM began assembling M1 carbines.

The bra manufacturer, Maidenform, fought hard to have women's bras declared a wartime essential, not a luxury. But to hedge its bets, it began producing slings for homing pigeons used to transport messages behind enemy lines. Interestingly enough, the slings looked just like the cups of women's bras.

The miracle drug that saved so many lives during World War II, penicillin, was made by Charles Pfizer & Company of Brooklyn.

The piano manufacturer, Steinway & Sons of Queens began manufacturing glider wings – the construction of piano rims and glider wings being very similar in nature.

The American Red Cross, which was given space in the two ground floor galleries of the historical society, produced four million surgical sponges for the war effort.

The war touched the lives of New Yorkers personally. Over 900,00 New Yorkers served in the military. And over three million men and women shipped out through New York's harbors.

Military training camps sprang up throughout the area, and nightclubs and theaters opened their doors to the droves of servicemen and women passing through.

The American Theater Wing, a wartime service organization played an important part in several areas. The first was its efforts in putting on War Bonds drives, generating millions of dollars for the U. S. war chest. They also organized speakers' bureaus that brought the message of the war, why it was being waged, and how American dollars were being used to fund it, to the American public.

Another successful arm of the American Theater Wing was the Stage Door Canteen. The Canteens were composed of Broadway and Hollywood entertainers and other personnel, and employees of broadcasting entities. These performers and others entertained thousands of uniformed soldiers in the Canteens and injured and recuperating soldiers in hospitals throughout East Coast hospitals.

Another program that was utilized during the war effort to boost morale was a series of Vaudeville-like programs put on with Broadway and nightclub singers, dancers, comedians, and musicians. These shows were put on during lunch breaks at defense-related factories and plants. These productions were the only performing that Laura did during her sojourn back in the United States. The audiences loved her but she was still a pariah to Broadway producers and stage managers.

Just because Laura was not welcomed with open arms by the theater district does not mean that she was treated the same way by all of New York. Thousands of Parisians had fled to New York ahead of the German invasion. Laura and Françoise made contact with artists, musicians, singers, dancers, and actors who they had met over the years in Paris. These friends invited them to their art show openings. They welcomed them into their homes and salons. They entertained them backstage after their performances. They invited them out for dinner and the theater, which Laura and Françoise had to decline unless their friends were paying, because the Goldmans just did not have the money to pay for such entertainment any longer. Between their work and Françoise's Jewish relief efforts, they were a very busy couple. All-in-all the couple had a very active social life. But through it all, Laura could not say that she had a real true friend in all of New York.

Chapter 23. Marcella

In the spring of 1942, Marcella brought home the man of her dreams – Lieutenant Carl Williamson. Tall and good looking. And white.

Trained in classical ballet from the age of six, Marcella had spent twelve years studying under some of the best instructors for those who did not intend to go into ballet professionally. At one time she toyed with the idea of auditioning for a position as a can-can dancer at the Moulin Rouge. Most of the can-can dancers were ballerinas. That is what gave them the ability to perform such high kicks and to remain on the balls of their feet and on their toes throughout most of their performances.

It was her father who put the kibosh on her performing. Marcella had been in her terminale, the last year of what Americans called high school. Françoise took her for a long walk down the Champs-Élysées one Sunday afternoon. He implored her to continue her studies by attending the Sorbonne and majoring in Art History. Having been dragged to every major and minor museum throughout Paris, most of France, and quite a bit of Europe, she was very well prepared for a career in the arts. Besides which, she loved art for art's sake and her father thought she had a real flair for writing. He reasoned that she could write about art

– that she could make an excellent career sharing her perceptions about art with the world. Marcella dearly loved her father and usually listened to his advice. She did so this time. At the age of 17, she enrolled in classical art appreciation at the Sorbonne.

The Sorbonne, in the historic soul of the Latin Quarter, had been built on the original foundations of the medieval Sorbonne which dated back to the 13th century. One of the first universities in the western world, it was founded for a small group of religious students. With studies in Arts, Civilizations, Humanities, Languages, Literature, and Social Studies, it produced such philosophers as René Descartes, Jean-Paul Sartre, and Simone de Beauvoir, among others. Rich in heritage and also in quality of learning, the Sorbonne encouraged its students to think for themselves so they could become responsible leaders in their fields of endeavor.

Marcella took her degree in Art History and Appreciation when she was barely 21. By the time she received her diploma, she had been published many times in various art publications. It was on the strength of these articles and her educational credentials, of course, that she was able to secure a job in the acquisitions department of the Louvre. Her writing showed her attention to detail in the art that she reviewed for her articles. Her employers reasoned that because she was not an artist, she did not come with preconceived notions about light, texture, brush work, who was or was not a master, or anything else. They thought that with the right guidance she would be able to judge art independently for its own sake. They were right. She spent her days among not only the old masters, but soon-to-be masters, as well.

Marcella had been working at the Louvre when she and her family fled Paris. After settling in New York, she got a job at the Metropolitan Museum of Art, again in the acquisitions department. With her credentials, the Met was thrilled to have her.

From her very first acquisitions of minor works by classically trained artists for the Louvre, she was recognized as a future leader in her field. The curators of great museum had considered themselves lucky to get her. Her bosses at the Met felt the same way. To show their faith in her talents, they offered her a handsome salary. She accepted the job, not for the salary, but for the opportunity to work in another one of the top museums in the world. It was because of her excellent income that she and her parents were able to live in such nice accommodations in New York.

Marcella spent her evenings at the theater, not as a spectator, but as a performer. She had inherited her mother's love of performing. She too, could sing and dance. She was very deeply involved in community theater, performing in church basements, recreation centers, school gymnasiums, and anywhere else the troupe of actors she performed with could erect a stage and scenery and place chairs for the audience. Although she did a mean shuffle-ball-change, her specialty was ballet, not tap.

Having completed her studies at an institution that encouraged public speaking she could speak to anyone on many different subjects. She had given many speeches on art and art history so she was poised in front of a crowd where she was the center of attention. She had especially become self-informed about all matters of the war in Europe. At parties, she was regularly asked her opinion of how things were going as if she were there and had a special insight into the day to day military operations. Once people found out her brother was an aide on the staff of General de Gaulle, her opinion was especially sought out.

In April of 1942, Marcella was invited to the home of one of her new friends she had met at work - Caroline Williamson. Caroline wanted Marcella to meet someone special. Caroline's twin brother, a Navy pilot, was home on leave prior to being deployed on an aircraft carrier bound for Europe. According to his sister, he spoke French fluently and was mad about all things French. The sister reasoned that he would find Marcella interesting to talk to – no more than that. The brother's name was Carl.

Carl and Marcella hit it off right away. Carl later joked that Marcella had him as soon as she said, "Bonjour, mon nouvel ami."

With the two of them conversing in both French and English, sliding from one language into the other seamlessly, Carl completely monopolized her time at the gathering. And no wonder. She was a stunning beauty. Tall and slim, a dancer by training, she carried herself as only a dancer can do, upright, with no slouching in her posture whatsoever. This gave everyone the sense that she was full of self-confidence even in those times when her confidence was at its lowest. Her hair was honey blond like her mother's and she had Laura's hazel eyes. In fact, she looked like a younger version of her mother.

Marcella and Carl were married six weeks after they met in a beautiful ceremony in Carl's parents' Upper East Side home. They had a one week honeymoon before Carl was due to ship out. This rush to the altar was not unusual during the war. Many couples, unsure about their futures, sought to cling to any sense of normalcy they could. To Carl's parents, the fact that Françoise and Laura were in show business was more of a problem than their Negro and Jewish ancestry. Marcella and Carl spent their honeymoon at the Waldorf-Astoria Hotel away from the cares of the world. When it was time for him to ship out, the entire family went to the docks to see him off. He was magnificent in his Navy Lieutenant's uniform. Marcella held up very well until his ship, the USS Ranger, was out of site. She had steamed out of dry dock in Norfolk bound for Quonset Point, Rhode Island where it was to be outfitted with new planes, stopping in New York to pick up the pilots of those planes.

As the ship sailed away, Marcella broke down and cried on her father's shoulder. "We'll pray for him," was all that he could say to comfort her.

Chapter 24. Henry

One day Laura's brother Henry came to call.

What Laura did not know, what Henry did not tell her, was that he worked as a waiter at a leading mobster hangout. The pay was excellent and he had plenty to eat, but the work was dangerous.

Laura answered the buzzer from the vestibule on the first ring, "Yes, who's there?" she inquired.

"It's your brother, Henry."

"Who. Who did you say," she asked incredulously.

"Your brother Henry."

"Come on up," she replied, still shocked. "I'm on the seventh floor,"

She was waiting at her open door when he stepped off the elevator. She watched him as he walked toward her standing in the open door of her apartment. He had his hair conked - slicked back and wavy. Like his older brother Charlie, he was a gambler, too. He was dressed in the gangster clothes of the day – a custom made suit with extremely wide lapels. He wore a wide silk tie with a diamond tie stud that was shaped like an eagle or a hawk, Laura could not be sure which. His heavy gold cuff links, rings, and watch glittered each time he waved his hands in the air, which he did often. To finish his look he had on a gold chain that attached to his wallet. He called the wallet, a "pocket book". The other end of the chain was attached to his belt loop. His shoes were polished so highly you could literally see your face in them. Laura could tell he was flush and had been for some time. He was no longer thin as a rail as she had remembered him from childhood, but looked well-fed and fully filled out.

They hugged. "Hello, Henry," she said. "It's so good to see you. To what do I owe the pleasure?" she asked as she showed him into the living room of the apartment.

"Why, I just wanted to see my sister, that's all," replied Henry.

"Henry, don't try to bull shit me. You've been in New York for almost a year. Randolph wrote me and told me you were here. Why did you wait so long to get in touch with me?"

"Oh, Laura, you know me. I'm a rambling man – like a rolling stone. I just now slowed my roll enough to think about getting in touch with you."

"Well, if you've come with your hand out, you needn't have bothered. Françoise and I have nothing. Were it not for the generosity of his family, we wouldn't even have decent jobs. And my daughter's the one who pays for our apartment."

"Well, I did want to touch you for a loan. I've got a chance to get into a high stakes game, but I need backing."

She knew it. Same ole Henry. "Poker or craps?" she asked.

"Poker."

"How much are you touching me for?"

"A thousand."

"Oh. That's a big touch. What makes you think I've got kind of money? Françoise and I left almost everything we had behind ."

"I'm hoping. That's all. Whatever you can spare would help. I can't say when I'll be able to pay you back, but I will. You know I will."

"When do you need it?"

"By this weekend if you can manage it."

"Come see me on Friday," she said. She would have to explain it to Françoise somehow. He would be angry but he would forgive her. He knew she had a soft spot in her heart for her good-for-nothing brothers.

On Friday, Henry came to see her. She gave him a thousand dollars in ten one hundred dollar bills. Except for when he came to repay her on Tuesday of the following week, she never saw him alive again.

"Never again, Henry," were her parting words to him.

Six months after Henry came to visit her, she received a telegram. Henry had been killed. She was asked to contact the New York City detective, Rob Herlinger. When she spoke with Herlinger, she was told that Henry had been caught in the crossfire between mobsters fighting for control of drugs and prostitution. In his capacity as a waiter, Henry had been serving drinks when one mobster opened fire on another. Herlinger said that Henry had given her as his next of kin at the restaurant. That is how the detective had been able to locate her to notify her of Henry's death.

Laura wrote to her sisters and brothers about their brother Henry's death. None were able to send her any money to aid with the burial expenses. She paid for a simple graveside funeral and had him buried in a simple coffin. She, Françoise, and Marcella were the only ones in attendance.

Although an infamous womanizer, Henry had never been married, never letting one woman pin him down long enough for her to get him to slip a ring on her finger. He also, to his knowledge, had never had any children, which he maintained was a good thing since he further maintained that he was not good father material.

When Laura cleaned out Henry's one room furnished apartment, she found hidden beneath the floorboards, covered by a beat-up chifferobe, a coffee can with almost $12,000 in it. She kept the money and sold everything else. This money became her "cushion" and she never again had less than $12,000 throughout the remainder of her life.

Chapter 25. Françoise

In 1943, a production entitled *Away We Go* was the first musical written by the team of composer Richard Rodgers and librettist Oscar Hammerstein II. Rodgers, working with Lorenz Hart, had produced over two dozen musicals including *Babes in Arms*, *The Boys from Syracuse*, and *Pal Joey*, and the words to songs *Rose-Marie*, *The Desert Song*, *The New Moon*, and *Show Boat*. He had also written musicals, songs, films, and a song that was to become significant in Laura's life, *The Last Time I Saw Paris*.

Away We Go was based on a largely unsuccessful play by Lynn Riggs called *Green Grow the Lilacs*. The play had dual plots – the main plot being the romance between cowboy Curly McLain and farm girl Laurey Williams, and the secondary plot between cowboy Will Parker and his girl Ado Annie. The play eventually wound up in summer stock as a musical with traditional folk songs and square dance numbers where it was seen by producer Theresa Helburn who saw it and thought it might work as a Theater Guild production.

Helburn contacted Rodgers and Hart, but Hart, who by this time had become a serious alcoholic, decided that he did not want to work on the project, and headed off to Mexico. That left Rodgers without a collaborator. Oscar

Hammerstein found out that Rodgers was seeking someone to write the book for the project. Through much machinations, it became known to Rodgers that Hammerstein would like to work on the project. Rodgers asked Hammerstein to come into the project with him. Their preferred writing styles meshed beautifully. Hammerstein, having set the machine in motion, eagerly accepted the offer. Hammerstein preferred to write a complete lyric before it was set to music, and Rodgers preferred to set completed lyrics to music.

The show found itself without a backstage manager and no matter how good a show is, if the backstage is a shambles, the production will be a disaster. Someone has to keep things moving backstage in order to keep things moving onstage.

The show was preparing to go on the road to New Haven for its preview. Françoise was approached by one of the show's backers who suggested that Françoise apply for the position. Françoise had extensive background in all aspects of theater productions - from sweeping up stages when he was barely seventeen, to producing shows, designing sets and costumes, and managing show people in general. He was given the position. Again, Françoise got Laura a position as assistant to the wardrobe mistress. They went to New Haven to the Shubert Theater on March 11, 1943. Although the show was acceptable, all involved could tell that it was not going to be a major hit.

When they went to Boston for the Boston preview, Françoise and Laura were on the same train but they might as well have been miles apart. The producer, director, composer, librettist, and Françoise the stage manager, kept their heads together constantly. There was something indefinable wrong with the show and they were frantically trying to figure it out and fix it before they took it to Broadway.

The final changes were made to the show in the Boston preview with a reworked minor number. The song *Oklahoma* was redone with the title of the song becoming a chant. Coupled with a massive eight part choral, this gave an interesting twist to the same ole bit. The new staging had the chorus coming down to the footlights in a V formation extending the song to include a spelling of the name "O-K-L-A-H-O-M-A" ending with a *ritardando* leading into one last iteration of "Oklahoma!" At the song's conclusion, the audience took to its collective feet, clapping and cheering.

In the post-production meeting that night, a decision was made to change the name of the show to *Oklahoma!* The show opened at the St. James Theater on March 31, 1943. And the rest, as they say, was showbiz history. A hit was born, as was a new star - Celeste Holm.

The entire cast, crew, and executive staff reveled in the success of the musical hit. The show ran for over two thousand performances. Sadly enough Françoise, did not endure for the run of the show.

The information coming out of France concerning the Jews was dire. Even before being requested by the Germans, the Vichy government had begun its persecution of Jews in France – both French Jews and immigrant Jews. The laws, called Statut des Juifs, passed on October 3, 1940, took away many Jewish rights. Included among these rights were the right to own businesses and limited Jews' access to public parks and cinemas and most professional activities. It also limited their right to purchase rationed goods until the afternoon hours when most supplies had run out for the day. In addition, it established a curfew for all Jews. Further decrees passed on June 1, 1942 required Jews to wear yellow arm bands with the star of David and the words Juif written on them. As hard as it was to learn these things about the Jews left behind in France, it was even harder to learn that they were being deported to concentration camps in Auschwitz – the death camps.

The word leaked out of France was horror personified. On July 16, 1942 some 13,152 men, women, and children were forced out of their homes. The Vichy French government set up a camp at Drancy, just outside of Paris. This camp saw more than 7,000 people housed in a facility set up to house 700 people. In all over 70,000 Jews were transported from Drancy to Auschwitz where all but 2,500 were gassed upon arrival.

Françoise and his relatives were mortified at the news and angered beyond belief. Each day Laura gave thanks for their safe escape from France. Each day she prayed for safe deliverance for those in peril. And the war dragged on.

Between his job in the theater and his efforts with the American Jewish Joint Distribution Committee, Françoise did not have much free time any more. He and his relatives and friends raised money to send to Europe to help those few Jews lucky enough to escape the reign of horror. In addition, they sponsored those fewer still who were allowed immigration into the United States. During the beginning of the war United States officials said they feared that European Jews could be blackmailed into spying for Germany, and so the US was stricter in the number of Jews they allowed in. American Jews openly challenged this, what they considered to be, anti-Semitic policy. Although thousands of Jews were admitted into the United States, the US did not pursue an organized rescue policy for the Jews until much later in the war.

Laura noticed that Françoise complained of being tired more and more frequently. She urged him to rest but he always had somewhere to go, some group he needed to speak to, some fundraising event he needed to attend in order to raise funds for the JDC.

Françoise spent many hours in this pursuit. Laura did not mind, in fact, she supported him in his efforts. Because she was a shiska she was not accepted into the female society of the other Jewish wives. Not having any friends in the theater, she was very lonely indeed. Then one day as she was walking down Broadway, she happened upon a woman who she recognized slightly. It was Lucille! They had lost touch over the years. Many years before, Laura's letters to Lucille had been returned marked "Return to Sender. Addressee unknown." Laura had asked after Lucille when she visited in St. Maurice but Lucille's mother had passed away and there were no other relatives of Lucille's left in the township. No one knew how to get in touch with her.

Suddenly, there on the streets of New York, they found one another. They embraced and went to a local café to sit and catch up on old times. It was this one dear friend in New York that Laura came to rely on for comfort and understanding during her stay in New York for comfort and understanding. Lucille, oddly enough, had wound up in the same position as Laura. She, too, was a wardrobe mistress in a local revue. Life for her too was hard, but as the two old showgirls commiserated, they had no regrets as it was still better than the life they would have lived if they had remained in Louisiana.

One Sunday night after they returned home from the theater, Laura noticed that Françoise's footsteps seemed to be particularly heavy. They walked slowly through the darkened streets. It took them twice as long to get home as it normally did.

As they let themselves into their apartment, Laura said, "Françoise, you look tired. You didn't sleep well last night. Are you coming down with a cold?" She reached over to feel his forehead.

"No, I don't think so," he replied wearily. "I'm just tired. Bone tired."

"Why don't you go and get in the bed? I'll bring you some dinner," she said to him.

When she came into their room with a tray twenty minutes later, he was already asleep. She left the tray on the nightstand on his side of the bed while she went into the bathroom to run herself a bath.

When she came out, she saw that he had eaten a small amount of the soup and was asleep once again. She went back into the bathroom and got into the tub. When she came out the next time, he was still asleep. She took the tray into the kitchen, ate a light meal herself, washed out the dishes, and returned to the bedroom. She turned out the lights and went to bed.

Françoise passed away quietly in his sleep during the night. He had suffered a massive heart attack. He had none of the warning signs or symptoms. He just went. The day was Monday, May 8, 1944. It was also the day that Laura became a great-grandmother. Randolph's eldest grandchild, a boy, was born to his middle daughter Mirtice. They named him Jessie after his father.

When Laura had awakened in the middle of the night to find Françoise unresponsive, she knew instinctively that he was gone. She immediately called his rabbi, who said to her "Baruch dayan emet," Blessed be the one true Judge. By custom, the rabbi did not come himself but sent the chevra kaddisha, those whose job it was to care for the body of the dead. They were responsible for Taharah, the ritual cleansing of the body required by Halacha, and preparing it for burial in accordance with Jewish custom. They wrapped Françoise's body in a tachrichim (a white burial shroud). This simple burial covering was purposely kept simple to avoid distinguishing between the rich and the poor in death. Françoise was also to be buried with his tallits (his prayer shawl), rendered ineffective by cutting off one of the fringes. Françoise's body was not embalmed and there were drilled holes in his coffin, a simple pine box to allow contact with the earth.

Although it was traditional to bury the body within 24 hours, Laura insisted they wait three days – to allow her son Randolph time to arrive from Louisiana so that he could attend the funeral. Françoise's sister Jokima was furious at this delay, saying that k'vod hamet (honoring the dead) was not being observed. Laura stood her ground. They had Françoise's funeral services at the synagogue where he had attended since moving to New York. Laura had him buried at The Woodlawn Cemetery in the Bronx, New York. She had a star of David etched on his tombstone so all who saw his grave would know that in the end, he was proud to be a Jew.

Françoise was 67 years old when he died. He and Laura had been together for 33 years. Many things had happened over the years that made Laura wish she had never gone into show business. Françoise being in her life was not one of them. He had been a good husband and lover to her. He had always been attentive to her needs and he had told her nearly every day of their lives together that he loved her. For her part, Laura had loved him just as much as he loved her. He and the children were her whole life. While she loved the grease paint in her veins, it was secondary to her love for her family.

Because Françoise was looking out for her even after death, he carried a life insurance policy which gave her the ability to give him a proper burial with enough left over to give her some protection in life.

Adrien, understandably, could not come. Randolph caught the train to come be with Laura and Marcella. He stayed for a week before he had to return to his job as a bakery delivery driver.

Françoise's sister and her family, who had fled France the year prior to the invasion by the Nazis and lived in New Rochelle, were in attendance at the services at the synagogue and the burial at the cemetery. They barely spoke to Laura. They had never approved of Françoise marrying a shiska. It wasn't so much that she was a Negro. Being from France, they did not mind that as much as they minded that she was non-Jewish, especially since Jokima had tried so hard to introduce him to a nice Jewish girl.

Nearly a hundred of the show people Françoise had worked with, some back in France, but most in the United States, also attended the funeral. Their artist friends from Paris who had become their social circle in New York came. There wasn't a vacant seat in the synagogue.

Laura returned to her job as assistant wardrobe mistress a month after Françoise death. Exactly one year later on the anniversary of his death, victory was proclaimed in Europe.

And standing beside her through her ordeal was her dear friend Lucille.

Chapter 26. The War on French Soil

When France surrendered to Germany on June 24, 1940, Germany then occupied three-fifths of French territory. They set up a new puppet government on July 10, 1940 in the city of Vichy, and the puppet Vichy government controlled the rest of France. The Vichy government was headed by Henri Philippe Pétain, who had been a general during the Great War. On June 17, 1940, Pétain made an appeal to the people of France to cease fighting and to obey his government.

Those French people who were still in occupied France who resisted and harassed the Germans at every turn were simply called The Resistance. But there were other French people who refused to accept the defeat of their country. Those who could, escaped and continued their resistance on foreign soil – most notably from Great Britain. Acting Brigadier General Charles de Gaulle, Undersecretary of State for National Defense and War in the Paul Reynaud government, and a few senior French officers founded a new government in exile. They called themselves La France Libre (The Free French).

De Gaulle gave a memorable speech on BBC Radio the day after Pétain's speech, telling the French people "La France a perdu une bataille, mais la France n'a pas perdu la guerre" meaning "France has lost a battle, but France has not lost the war". The speech only reached a few French cities but news of it spread throughout the underground resistance. De Gaulle's later speeches reached many more people on French soil, helping to steel the resolve of those left in France who opposed the Vichy government.

De Gaulle's openly disagreed with both the Churchill's government ministers and representatives from the United States. Because of these disagreements, he was initially left out of plans to retake France from the Germans. Additionally, both the British and the Americans objected to the fact that he was not an elected representative of the French people. The Army of Africa based in Algiers was led by General Henri Giraud. De Gaulle relocated to North Africa, one of the few free areas of France, where he joined forces with Giraud.

Against objections of his ministers, Churchill made the decision to inform de Gaulle of the invasion plans. A carefully constructed decoy plan had been surreptitiously leaked to the Germans. Fearing that the French coding system could be broken, Churchill decided not to risk sending a message to de Gaulle. If a message was intercepted and decoded by the Germans, Operation Overlord, the true plans for the retake of France, would become known to the Germans and could be thwarted before it could be launched. In the end, against the advice of his senior staff, Churchill personally sent two planes to bring de Gaulle and his staff to Britain so de Gaulle could be informed of the D-Day plans. After all of that, de Gaulle refused to endorse the plans and returned to North Africa in a huff.

In the part of the operation was called Operation Dragoon, La France Libre and the troops in North Africa under General de Lattre de Tassigny, did participate in the landing in the south of France. This mass of troops, known as the French First Army, helped to liberate one third of France and joined the Allied forces in liberating the rest. On June 14, 1944 de Gaulle returned to France and set up a government in Bayeux. Adrien was with him as one of his aides.

Chapter 27. The Liberation of Paris

Paris was not as heavily bombed as some other European cities. Bombed by the British and the Americans near the end of the war, it suffered bombing raids nonetheless. Most of the bombings took place in working-class districts of Paris, targeting the many factories located in those arrondissements.

The worse bombing took place on April 21, 1944 at Porte de La Chapelle, in the 18th arrondissement. Missing the La Chapelle marshaling yard, accompanied by air raid siren after air raid siren, bomb after bomb was dropped on non-military targets, killing over 600 civilians and wounding almost 400 more. Many houses on the Rue Championnet, near Montmarte were reduced to rubble. Attempting to bomb the Renault factories located in the 16th arrondissement, the Billancourt section was also bombed. The 14th and 18th arrondissement and the Plaine St Denis area were evacuated. The deeper metro stations were used as bombing shelters but they could not contain everyone. Some people took shelter in their basements only to have their houses collapse on them.

The liberation of Paris began on August 11 of 1944 when nine French Jews had been openly arrested by the Paris police. By the 16th of August, newspapers speaking out against the arrests in particular and the puppet French government in general, were published. Food was in short supply but sidewalk cafes were crowded with onlookers hoping to get a whiff of which way the winds of the provisional Vichy government were going to blow. On the 18th, more than half of the railroad workers went on strike and paralyzed the city. The regular police disappeared from the streets. There were several spontaneous anti-German demonstrations and members of the Resistance appeared armed in the streets. By the following day the Resistance had taken over the police stations, city buildings, government offices, newspaper buildings, and most importantly, the Hôtel de Ville – City Hall.

With concern that communists would fill the vacuum when the Germans pulled out, General Dwight Eisenhower agreed that de Gaulle and the French First Army should be the first to enter Paris. They marched into the city on the 25th of that month. On that day, Charles de Gaulle, President of the Provisional Government of the French Republic, took over the War Ministry on the Rue Saint-Dominique. De Gaulle gave a stirring speech to the crowd from the balcony of the Hôtel de Ville. The following day there was a victory parade down the Champs-Élysées while German snipers shot at the troops as they marched by.

On the 29th of August there was a combined Franco-American military parade to celebrate the arrival of the U.S. Army's 28th Infantry Division. Ecstatic crowds greeted the armée de la libération with men, women, and children alike climbing onto the cars and trucks of the liberators. Wine flowed freely on every street. Even the children drank wine that day to celebrate the liberation of their city.

Other Allied forces arrived the following day. A few days later, General Leclerc's French Armored Division entered the city. It took six days of hard fighting, with the Resistance playing a major part, to totally recapture the capital city from the Germans.

The German garrison stationed in Paris, headed by German commander General Dietric von Choltitz, surrendered. It was said that von Choltitz ignored Adolph Hitler's direct orders to leave the city in rubble. Hitler is reputed to have placed a phone call to von Choltitz at the last hour demanding to know "Brennt

Paris?" meaning "Is Paris burning?" Whether this actually took place or not, only von Choltitz knew for sure. But this is the word that reached American shores and Laura and her Parisian friends reveled in the news that their beloved city was not destroyed.

The Germans fought with determination in the rest of France until the end of '44. Finally, after four years of occupation, the Allied Forces, the Free French, and the Resistance liberated all of France.

Laura, along with the rest of the world, followed these events with her heart in her mouth. She knew so many people who were fighting in the war, both French and American, family and friends. Some of those she had known would never return to their loved ones. Some would return badly injured. Others would come through unscathed, but would never be the same as they were before they left for the war.

But it was finally over. The only bittersweet note was that Françoise was not there to share the good news with her.

Chapter 28. Return to Paris by way of Louisiana

When Laura, safely in New York, heard about the liberation of Paris on the radio, she wept. Oh how she wished that she had been a part of it. She knew in her heart that if she had remained in France her child and her husband would surely have been sent to work camps, or worse – to the ovens. Still, she would have liked to have been in the city on that glorious day.

She began making plans to return. At this point she was blocked by the US government. The war was not officially over. She was further dissuaded from returning by being informed about how bad conditions were there. She was informed that there were many destroyed buildings and no support system was in place. Food was in short supply. There were few jobs especially, in her type of work. Laura put her name down anyway to be one of the first to be allowed back in. To make her case, she secured letters of recommendations from Josephine Baker, Maurice Chevalier, and just about every French entertainer and minor official she had ever known. She cited the fact that she owned a house in Paris and she could secure for herself a small annuity which would support her. She had Adrien in his role of minor military official intercede with de Gaulle. de Gaulle sent word back that it was not advisable to return at that time. Laura wrote to friends in Paris. They confirmed what Laura had been told by the government. Laura gave up her dream of returning to Paris. For the time being.

France did not resume issuing visas until the following year. On August 20, 1946, two years after the liberations, a notice came in the mail that her visa had been granted. Laura thought about it day and night and finally, against all advice, in the summer of 1947 decided to return to Paris. By this time, Mirtice, one of Randolph's daughters, was expecting her second child. Laura decided to wait until the baby was born in October. This would give her time for a trip to St. Maurice. Arriving in Paris in August would have been hot and most unpleasant with almost all small shops and all theater productions closed down. By the fall however, the weather would be cooler, and the city, especially the theater, would be doing business as usual. Laura was itching to get back on stage, if that were at all possible. If not, well she was one of the best damned wardrobe mistresses on Broadway. Surely she could find a job doing the same thing in Paris.

Laura remained with *Oklahoma!* until she left to return to Louisiana to await the arrival of her third grandchild. Immediately after the child was born she was planning on returning to Paris. She knew this would probably be her last trip back to Louisiana. She made the most of her time there, visiting with friends and family, some she had not seen for over forty years. The baby was born on October 27th. The parents named her Celestine, after Laura's middle name.

During this trip, thanks to Randolph, she was finally reunited with her two eldest sons – Marvin and Chris. Their father had taken them to Florida when they were two and three years old and had passed them for white and she had not seen them since.

Some years before, during a trip to Louisiana, Marvin and Chris had visited with their father's sister Muriel. She had mentioned that she knew their mother and they had two brothers who still lived in Louisiana. After much pressure from Marvin and Chris, Muriel reluctantly gave them their brothers' names and what she knew of how to get in touch with them. They had located Randolph, now living in Minden, a small town in north Louisiana. Randolph had passed on their addresses to Laura. She had written to Chris and Marvin that she was going to

Louisiana for a visit before returning to France. Her two sons drove from Florida and met her at Randolph's house. Although there were hugs and kisses all around, she did not know what to say to them, nor they to her. The two days they were together were very awkward ones. The first thing they told her was that their father had told them about their Negro heritage only after they were adults. They also told her that their father had always told them that she had abandoned them.

When they were ready to leave, Marvin asked Laura if he could have a word with her. They went into a back room to talk. Laura could tell his heart was heavy. "Mama," he began. "Are you really in show business? Papa told us you worked as a house maid. If you really had all you say you had, then why didn't you come to see us in all that time? All these years I thought it was because you didn't have the money to find us. I used to daydream that I would come home from school one day and you would be there." There was a catch in his voice. Laura could tell that Marvin was very near tears.

Laura squared her shoulders. It was not as if she had not been expecting this. She began, "When your father left and took you with him, I was working as a maid in a restaurant. I cleaned and swept and helped old ladies out to the outhouse. Yes, that's true. But since I left here, I've never worked as a maid again. For a while, when I first went to New York, I was a waitress but that was as close as I came to waiting on anyone ever again."

"I didn't come to see you because I didn't know where you were. Your father hid you from me. If you hadn't gotten in touch with Randolph, we wouldn't be here together now. " She sighed.

Tears were beginning to stream down her face. It was some moments before she went on. "It was for the best, Marvin," she said choking back the tears. "Look at you. You're more white than Negro. You got to go to school and even to college. You're a professional man. Tell me truly, aren't you glad you were raised as white instead of colored? If I had thought for one minute that you were being mistreated, I would have moved heaven and earth to find you. But I knew from your father's sister that you were being well taken care of. I went to see her every time I came to Louisiana. She showed me many pictures of you growing up.

I saw you in your cap and gown when you graduated from high school and also from college. I saw you in your wedding pictures and also pictures of your children. But she would never tell me where you were. All she would say was that you were in Florida. That was all I could do to keep up with you."

She paused. It was some time before she went on. Marvin did not say anything. His face was impassive.

Laura resumed. "I know you probably hate me. I understand that. I came to terms with that years ago. That's okay. I can live with your hatred. I didn't have any choice in the matter. Your father took you and left. I suppose I could have pressured your aunt and got her to tell me where you were, but what if she hadn't? She would have cut me off from even the second-hand knowledge I had about you. Over the years I came to realize that you probably had a better life than any I could have given you. It was better for you the way it was."

After his opening question, Marvin had not said a word. He had just listened. When she finished he nodded his head, let out a very deep breath, and walked outside to where Chris was waiting in the car.

Laura followed him outside. She waved to them as they pulled away. She was drained. Randolph walked over to her and put his arm around her. She laid her head over on his shoulder. She wrote to Marvin and Chris frequently after that and they wrote back, but she never saw them again. They continued to pass for white until the day they died. It would be left to their grandchildren to discover the truth about their heritage.

Laura returned to Paris right before Christmas. Marcella chose not to return to Paris with her. She had laid down her roots in New York and wanted to remain there. She and Carl were parents by this time. Their two children were being raised American. Not Negro-American or Jewish-American – just plain American. Laura shook her head. She knew Americans and knew that you could not be just an American unless you were white. You had to be a hyphenated American, as if to say, you were only partly American in some way.

The only way to be white when you had Negro blood in you was to deny your heritage, or have someone else do it for you. She and her sons were a living testament to that. Although she looked white, from the top of her blond head down to the pink pigmentation under her toe nails, in the eyes of Americans, she was just as Negro as the darkest Negro one had ever seen, with distinctly African features – wide nostrils, thick lips, kinky hair, dark pools for eyes. With her slightly French accent, with no hint of her Louisiana twang left anymore, she did not speak like most Negro Americans. Although she was polished and professional, able to hold an intelligent conversation with the highest of dignitaries, she was still considered to be inferior in the land of her birth. Yes, she missed some of the American ways and customs when she was back in France, but when she was confronted with racism in the states, she longed to be back where she had come to realize that she belonged – in France, where the color of your skin was immaterial.

Chapter 29. Joyeux Noel en Paris

Laura arrived back in Paris at the beginning of December in 1947. She came by ship so she could bring all of her things from her New York apartment with her. Adrien met her at the dock in Le Harve. She was so glad to see him that she wrapped her arms around him and held him while she wept. Finally, she let him go and just looked at him. Her son was now a man. He was fully filled out and he looked just like Françoise.

On the drive to Paris, he told her about the house. After they had arrived in New York, Françoise had a letter sneaked into France. In it, he had arranged with one of his friends to have the house rented out in their absence. The rents had been collected by a Paris rental agency and after peace was declared, not knowing that Françoise was deceased, sent to him at his relative's address, which Françoise had left as his address of record. When the letter with the check was received at his relative's, it was then given to Laura as Françoise's spouse and heir. In the statement that accompanied the letter and the check there was an accounting down to the last penny. It amounted to over several thousand dollars. Since the check was in Françoise's name, Laura took the check to the bank which had handled

Françoise's estate. They returned it endorsed over to her. The bank wrote a letter to the rental agent in Paris and after that the checks came in her name.

She had written to Adrien, now a lieutenant-colonel in the French army, and he had checked the house. He wrote back that the roof had leaked over the back porch and rain water had ruined the walls and floors in the back of the house and the plumbing made a horrible racket. Other than that he assured her the house was as she and Françoise had left it. He had arranged with the rental agency to have the apartment on the second floor vacated and the furniture moved back from the basement. It took six months, but he had finally written to Laura that all was in readiness for her return.

Françoise had left a will and in it he had specifically left Laura the house and all its contents. Everything else was divided between the three of them - Laura, Marcella, and Adrien – 25% of his total assets to each of the children, and the rest to Laura. When they had first fled from Paris the stocks and bonds were worthless but now they were steadily recovering their pre-war value. The real estate they had owned was lost due to the heavy taxes that the Germans put on the French after their takeover. The Germans had taken valuable property right and left. Millions of dollars in choice commercial real estate was gone. The stocks and bonds that Françoise had accumulated while in the states were starting to pay dividends. Laura was not exactly down to her last sou, but she was certainly not the millionairess she had once been.

None of this was money Laura could spend. Françoise had made her promise many times over the years, that she would not touch the money that was in investments. That money would be for her old age – when she was too old, sick, or tired to work any longer, that as long as she could, she would continue working. That is why they had lived so frugally and went to work as soon as they got to New York – so there would be something for her when she could no longer provide for herself, not their carefree spendthrift days of days gone by.

Françoise had also left an insurance policy. After paying for Françoise's funeral there was some money left from that. And the money from the rents. All of that was hers to use as she pleased. And she had the money from Henry.

Although not flush, she was certainly comfortable. She had enough to see her through the rest of her life, providing she did not indulge in reckless spending.

When she arrived in Paris, she found everything as Adrian had said. Although shabby, all of her possessions were intact. Laura made a mental note of what survived storage and what needed to be replaced. She retrieved some large shawls stored in a trunk and draped them over the sofas and chairs. That would have to do until she could get them recovered.

The roof had leaked over the back porch and rain water had ruined the walls and floors in the back of the house and the plumbing made a horrible racket. She set about having these repairs made. All of the walls were dingy, no longer bright and sunny the way she had kept them. She had all of the wall paper replaced in her apartment on the second floor and the apartments on the upper and lower floors as well. She had the whole house repainted inside and out. She settled back and looked at her handiwork. The repairs had cut into her capital but she thought it was worth it to restore the house to its pre-war condition. Françoise had loved that house. He had bought it with his own money, not inheritance money, and he had been able to hang onto it through ups and downs in his financial position. That house had been his port in the storms that swirled around him. He would be proud that she was taking care of it so well.

The week after returning home, Laura went into the garage and uncovered her Duesenberg. She tried to start it but the engine would not turn over. It had gas in it, but it would not crank. She sighed, got out of the car, replaced the tarp, and went back into the house. The irony of it all – a $35,000 car that would not start. She bet herself that if it were a Ford it would have cranked right up. She would look into getting it in running condition after the holidays.

The Christmas lights were already up when she arrived in Paris. The 200 trees from the Place de l'Etoile and the Arch de Triomphe to the Place de la Concorde, all along the Avenue de Champs-Élysées, were completely covered in lights. From hotels, to shops, to the grands magasins, to the Hôtel de Ville, to private residences - all had broken out massive numbers of lights, as much to celebrate France's liberation from Germany occupation as to celebrate the holiday season. The lights twinkled and seemed to dance in the crisp December night air.

Laura went out each evening just to look at them. By day, she worked on decorating her apartment – something that in the years before she left Paris, she hired others to do for her. The Christmas decorations were stored in the attic. There were over two dozen boxes of them, everything from crèches, to miniature towns that used to delight Marcella so, to decorations exclusively for the tree. There were over a dozen Père Noëls alone.

She could not manage dragging a Christmas tree home by herself so she paid to have one delivered and set into its stand. She could have waited until Adrien came to visit her but she did not want to get into a pattern of leaning on him. She wanted to do for herself for as long as she could. She was healthy. There was no reason why she could not. So she selected a tree that was twelve feet high paid to have it delivered to the house. As soon as she saw it in the parlor, or as they said in the states, the living room, she vowed that the following year she would get an even taller one – fifteen feet.

When she finally got her tree decorated, she treated herself to vin chaud at one of the Christmas markets. Careful not to resume her old spending habits, she vowed that going out to eat in restaurants would be the exception rather than the norm. She did allow herself to shop for original Parisian Christmas gifts for her children and their families. She had to get their gifts off to the states quickly or they would not arrive in time for Christmas.

Christmas had always been a joyous time for the Goldmans. Because Françoise had been a non-practicing Jew throughout most of their marriage, he did not object to the Christian way of celebrating and decorating for Christmas. And because Laura did not have very much in the way of Christmas as a child, she went overboard, more for herself than the children. There had been plays and concerts and gifts for all. She would begin her shopping each year in early December in order to get her gifts to the states delivered by Christmas day. This year she sat down with a pen and paper and very carefully calculated who she would be able to send something to and who she would have to drop off her Christmas list.

Christmas cards were a different matter. She went to the Stern Engraving Company located in the Passage des Panoramas between Rue Saint-Marc and Boulevard Montmarte, in the 2nd arrondisement and selected one with a Parisian theme and ordered one hundred. Then came the hard task of addressing them. This was also a good method to notify everyone that she was back in Paris. One hundred proved not to be enough. She went back to the stationery store and ordered a hundred more.

There were plenty of free things for her to do in Paris to enjoy the magic of Joyeux Noël. On Sundays she attended mass at Notre Dame. They had their classic Christmas tree set up in the square. In the evenings they had a light and music show every hour inside the nave of one of the chapels. She attended the children's choirs' performances and listened as their clear pure voices filled the cathedral. As they sang, she reminisced about her own sojourn in the Evergreen Baptist choir.

On the Saturday before Christmas, she went to the Monteverdi Vespers concert – a Christmas concert that had been happening since 1610. The Marian Vespers of Claudio Monteverdi was a high point in Renaissance choral music. A special seating structure had been built on the square in front of Notre Dame for visitors to sit and listen to the music, which afforded a different perspective on the cathedral's beautiful stained glass windows. She was so moved that she wept from the sheer beauty of the musical offerings.

And no Christmas would be Christmas without going to see a performance of The Nutcracker Suite at the Garnier Opera House and Handel's Messiah at the more than a dozen locations where it would be performed throughout the holiday season. She chose the performance given at Basilica du Sacré Coeur. Even with no family around her, this Christmas seemed more like Christmas than any in a very long while.

One night she walked over to the Hôtel de Ville so she could see the decorated carousel. Careful to watch her money, she spent only a few francs the entire evening - to have a crepe and a cup of vin chaud.

Several times she went to see the decorations in the Grand Magasins. Her favorite of all the store decorations was in the Galleries Lafayettes on the Boulevard Haussman. All of the store's exterior windows, eleven of them, were decorated with elaborate themes by a new fashion designer who was destined to be a success - Christian Dior.

For his initial season Dior had designed an iconic Bar jacket. The style was such an instant hit that Galleries Lafayettes decided to carry Dior's entire line of clothing, dresses, suits, shoes, purses, and scarves, along with the other branded items he planned on adding to his line. The store windows were a reflection of the season's offerings created in miniature for 74 two-foot high puppets executed by a master puppeteer.

The puppets were depicted going strolling along Avenue Montaigne in front of the Dior couture house, walking by the Tour Eiffel and the Opéra Garnier, getting into a hot air balloon, going ice skating, standing in front of a music stand, and at a funfair, just to name a few of the scenes. Crowds gathered around the windows three and four persons deep in order to enjoy the unique window dressings, the tone of which set the standard for other department stores' Christmas window dressings for over 50 years to come.

When Laura went on these strolls about Paris, she deliberately left her purse at home and only took a few francs with her so she would not be tempted to spend too much. She got great ideas for her Christmas list, which this year only included her children, grandchildren, and now her great-grandchildren. All of them would get something from her from Paris, including Mirtice's new baby girl, Celestine. Everyone else would get a Christmas card.

She wished the car was running so she could take a drive out to the countryside, maybe up to champagne country to take in the holiday decorations there and pick up a case of Moet & Chandon.

She wished that she did not have to watch every penny – that she could purchase a Christian Dior gown for herself.

She wished for so much, but most of all she wished for Françoise to be there to enjoy it all with her. But those things could not be, so she put them all out of her mind.

The climax of the Christmas season was midnight mass at Notre Dame and the late-night feast called Revellion. Although cooking only for herself, Laura put on the dog. She had puff pastries from Picard, fresh oysters from the Brittany coast (she preferred hers fried), fois gras from Dordogne, caviar from Petrossian's, roast chicken, a ham, and traditional (for her family at least) Louisiana gumbo – made with chicken, pork sausage, shrimp, crab meat, and of course, okra – all served over long grained white rice. She had brought back her own personal store of roux, gumbo file, and Louisiana Hot Sauce purchased during her last trip to her home town.

For dessert, she had the traditional cake, the Buche del Noël, or Yule Log. This she bought already baked. She would be eating for a week on all that she prepared.

Laura had never been much of a cook. That is until she was forced to cook for herself and Françoise in New York. Not being able to afford to eat out very much, and wanting to feed her husband well, she set about learning how to cook the food he liked to eat. She knew that Françoise, having grown up with French cooking, did not think it was undercooked and ill prepared as Americans did, who have a tendency to overcook their food. So she learned to make the roasted meats and chicken and the sauces used to embellish them, as he liked them.

For Françoise's part, he had complimented her heartily for trying to please him. So much so, that on their first Christmas in their new apartment in New York, he had gifted her with a new stove and refrigerator. The apartment did not come with these appliances and in order to get moved in as inexpensively as possible, they had purchased older, used ones. It wasn't long before Laura grew frustrated at trying to prepare meals on those antiquated appliances. Françoise, seeing how she was struggling to please him by doing something that was totally foreign to her nature, conferred with one of his female relatives, and together, along with a recently opened charge account at Macy's Department Store, got Laura the kitchen of a woman's dreams, circa 1940. Laura, having received so many expensive presents from Françoise over the years, including jewels, furs, cars, and even an apartment, thought the stove and refrigerator was the best gift ever. It reminded her of the Gift of the Magi, where each partner sought to do something wonderful for the other, only in her and Françoise's case, there was no tragedy.

Having become accustomed to a well-equipped kitchen, one look at the kitchen in her Paris apartment (her old-fashioned stove was little more than two sets of cooktops mushed together) and she was off to the appliance department of Le Bon Marche. She had come to appreciate a well-equipped kitchen during those seven years in the states. Since she had to be in the kitchen to do her own cooking from now on, she was determined to make it as painless as possible. Her Christmas present to herself was a new refrigerator and cook stove, now called a "range" by all sophisticated women. She gifted herself weeks early so that she would have the new appliances to cook the holiday meal on. She opted for a 42 inch range, with double ovens, double broilers, and a warming compartment on the side. She found a French brand that suited her needs.

Because French refrigerators were so notoriously small and Laura had been used to the oversized beast in her New York apartment, she had an American refrigerator, a Frigidaire, shipped to her from Macy's and had it outfitted to use with the French electrical system. There was a company that did this as a specialty. The refrigerator was the latest and greatest model to come out, with a larger than normal freezer compartment.

So Laura got what she was looking for – freedom from having to go to the market every day in order to have fresh foods available to her and a convenient way to cook that fresh food.

Then she had a cabinet maker come in and make her something that few Parisian kitchens had – built-in cabinetry especially designed to hold all of the modern appliances that women needed to produce the meals by themselves that they used to hire two or three people to cook for them. By the time she finished with her kitchen, it was a chef's dream.

Life was good and she was ready to live out the rest of her years in retirement inside the house that she had loved since the moment she had first set foot inside it.

Around 10 AM on Christmas Day her doorbell rang. The caretaker and her family were away for the day, so Laura went down to answer the door. It was Adrien! He had written to her earlier in the week and told her he would not be able to come for Christmas, that he was on duty the entire week. He had managed to get leave after all and had surprised her. Adrien had a key to the house and her apartment, but he chose to ring the doorbell. Laura sensed that something was up. He had with him a tall leggy blond who clung to him like a cheap sweater. Her name was Charlotte. He introduced her as a mannequin.

Laura invited them to come upstairs and into the living room. Thinking that she would be spending the day alone, she had fixed herself breakfast and had changed into a peignoir set that Françoise had given her years before that she had to leave behind when they fled from Paris. She had retrieved it from one of the many trunks stored in the basement and had taken it to a dry cleaner where they had presented it to her almost as good as new. She fixed mimosas and served them while she went in to change. After dressing she discovered Adrien and Charlotte had almost polished off the bottle of champagne. She was just in time to get the last corner. Adrien opened another one.

"To Mother and her return to Paris," was his toast.

"To us being together," was her rejoinder.

They all retired to the dining room where she had laid out the remainder of the food from the feast the night before.

"If I had known you were coming I would have cooked something special for today," she apologized.

"Don't be silly," said Adrien as he hugged her. "This is just perfect," he said as he spied the gumbo. It was one of his favorites. "It's plenty. I just wish Dad could have been able to return also. But here," he said as he shook the memories from his mind, "Let's be thankful for those who did return."

They all sat down and began their feast.

"This was the perfect ending to a perfect year," thought Laura to herself. She agreed with Adrien that the only thing missing was Françoise. Oddly enough she had never thought ahead to their old age and which one of them would go first. She had never let her thinking go there. Now she wished she had. Then this day would not have been so devastating to her – the first Christmas back in Paris without Françoise. There would be many more of these firsts to come over the years. She dreaded each and every one. Her motto had always been "never suffer future pain" meaning don't dread something for days, weeks, months before it ever happened. But looking into the future without Françoise was something she could not stop herself from doing now.

At five o'clock, with Adrien citing the need to return to duty before his leave was up at midnight, he and Charlotte got up to go. At the door he leaned in to kiss his mother on the cheek. He said to Laura, almost in a whisper, "I'm getting out before this time next year. I haven't decided when, just yet."

"Wonderful," she replied "Maybe I'll get to see more of you when you do."

"Us," was his reply. And that is how her youngest son told her of his intentions to marry. And it was about time. After all, he was 36.

As she went to her bedroom after seeing Adrien and Charlotte out the front door, Laura thought to herself, "I've made it through my first Christmas back in Paris without Françoise. And my son was here to help me. I was dreading this, but I made it through. Maybe I can make it through the rest of what I'll have to go through. Maybe."

New Year's eve found Laura on her knees at Notre Dame praying for strength. The Christmas cards she sent out had brought many in return, some of them with invitations to come and visit, others to come and stay, and some to just come and party. After New Years' prayers she went to a private party at the estate of a friend who lived right outside of Paris. Her car was not running so they had someone come by to pick her up. They swore it was no bother. They insisted she spend the night so she took a small overnight bag with her. She danced until dawn. They even asked her to sing. She obliged them with her rendition of "The Last Time I Saw Paris." There were tears in the eyes of the listeners when she finished. With the sun already up, she retired to one of the guest bedrooms upstairs. "1948 is going to be my year," she thought to herself as she drifted off to sleep.

Chapter 30. Return to Show Business

Jules Etienne had been Laura's stage manager. He had been with her many years before she, and Françoise, and Marcella had to flee before the Germans. He and his devoted wife Marie chose to remain behind in Paris and face them. Jules had been imprisoned by the Germans for about a year before they released Jules.

When he heard that Laura was back in town, he went to her house. She had sent a Christmas card to him where he used to live but it was returned to her marked "Retour à l'envoyer" as did quite a few others. She was on her hands and knees scrubbing the bathroom floor when the doorbell of the apartment rang. Whoever it was had gotten by the caretaker so it must be someone who knew her. She went to the door to find Jules standing there.

"Jules! Why how nice to see you. Do come in." They hugged and kissed as only long-lost friends can do.

"You look as if you have been cleaning," he said.

"I have. My apartment was rented out while Françoise and I were in the states and the floors look like they haven't been cleaned properly in all the time I've been away. I keep scrubbing them, but the dirt's ground in. I can't get them clean."

"Doesn't your maid do that kind of thing?" he asked.

"I can't afford a maid. I'm living on a shoe string," she admitted. "Françoise left me a little money. Just enough to live on but not enough to have servants. Besides I got used to doing things for myself while I was living in New York. But enough of my misfortune. Come in and let's catch up." She showed him into the parlor. "How is Marie?"

"Marie died four years ago," said Jules sadly. "We were barely keeping body and soul together and she got sick with the flu. There was very little food because of the rationing and we were both half hungry and sickly most of the time. If she had been healthier then maybe she could have survived, but she was too weak, and well, she didn't make it. I heard about Françoise. I'm sorry."

"And so am I. About Marie. Well, it seems that both of us are left to weather this storm by ourselves. But we can make it. I know we can. Others have before us." They chatted on and on about their personal war stories.

In a pensive mood Jules related to Laura the day he thought the Germans were going to kill him. "The guard walked to my cell," he said. "He opened the door, and told me I was free. I thought they were setting me up to murder me, then I realized they wouldn't have had to go to such an elaborate ruse to do so. They could have slipped something into my food or merely taken me out into the courtyard and shot me. With no explanation of why they had held me or why I was being freed, they just released me."

"And poor Marie," he went on, "Never having worked a day since we got married, they ordered her to work as a shop girl. She was on her feet for ten hours a day. They didn't know what to do with me. I found what work I could but non-sponsored work was hard to come by and I couldn't get anything in the few theaters that remained opened. We were lucky not to be forced to work in the arms factories or other factories where they were making materials to use against our own people and those trying to help us as the Germans forced other French people to do. Maybe it was because of our age, but other than the time they locked me up, the Germans and the Vichies left us pretty much alone."

He had finished off the drink Laura had poured for him. She got up to get him another. After she sat it down before him, he picked it up, drank from it, and said, "Françoise always had good liquor in the house. Here's to Françoise," and raised his glass.

"To Marie," rejoined Laura.

Jules went on with his story. "Oh, listen to this. For a while I worked as a waiter at Maxim's." He laughed. "I was the worse waiter ever. I broke so much china that I should have paid them to work there. I finally landed a job as the house guard at a cheap burlesque theater. I was the 'Pops' who sits at the back by the door to keep the undesirables out. Imagine that. After all my years in show business to wind up as a house guard." His eyes became a little misty.

Laura went out to the kitchen to prepare a little nosh for them.

When she came back Jules was noodling at the piano. He started playing the cue music for "Mon Homme" ("My Man"). Laura broke into song.

"Kid, you've still got it. Have you thought about performing again? I'm not Françoise but I can probably get you some bookings. They won't be what you were used to but if times are as tight as you say they are, it could make things a little easier for you."

"Oh, I don't know, Jules," said Laura with reluctance in her voice. "I've thought about it, of course, but I don't know if I have the mental energy for what it would take. Just the energy to get started is more than I can bear to think about. But I'm tired of living like this. I've worked too hard all these years to end up like this. I don't deserve this. Let me think about it." She mused. "If I did, and that's a big if, then how would I get started? Françoise took care of all my bookings, and everything else. I was a pampered prima donna. I don't even know how to read a train schedule." Then something snapped inside of her. "What the hell! Let's give it a try. What do I do first?"

"First, I find someone to represent you. I think I know a couple of people who might be interested. Let me go have a talk with them. Is your telephone working? I tried to call you earlier but Central couldn't find a number for you."

"No, the phone isn't on. I didn't see a need for it and it's such a big expense. But if I'm going to do this, then I'll have it turned on again. How can I reach you?" she asked him.

"Here's the number of the phone in the hallway of the boarding house where I live. I lost the house Marie and I had together. The taxes under the Germans were crushing in order to repay their reparations." A cold hard look came over his face and quickly faded. He smiled a little.

"Oh, I'm so sorry to hear that," she said. "Françoise never told me much about financial matters. The office buildings and apartments we used to own, well they were lost during the occupation. This is all that was left of the real estate we once had together. I don't know how he managed to hang onto this one, but he did."

Jules patted her on the arm. "I know," was all that he said.

When Jules left, Laura went into the basement and because she could not bring the trunks upstairs by herself, she unloaded each one, eight of them, and brought the contents, one load at a time, upstairs to a vacant bedroom and started going through them to see what could be salvaged that was usable to work into her act. Her stint as a wardrobe mistress was invaluable in helping her determine what could be reworked and how it could be done. She had little money to devote to this project and she knew that Jules had even less than she did. They would have to pull off this comeback on a shoestring.

When she finished, she had ten costumes that she could fit into that were usable, as is, without any alterations whatsoever, plus half a dozen long gowns that she had completely forgotten she owned, including a gold lame one that miraculously had not tarnished. It featured a high neckline and boning in the midsection to produce shapely curves. Not being able to afford anything more, it would have to do to be her finale gown, that is if she ever had another finale. She hoped that Jules could find her a spot singing at a little club or something. Coupled with her trademark fans, (she found four intact pair including her large white ones) which had also weathered the storm, she had her costuming all set. At least until Jules said yea or nay to one or all.

Several days later, Laura had just completed getting the phone turned on, when the ringing of the phone bell startled her. The house had been silent since her return with only the muffled voices of the tenants above and below to keep her company. It was Jules.

"Hi, Kid," he said brightly. "I've got good news. I found a booking agent, Henri Gauthier, who was surprised to hear you're back in town and wanting to work. He wants to meet with you this afternoon. Can you make it?"

"Why, yes. I think I can. What does he want me to do? Audition?" she asked.

"No, he didn't say so. He just said he'd like to meet with you," Jules answered.

"What time?"

"Can you be there by two?"

"Oui."

He gave her the name and address of the agent.

"Okay. I'll see you at two," she said. When she hung up the phone, her hand was shaking. Never one to be overly bothered with a case of the nerves, she had one now.

She dressed in her best suit and a hat which she had plucked from a giant hat box she retrieved from her basement. She went to meet the agent. She and Jules had not rehearsed anything, but Jules sat down at the piano and gave her the pickup for "Who's Sorry Now." Laura's voice, unused to singing professionally for the last few years, responded to the easy lyrics, lyrics she had sung over a hundred times over the years. Ones that she had made her own on an album she had covered in 1938. When she finished, Gauthier took a contract out of his top drawer, wrote in some figures and slid it across the desk to Laura and Jules. Jules looked it over briefly, and grinned.

"Sign it." He said to Laura. She picked up the pen and signed. It was the beginning of her comeback.

Jules and Laura walked out of Gauthier's office. He steered her into Café George V. Laura was glad Jules had chosen this particular restaurant. She enjoyed their chocolat chaud only slightly less than that served at Les Deux Margos, which on the Saint-Germain-des-Prés, was too far away to go just to get a cup of hot chocolate. They sat down and both let out their breath at the same time.

Jules started laughing. Laura started crying.

Jules spoke first, "We're on our way, Kid. What do you think?"

Laura answered, "I think I'm in a dream but don't pinch me and wake me up. You don't know how I have longed for this during the years in the states. I don't care if we get last billing in a burlesque house, I'm just glad to be back!"

"So am I, but we're not going to be playing any burlesque houses,' said Jules emphatically. "The first thing we need to do is get you a voice coach. I've got someone in mind - Stanislaw Levinsky. They say the war broke him but I think differently. I know he'll work cheap. We can use your house as a rehearsal hall for the time being. I'll get someone out to tune the piano."

The waiter came and they ordered - chocolat chaud with patisseries for Laura and café for Jules. When they were served, Laura had to remember the strange lip in the middle of the saucer that could upset the hot liquid. They were still using those damned saucers that had so embarrassed Laura the very first time she sat down and had chocolate chaud at that establishment.

"What else?" asked Jules. "Oh. What have you got to wear?"

She told him about her finds in the trunks.

"Good," he said enthusiastically. "There's got to be something we can use. We'll probably have around forty minutes to fill. You'll have time for one costume change. So we'll need four costumes – two for the stage and two evening suits for you to wear to walk into the theater and leave again. From now on, every time you walk out of your house, you've got to be dressed to the nines. No running out with your hair all amuss to pick up a paper or something from the market. Hire a maid to do your running around for you."

"Now when have you known me to run out with my hair amuss?" she asked with amusement.

He chuckled. "Never. You're always picture perfect when you walk out of the door. We're going to need a wardrobe girl. We can get someone from one of the university drama departments to do that. How much money do we have to work with? You got any?"

"About ten thousand US. That's Françoise and my entire nest egg." She had a lot more than that but she was not about to tell anyone except her children her true financial position.

"That's more than enough. Oh, say, what happened to your car? Did you sell it before you left town or what?"

"No, it's in the garage. I tried starting it when I first got back but couldn't get it to crank."

"Probably just needs a battery, maybe spark plugs. And the petrol is probably stale. I'll take care of it. We'll hire you a driver for opening night. It'll be just like old times."

"Yes, but without Françoise," she said sadly. "I don't know if I can pull it off without him. He was there from my first independent performance in Paris."

Jules reached over and covered her hand with his. "The show must go on," he said quietly.

"Yes," she said. "The show must go on." To her amazement, she did not cry. Instead, she drew herself up to her full height of five feet eight inches. "I've got work to do. Will you be over tomorrow?"

"Yes. I'll be there at noon. Have some lunch ready for me, will you? I've got to get moving, now. I'll see how much I can get done today."

With that, he signaled to the waiter, paid up, and they left, each going their own way.

Laura could have stopped incorporating a strip tease in her act when she turned 40. Her career had been far enough advanced that she did not have to take her clothes off to get her act on the bill. Her voice and dance routine had been polished and sophisticated, but audiences had loved her act and she made damned good money, so she had kept stripping. Besides, she really enjoyed being the exhibitionist. But those days were over.

She would have to stage a comeback on the strength of her singing and dancing alone. After her car wreck, she had found it nearly impossible to tap.

Gradually, she had regained some proficiency but never footwork like she had as a young hoofer. She wondered if she could even do a two-step now. She still had footwork, only today they called it modern dancing. She called it strutting her stuff. She could do that in her sleep.

She needn't have worried. Jules found an excellent dance master to work with her. Before they were even introduced he blurted out, "Let me see you Fox Trot". He grabbed her and because there was no music she had no way of knowing if she was in step or not. "Okay," he said as he released her abruptly, "Now let me see you waltz." She waltzed by herself for him to an imaginary tune in her head.

"You move beautifully," he said matter-of-factly. "Yes, we have something to work with." He turned to Jules. "I can teach her. I won't have her doing any tap steps, just a little modern dance with boy dancers for support. The girls will be there as backdrop and to fill the eye. With hard work, it's possible. I'm thinking about a lift for the finale." He spoke about her as if she were not even in the room. Abruptly he turned to her, "Can you do a lift?"

"Yes," stammered Laura. She had not been this nervous since she first started out in show business. She took a deep breath and regained her composure. "I've done many lifts over the years, but mind you, I haven't been on a stage for seven years. It's been longer still since I've done a lift, maybe 10 years or so, but I can certainly give it my best effort. I'll need a strong, young man though. Do you have anyone in mind?" She was feeling herself beginning to take charge of the situation.

"Yes, I do," he answered. "I'll have him look you up. Let me know how it goes. His discipline is kind of shaky. We'll see if you can whip him into shape."

Laura held up her hand. "Oh, wait. Now you have me worried. I don't need any problems," she said.

"If he doesn't work out, we'll find someone else."

"Okay," she agreed. "Have him contact me. I can always say no."

Laura met David Emery the next afternoon. Jules brought him over for her to audition. The dance master gave them a set of choreographed steps to perform.

David hit all his marks on the third try. After five tries Laura was still trying to hit hers. David stepped into her and guided her through the routine. Then the dance master gave them another set of steps to perform. Again, David hit all of his marks on the third try while Laura was still struggling with hers. Again, he stepped into her and guided her through the routine. Then they put the combination together. This time Laura let David guide her through the routine the first time. By the third time she had it. Wow! Was he good. "He should have been the dance master," she thought to herself.

At the end of the audition, she motioned for David to sit down at a table and talk to her. She asked him about his performance background. He had come prepared with stills, handbills, and clippings. She looked at all the pictures and read through his press notices.

After she finished reading, she settled back in her chair and said, "Now, tell me why they say your discipline is kind of shaky. What is it I need to know about you?"

"Well, ma'am, I missed a few rehearsals."

Laura was all ears. "Tell me about it."

"I was young. I was in love. Things weren't going well. My girl left me and I kind of went off the deep end."

"When was that?"

"Two years ago."

She sat for a moment. "Okay. Let me think about it." At length she said, "Convince me I can trust you," she said.

"I can't," he said solemnly. "All I can do is tell you is that I have my head on straight now."

"What happened to the girl?" asked Laura.

"We didn't get back together. I'm seeing someone else now."

"I've always tried to work with partners who're married. More stability. More to lose. Any chance of your getting married anytime soon?"

"No."

"Okay. I'll let you know in a day or two. I suppose you can lift?" she asked.

"Yes ma'am, I can," he said emphatically. He got up from his chair and extended his hand to her. She took it and guided her out onto the practice floor. "Just let yourself go and I'll be here. I've got you," he said, almost in a whisper. He led her into a pirouette and then suddenly, she was flying. He held her high overhead with no trembling in his arms. She arched her back and took a deep breath, knowing that she was secure in his hands, arms, shoulders, and legs. He had her.

He sat her onto her feet. "You're hired," she told him. "But I'll fire your ass in a New York minute if you let me down."

"Thank you, Miss Boullt. I won't disappoint you," he replied. And he never did.

Chapter 31. Randolph Passes Away

Laura had returned to the states approximately once every two or three years or so during the '20's and the '30's. On each trip back, she made the dreaded trip to Louisiana to see her family. For weeks after she returned from each trip, she was depressed and withdrawn. Having to face the demons from her past haunted her for weeks.

While in New York, she had vowed to try to make it home every couple of years. She had made it there in '42. Then in '44 Françoise had passed away. Life became tougher for her after that and she did not make the bi-annual trip anymore. She did not go back until '47.

It was no different this last time. Depression had hung over her all through the Christmas holidays. There were many things that could have contributed to her depression, being without Françoise, being back in Paris and seeing the destruction the war had taken, feeling the emptiness of friends who would never return, not being in show business anymore, all of those things could have contributed to her depression, but deep in her soul Laura knew that it was that damned trip to Louisiana. Were it not for the fact that her sons were there, she would never go there again.

Laura had just returned from the states and had just signed contracts for shows beginning in June and as happy as that made her, that ole Louisiana depression lingered in the back of her brain. But she did not let it get her down. She had a goal in mind and she was not going to let a little bout of depression stop her.

A few weeks after she and Jules started rehearsals, she received a cablegram from Lida, Randolph's wife. Randolph had suffered a cerebral hemorrhage and had passed away. The funeral was to be in a week to ten days. Laura immediately placed a trunk call to Lida to assure her she would be there. Randolph and Lida did not have a phone, so Laura called Hamp. He told her that Lida and the girls were not in Louisiana. They were in Los Angeles at Charlie's house. She placed a person to person trunk call to Lida at Charlie's. Lida was evasive. There had been no exact time set for the burial as yet but she was hoping to have it a week from that Friday. It was Wednesday.

The only way Laura could go there and be back in time to prepare for her opening show was to fly. She had not been on a plane since they had flown out of Lisbon in '40. She made arrangements to fly from Paris to New York and from there to Los Angeles. It would cost a lot to do so but she felt she had to be there for her son in death even though she had not been there for him in life.

When she arrived in Los Angeles she was picked up at the airport by her brother. She noticed a strange quietness about him. He didn't rattle on the way he normally did. She knew something was going on. She was determined to find out what it was from Lida.

The next day Laura borrowed Charlie's car and asked Lida to go to the store with her. As soon as the two women got in the car, Laura asked point blank, "What happened to my son?"

Lida started crying. The story she told was so hideous that Laura wanted to scream - but did not.

On a trip home to Louisiana at Christmas, Charlie had begged to be allowed to take Randolph and Lida's youngest daughters, Johnnie and Laura, out of rural

Louisiana and give them a better life, he said. Johnnie did not want to go but Laura did, so they agreed to let her go with her great uncle.

Each time they talked to Laura on the phone, something seemed off to Randolph and Lida so they sent Johnnie to bring Laura home. Something horrible was happening. Their uncle had Laura sleep in his bed every night. Johnnie was young, but not so young that she did not know what that was all about. Johnnie had immediately placed a call home to her parents to tell them to come right away. Although they did not really have the money to do so, they both went out to deal with the trouble.

After Randolph had been informed of what was going on by Johnnie, he had confronted Charlie. A fight had ensued and Charlie had struck Randolph in the head, knocking him down.

The following day as they were preparing to leave, the two men had started to fight again. They were in the front yard with a cab waiting at the curb. This time, Lida reported, Randolph had grabbed his head and fell to the ground and passed out. A neighbor had called for an ambulance and they had taken Randolph to Mount Sinai.

The doctors there had broken the news to Lida. Randolph had suffered a cerebral hemorrhage – a stroke. There was nothing they could do but make him comfortable. Lida explained they had no money for hospital bills or anything else. The doctors told her that since Randolph had served in the military they could transfer him to the Veteran's hospital. She was told there was a surgeon there who was perfecting a technique for dealing with brain disorders. He had successfully performed brain surgery on returning soldiers after the war. The county would pick up the cost of the ambulance to transport Randolph. Lida agreed to have him moved there.

At the Veteran's hospital, they performed surgery to remove blood from around the brain and to fix damaged blood vessels. This was experimental surgery to be sure with no guarantee that it would work or that Randolph would not be permanently paralyzed should he survive. He lasted five days, expiring on April 28th.

Lida had sent off the cablegram to Laura right away.

"I'm stuck between a rock and a hard place," said Lida. "I need to return to Louisiana and take my girls with me but I have no money. I had to pay the hospital all I had in order for them to release Randolph so he could be moved to the Veteran's hospital. I have tickets for the return trip home but no money for meals or anything else. I'm thinking that maybe I should cash in the train tickets and go by bus."

Laura was prepared for this. She opened her purse, took out $300 in twenty dollar bills and gave it to Lida. "Keep the train tickets," she said. "After the funeral I'll personally see to all of you getting back home. For now I just want us out of Charlie's house. That bastard."

Laura placed a call to the only person she knew in Los Angeles - Marcelle de St Martin. Marcelle came to Laura within an hour of receiving her call. The two women sat out in Marcelle's car and talked.

When Marcelle left, Laura came back into the house and told Lida, "Get the girls ready. We're going to stay with a friend."

Marcelle put them all up for the next week, taking time off from her job at the studio to drive them back and forth to wherever they needed to go.

Hamp arrived from Louisiana by bus the day after they went to Marcelle's. He was accompanied by C. J., Randolph's eldest surviving child, Ladine having died from diphtheria when she was only three years old. There had been no way to let them know what Charlie had done to little Laura, so the two men went to Charlie's house expecting a warm welcome. Laura knew they were expected and so went to Charlie's house that night to tell them the horrible news. They said that Charlie had picked them up from the bus station and dropped them off at his house and they had not seen or heard from him since. They did not know where he was or when he was to return.

Marcelle had found the name of a hotel in downtown Los Angeles that would put the two men up and Laura paid for them to stay there for the duration of their time in Los Angeles. She made both of them promise that they would not approach Charlie at all. Hamp was particularly notorious with a switch-blade knife, having killed a man with one, he claimed in self-defense, some years previously. The last thing she needed was for one of them to go to jail for trying to take revenge on Charlie.

Adrien and Marcella arrived by plane the day before the funeral.

With Marcelle's help Laura and Lida had been able to secure a burial plot for Randolph in the Los Angeles National Cemetery (commonly called the Veteran's cemetery) in West Los Angeles at the corner of Wilshire and Sepulveda. The small family was there, Laura, Lida, young Laura, Johnnie, C. J., Marcella, Adrien, and Hamp. And Marcelle. She stood by Laura like a rock. They laid Randolph to rest there in a beautiful mahogany coffin that Laura had paid for.

It was decided that the two men would return with Lida and the girls on the train. The morning after the funeral Marcelle took them to the bus station to cash in their tickets. The following day she took them all to the train station where she and Laura saw them off to Louisiana. The day afterwards, Marcelle drove Laura, Adrien, and Marcella to the airport and put them on a plane to New York, with Adrien and Laura going on to Paris.

The two friends embraced as sisters, with Laura expressing her undying gratitude for all that Marcelle had done for her and her family. They parted with each of them near tears. This would be the last time they would ever see each other. Marcelle handed Laura a portfolio she had brought with her from the car. She told Laura not to open it until she got on the plane.

After the plane was airborne Laura asked for a glass of champagne but she did not touch it. Numb from the previous days' events she just stared out the plane window. Eventually she remembered Marcelle's portfolio. She got it from the overhead bin. In it were drawings for six costumes. There was also a note from Marcelle. "For your upcoming show and the one after that for I know the first one will be such a success that you'll be putting on another soon afterwards." Tears rolled unrestrained down Laura's cheeks. She realized that someone may become concerned if they should see her crying so she took a handkerchief from her handbag and dabbed at the tears, trying not to smudge her makeup.

"Ma'am, are you alright?" The gentleman in the seat next to her inquired.

"Why, yes, thank you," she replied.

"I just noticed that you haven't touched your champagne, that's all." He lied. He had noticed her crying and was trying to be polite by not mentioning it.

"Oh," she said. "I've got something on my mind. I buried my son a few days ago."

"Oh, ma'am, I'm so sorry to hear that," he sounded really sincere about it. "I didn't mean to intrude on your sorrow. Again, pardon me ma'am, but have I seen you somewhere before? Are you a movie star or something?"

"No, I'm not a movie star, but I am a performer. I perform primarily in Europe. And yes, I've been in a few movies – all French. I doubt if you've seen any of them. They were mostly forgettable."

"Why, you're Laura Boult! I've seen your show! I was in Paris in '38 and you performed at the Follies-Bergère. You were wonderful. But listen here. If you need anything while you're in New York, please look me up." He gave her his business card.

"Thank you but I'm only changing planes there. I'm on my way back to Paris. But thank you for your kindness."

"I'm due to go to Paris in the fall. Will you be performing then?"

"Yes, I have several dates booked for the fall. Here, let me tell you who to contact who can tell you exactly where I'll be and when."

He took out a notepad from his breast pocket. She gave him Henri's name and address. "I've been so busy getting my show together I haven't been keeping up with all the engagements but if you write to the booking agent he'll send you a list of my show dates. I figure I'll get it all fixed in my mind a few weeks before I'm supposed to be somewhere. I used to not keep up with it at all. My husband was my manager and he would tell me where I was supposed to be but he died a few years ago and now I find I have to do these things for myself."

"Oh, were you out of show business for a while?"

"Yes, during the war. My husband was Jewish so we left Paris just ahead of the Nazis getting there. I wasn't able to get any bookings in New York. I just got back to Paris in December."

They chatted on a while longer. Finally, he said, "You look really tired Miss Boult. Why don't I let you get some rest."

By then she had drained her champagne glass and he had ordered her another. She closed her eyes and before she knew it she was being awakened by the stewardess with a dinner tray. They were somewhere over the Midwest. Only since the advent of the Boeing Strato-cruiser was it possible to make this long trip across the states non-stop. She was so glad for it because she did not know if she possessed the mental reserve to deal with changing planes in mid-America. She had not realized how little she had eaten in the last few days. The meal consisted of veal parmesan, potato puffs, and green beans with chocolate cake for dessert. She ate it all and immediately fell asleep again.

When they touched down, she said goodbye to her seat mate. He assured her he would come see her when he came to Paris the following year.

After Marcella parted with them at Idlewild Airport, Laura and Adrien went into the restaurant. He ordered a scotch for himself and champagne for her.

"Mother, you look exhausted," he said, looking concerned. "Have you even slept since this all began?"

"Well, I slept briefly on the plane, but no, son, to tell you the truth, I haven't had very much sleep at all. And also, to tell you the truth, I am exhausted. I'll sleep on the way back to Paris." Quietly, almost to herself she said, "Maybe I shouldn't have come. But if I hadn't I would have hated myself for the rest of my life."

Adrien said nothing. Without prompting, she told him the story of how she had abandoned his four older brothers, a story she had meant to keep from him and Marcella for the rest of her life. When she finished, he covered her hand with his. "You did the best you could, Mother. It was a different day and time then. There was only so much you could do."

"That's what I tell myself, but in my heart, I know I should have stayed with them and I should have looked for Marvin and Chris. I should never have given up on finding them. Oh, I have made a mess of my life."

"Mother, how can you say that? Look at me and Marcella. We wouldn't be here if you hadn't done what you did."

"Yes, that's true, but you don't know how this eats away at my insides, and always have."

"But yet, you've never talked about it for all these years."

"I didn't want my burden to be anyone else's burden. It was a cross I had to bear alone. Your father knew and sometimes when I would get weepy for no reason he would hold me while I cried and tell me that God has forgiven me even if I couldn't forgive myself. Eventually, I would stop crying, but the pain was always there."

When they finally touched down on the last leg of their very lengthy flight, Laura was emotionally and physically drained. Jules met them at the airport in the Duesenberg and drove them home, dropping Adrien at his apartment first. When they got to Laura's house, Jules took her key and opened the door for her. She went into the parlor and sank down onto the sofa. Jules quietly let himself out but not before telling her that he had brought her food from Maxim's and put in in the oven.

"Thanks, Jules. I appreciate all you've done."

"I'll let myself out and put the car away."

"Thanks, again. I don't know if I even have the strength to go down the stairs and back up again." He kissed her goodbye on the cheek and left.

After he left, she sat on the sofa for a long time. Suddenly the flood gates opened and she started crying, a gut-wrenching cry – the first time she had done so since she got the word of Randolph's death. She cried for Randolph. She cried for Lida. She cried for little Laura, for Johnnie. And she cried for Mirtice who Laura had found out was trapped in a loveless brutal marriage. But mostly, she cried for herself. There were two parts to her life. The Louisiana part was dysfunctional and was out of sync with the Paris part, which up until the war, had been nearly perfect. "Why must life be so painful and full of turmoil?" she asked herself.

Finally, the tears subsided. She got up from the sofa and walked over to the bar. She opened a bottle of Moet & Chandon. She took the glass and the bottle to her bedroom. Kicking off her shoes she lay down on the bed. She polished off the glass and poured herself another one. By the time she was sleepy she had finished the whole bottle. She had not done that since she used to celebrate with Françoise.

Oh, how she missed him. If he were here, he would kiss her and stroke her hair and tell her he would make everything all right again. But Françoise was not here anymore. She was on her own. This was scary and she was scared. She did not know if she was going to be able to do this. Before Randolph died she had all the confidence in the world. On the trip across the ocean and back she had too much time for reflection and the future that loomed before her scared her out of her wits. She fell asleep crying.

Chapter 32. Laura's European Tours

Laura awoke with a banging hangover the next morning. It was already 10 o'clock. She struggled out of bed and went into the bathroom. While a bath was drawing, she started unpacking. Her head was killing her. She found some aspirin in the medicine cabinet and took it.

"Okay, no more drinking for me," she thought to herself. "I can't handle it anymore."

After her bath, she went into the kitchen and remembering that Jules had left her some food, she looked for it and found it. That was her breakfast and lunch. She was starting to feel a little better. Around two her headache had subsided. She called Jules to let him know she was ready to work.

"I have drawings for costumes from Marcelle. Do you think we can find someone to do them in two weeks?"

"Sure we will if I have to sew them myself," he replied. He found a costume maker who promised to have them ready in time.

The following day and continuing for two straight weeks, they worked eight hours a day putting the finishing touches on her act.

On opening night Laura was thoroughly prepared. Her Duesenberg called for her at five. By six she was in her dressing room. When the stage manager sang out "Trente minutes a le lever du rideau" (thirty minutes to curtain), she was ready. At five minutes to curtain, he knocked, then stuck his head in her door. "Cinq minutes, Madame Boult."

"Je suis prêt," was all she replied.

Jules reached over and took her hand. "Break a leg, Kid."

"Thanks, Jules. For this night. For giving this back to me. For everything."

Adrien and Charlotte were there in the dressing room to wish her luck. "Do it for Dad," he said as he kissed her on the cheek. "He put his all into you, you know."

Laura was a "rock 'em, sock 'em, knock 'em dead hit". One of the papers said so the next day. They all more or less said the same thing. She was smashing! The theater management held her over for two additional weeks. She could not give them more than that because Henri had booked her into a European tour. When she received the check for her first week of performing, she went to Christian Dior and bought her first Parisian gown in seven years. She now had professional costuming, arrangements, choreography, and now new Parisian clothes to wear. She was ready to go on tour.

She played top theaters in ten of the largest cities in France, included among them Nice, Cannes, Monte Carlo, Calais, Lyon, Marseille, and Toulouse. She played two weeks on and two weeks off, returning by train to Paris in between show dates. All of her press notices said her show was stupendous. She was very gratified to be accepted back by her loyal fans.

It was time to set her schedule for the following year. Laura wanted to return to Britain, Scotland, and Ireland. She had played London and other venues in Great Britain for over 30 years. Her last performance in London had been at the Palladium in 1940.

The Palladium for many years had a resident show, usually a musical, but was able to offer one-off shows because of the way the theater was designed. The sets of the resident shows were lifted high above the stage in an area called the fly loft so that the sets of the off show acts could be wheeled in.

Val Parnell, the Managing Director of the Palladium since 1945 had a policy of headlining only big name American acts. Since becoming the managing director he had booked Mickey Rooney, Jack Benny, Frank Sinatra, Dean Martin, Sammy Davis, Jr., Ella Fitzgerald, Bob Hope, Danny Kaye, Judy Garland and anyone who was a big name in American show business, giving second bill to British and other European acts - except for Maurice Chevalier. Maurice, in his trademark tuxedo and boater hat, was a big name Hollywood actor. Maurice he booked as a one-man show.

Laura was not a big enough name for Parnell so he offered her third billing on a five act bill. Henri turned him down. As Laura racked up successes throughout Europe, Parnell repeated his offer several times. Each time Henri turned him down flat.

One day Henri called her up and asked her to come to his office to meet with him. He wanted to confer with her regarding several venues before accepting offers to play them.

When she had settled herself into one of his plush visitors' chairs, Henri said. "I have news for you. I've booked you into the Palladium."

"What? How is that news? Before Parnell, I played the Palladium every year for years. I won't take third billing," she replied. "As much as I would hate it, the Palladium just won't be in my schedule this year."

"I got you a one woman show. Honey, you're right up there with Judy Garland!"

Henri got his hoped for reaction from Laura. Her mouth literally dropped open. She had never expected to get star billing again at that theater in her entire lifetime as long as Parnell was there.

She squealed and jumped up from her seat, ran around the desk, and threw her arms around Henri. "Oh, Henri, you big wonderful doll, you. How can I ever thank you?!"

Then her mind immediately went to more practical things.

"But I must speak to Jules at once. I must get a completely new act together and I'll need new costumes. I have the designs for them already."

"But," sputtered Henri. "Don't you want to know the dates?"

"It doesn't matter," she replied. "Whenever it is, I'll be ready. But, oui, tell me the dates."

"Not for six months," was his reply. "Laura, it's only a one-nighter. You and Jules have plenty of time to put together a new act and break it in."

"That's fine. One night at the Palladium is better than a month anywhere else. It's the exposure. But it won't be a reworked or broken-in act. It will be all fresh, with fresh new modern songs. There are several that I've been rehearsing, thinking about putting into my current show."

"What are you working on? Anything I can mention in trying to book you for the rest of next season?" he asked.

"Why yes, there is. I've been rehearsing "Darling Je Vous Aime Beaucoup" by Anna Sosenko. I've got some great arrangements for it in a slightly slower beat than written. I was going to debut it in this fall's act but I think I'll debut it at the Palladium instead. There won't be a dry eye in the house. Oh, and "Les Feuilles Mortes" - Falling Leaves! I already have that one down pat. I sing it in both French and English. I heard Yves Montand sing it that way at a house party last month. Delicious."

"Great idea. They're both perfect for your voice," said Henri.

"Oh, I can't believe it! I've got to run now," she said as she hurriedly grabbed her purse and coat. "Call Jules for me and tell him to meet me at my house right away. Tell him the news. He'll know who else to assemble. Au revoir chérie," she called over her shoulder as she flew out the door.

Nat King Cole and the King Cole Trio opened for her. They had just charted with a song called "I Love You for Sentimental Reasons". The trio received a standing ovation, warming up the audience for Laura.

She and Jules put together a show-stopping act simply titled "Laura!". Together with her backup singers, a 10 piece orchestra, and 20 showgirls and male dancers she entertained the audience for two hours.

All of the London papers wrote up both acts as spectacular hits and praised Laura for introducing Nat to British audiences and for continuing to perform at her age. The paper stated, "Laura Boult still has the most spectacular gams of anyone in show business." To Laura, it was the pinnacle of her career, or so she thought.

In 1949 she performed in Nice, Venice, Florence, Milan, Naples, and Rome, as well as about a dozen venues in Paris and environs. She closed out the year by performing in Monte Carlo over the Christmas holidays. Her New Year's Eve performance was attended by the recently crowned Rainier the Sovereign Prince of Monaco and his consort, French film star Giséle Pascal.

Life was good.

Chapter 33. Chez Laura!

In 1950, based on the strength of her comeback, Laura was approached by a noted restaurateur. He wanted to open a restaurant with her name on it. This would also give her a home base to perform from when she was not on tour. She would not have to put up any money and her share of the profits for the use of her name would be 20% of the net. Except for the percentage, it was too good to be true. Jules and Henri negotiated on her behalf, and got her 20% of the gross. In addition, she got her regular contract price for per performance. Now that was a good deal!

Henri was happy because he did not have to search for engagements for her between tours and an added benefit was that he got the contract to keep the stage filled when she was not on it.

Jules was happy because it guaranteed them 48 weeks a year, and now they could hire a permanent band to back her and keep the dancers and backup singers on salary and not have to restage the show for each tour.

Laura was happy because she would get to do what she loved most without worrying about money.

They signed contracts in January of '50, closed the restaurant that was there and renovated, increasing the bandstand by 50%, and reopened in June of that year. The restaurant was an immediate success.

The restaurant was located in Montparnasse, the part of town where artists and others with like minds congregated after World War II. Laura's favorite late night hangouts were there. She frequently went there to wind down after a performance. Located on the left bank of the River Seine, Montparnasse had been the gathering place of artists and entertainers too numerous to mention from 1910 right up until WWII. So many moved away to the United States, just one step ahead of the Nazis - never to return. Those who did return welcomed others of like temperament. No one met a stranger there.

It was in one of the neighborhoods of the 14th arrondissement, on Le Boulevard Montparnasse, that the restaurateur found the perfect location for Chez Laura! The front of the building resembled an old mansion from the Art Deco period. The kitchen was strictly modern and up-to-date. They kept the prices in the mid-price range. There were several specialties of the house, included among them crepes, quiche, shrimp and crab dishes, chicken, pork, and beef dishes. Laura's contribution to the menu fare was gumbo. The gumbo was an instant hit, liked by Europeans who favored fish stews, and by Americans who liked hearty meat stews – her gumbo being a combination of the two. And of course there were desserts. All manner and kind were prepared each day, presented for the selection of the restaurant patrons on a push cart. It was not unusual that a diner could not decide which selection to make, so took two instead.

For the interior they decided to stick with the Art Nouveau period of the building's facade. The dining salon was done up with red velvet walls, chandeliers, white table cloths, and small table lamps. It was the re-creation of luxurious dining at Maxim's that Laura recalled from her heyday in Paris. With so many venues going ultra-modern, Laura wanted the restaurant that bore her name to evoke shades of the past. She accomplished her goal.

Recalling the midpoint of her career when several of the restaurants she frequented regularly provided meals to starving artists, Laura wanted to carry out this idea without actually trying to feed all of the poor starving souls of the city. Chez Laura! always kept a table for local artists on which was served soup, bread, a choice of a meat dish, chicken, or gumbo, cheese, a cheap wine, and a dessert - all for the price of a piece of artwork. There was also a similar table available for a veteran of World War II. This was a much kept secret and seldom used, but it was there and available to anyone who asked for it.

One stipulation was that a reservation was required, so that there was never any ambiguity as to whether or not the artist's or veteran's table was available or not. The other stipulation was that the recipient of the house's hospitality must be dressed for the occasion, either in appropriate daytime attire or dinner attire – no shorts, tennis shoes, jeans, kakis, or sandals.

And then the floorshow! Because of the size of the stage, Laura had to cut down the number of dancers in the act. They danced. They pranced. They sang both English and French songs. She went into the audience and chatted with them. She sat on the laps of good looking men, young and old, and sang to them, and their wives and girlfriends loved it. She made sure everyone who wanted one got an autographed picture of her. Enough could not be said about it.

Everything about the stage and dressing areas were designed to accommodate Laura. Everything was what Madame wanted. Laura's own dressing room had a star on it. When she was not playing the venue, management asked her permission to allow the headliner to use it. She agreed without hesitation.

Laura also had her own table. Preferring banquette type seating, there had been an entire row installed on the left wall as you walked in the front door. It's location was perfect - a place where Laura could see and be seen. She could confer with restaurant staff without disturbing patrons as the manager's office was located at the end of the banquette. It was here that Laura held court, reveling in her glories, past and present. When she was there, there was a steady stream of people going back and forth to her table, some to wish her well, some to get her well wishes. Some were there to pitch investment ideas to her, all of which she referred to Jules. And some who just downright begged. These she referred to Henri, who said "No" loud and clear as only a Frenchman could do it.

Chapter 34. Laura's World Tours

In 1951 Laura went to Hawaii, Japan and China and wowed them there, playing in about a dozen venues. Because of the distance she did the entire tour during the first half of the year without returning to Europe. For the remainder of the year she played venues closer to home and Chez Laura!

'52 saw her flying back and forth across the oceans, first to Africa, then back to Paris. Then to New York as a guest on Frank Sinatra's variety show. Then back to Paris, where she was in a stage production of Pygmalion, playing the mother in the first act. She had a six month run for that engagement. During that year she also appeared in two movies – one in Britain and one in France.

By now, her finances had recovered, and she had household help and a personal maid. She did not have to cook or clean for herself anymore, but enjoyed being waited on and catered to by others. From time to time she would shoo everyone out of the kitchen and spend hours there cooking all sorts of American or Americanized versions of French dishes. Her life was perfect.

It was around this time that it came to Laura's attention that Josephine Baker had overextended herself trying to maintain her estate, Château de Milandes in Dordogne, and her very large family. Although Laura had tried on several occasions to return the $10,000 Josephine had let Laura and Françoise have when they fled France, Laura went to her and this time begged Josephine to take the money – if not for her own sake then for her children. Josephine finally agreed and a large burden was lifted from Laura. That debt had been on her mind every since she had returned to France. Laura repaid not only the original $10,000 but a generous interest as well.

In '53 she went to South America. While there Jules dared her to go topless on the beach in Brazil. She took him up on his dare. From there she went to the United States. This time no one offered her a tour of the "Chitlin' Circuit." She played in theaters in New York where she stayed with Marcella and her family for two weeks, Chicago, Kansas City, Denver, Los Angeles, San Francisco, and several other large venues. Because of segregation she did not play any southern cities. While in Los Angeles she visited Randolph's grave. Marcelle had died the year before but Laura did not find out until almost a month afterwards. She paid a condolence call on Marcelle's husband and children while there. They remembered her from her week stay with them in '48. Hamp had moved out to California to be with his sons by then, and she visited with them also while she was there. It was a lukewarm reception that she received but that did not surprise her. Hamp had never forgiven her as Randolph had.

While in the states, she made a brief return to St. Maurice. She was only there for a few hours. That was all she could take. Lida was living in Minden, so she stayed two days with her. She was never so glad to leave anywhere. The poverty overwhelmed her and there was nothing she could do about it. She returned to France, as in the past, depressed by her Louisiana trip. It took her weeks to shake it off. She vowed never to return again, her reasons for going there in the past, her sisters and brothers and her children, all except Hamp, having passed away some time before.

In the fall of the year she appeared in the stage drama "Much Ado About Nothing," with a six week run.

The following year she made a tour of Spain and Portugal, headlining a star studded act culminating in performances in Madrid, Barcelona, and Lisbon that brought the houses down. Those were the major engagements of the year. With her vowing not to go out of the country anymore that year, Henri got her into three movies. But one was out of country - this time in Italy (a spaghetti western). The other two were in France (two romantic comedies). She did not star in any of these movies. She only had bit parts. But she could say that she had been in the movies. She filled in the rest of her schedule with local performances and a couple of TV dramas.

In 1954, against her better judgment she went to Germany. She reluctantly agreed to do it after Bob Hope contacted her and asked her personally to entertain the US troops stationed there. Since the USO gig would only pay her minimum she needed to finance the trip by playing other venues while there. She told Hope that she hated the idea of performing for the Germans and he assured her that there would be plenty of opportunities to pack any of her performances with American soldiers since, for various reasons, not all of them would be able to make it to the USO show. She had the tour added to her schedule.

At her first non-USO show, both the Germans and the Americans in the audience greeted her with a standing ovation. She was so overwhelmed that she had tears streaming from her eyes. Being the show-woman that she was, she quickly dried her tears and went into her performance routine.

On her way back from Germany, mostly as an excuse to vacation, she did one week shows in Ostend, Belgium, and Vienna and Innsbruck, Austria. Again, her shows were a hit.

After she returned from her German engagement she received a personally signed letter from President Eisenhower thanking her for her service to the armed services. Laura framed the letter and hung it on her study wall along with an autographed picture of her being given a kiss by de Gaulle upon the conclusion of a performance she put on for French soldiers. Having been banned from government-controlled TV and radio, de Gaulle, also ostracized from French politics, appreciated being given the opportunity to appear publicly at an event for the military, who he continued to champion him even in his exile status.

Late in '54 Laura decided she could no longer muster the energy to do it any longer. She had played every major city in Europe, North and South America, Asia, and Africa, some two or three times. This time she had not squandered her money. She had saved it and invested it wisely. She could have retired off her earnings after the first two years of touring but hearing Françoise's words in her ear each morning as she arose, she had kept going until she could not go anymore.

Too tired to perform any longer, she retired at the end of 1954.

She gave one last performance as a singer. Early in 1955 Josephine Baker asked her to be in a revue of the early 1920's at the Follies-Bergère. Laura did the entire act perched against a stool. Her part of the act lasted twenty minutes with her glamorous bevy of beautiful young men and women singing and dancing behind and around her – but never in front of her. No. She was always and still was, the star of her act. Her voice was clear and strong but she could barely span two octaves.

There were several acts on the bill that were meant to imitate and highlight performers who had worked in black face. Josephine, Laura, and other African-American performers, Eartha Kitt and Lena Horne among them, complained and the acts were pulled or reworked so as not to offend. Seen by some as an attempt to rewrite history, Laura did not think of it as such.

She explained in an interview given to a local newspaper, "This was an attempt to preserve with dignity the memory of those performers who were forced to perform in blackface in order to eke out a living in the theater and not an attempt to pretend that it never happened. Because it did. And those were big acts." Tears rolled down her cheeks.

After she stopped performing, she spent her days reading about French history and visiting with friends. She held a salon once a month but she no longer served champagne and caviar at those affairs. A good French wine, crackers, and cheese were the usual fare. Occasionally, she had good friends over for dinner but more often than not, it was they who entertained her. She watched her francs frugally, intending for them to last throughout her lifetime.

She had a garden planted in her backyard. The gardener took care of the shrubbery but she planted and maintained all of the flowers. To her, the garden took on a magical aspect. She even found herself enjoying digging in the dirt, something as a young women from Louisiana she would never have thought possible.

In her will she arranged for a little something for her grandchildren and great-grandchildren to remember her by. She made arrangements for the disposal of her house after she was gone. Adrien and Charlotte had been married for over ten years and had a magnificent home of their own, so they had no need of her house and Marcella lived in a fabulous apartment in New York and she had no intention of ever living in Paris again. Laura arranged for the house to be used as low rent housing for retired showgirls and other retired theatrical workers.

She went to the restaurant three or four times a week, although her stomach was more sensitive now, and she only nibbled at her food. Still a lover of authentic Louisiana gumbo, it now kept her up at night. She could eat the chicken okay but the sausage gave her heartburn. And she still, after all the years of living in Paris, thought that French food was undercooked.

She went shopping at les magazins, but only to lèche-vitrine – to window shop. She had so many clothes that she had converted an entire bedroom into a closet so she did not buy many clothes anymore. However, once a year she splurged and bought a designer gown, usually a Dior, and she always found herself somewhere special to wear it – usually during the holiday season. Also, once a year, she treated herself to a Chanel suit which she wore to church on Sundays. As she tired easily, she seldom went to the theater any longer, and like so many elderly people, television became her companion. Most of her clothes just hung in the closet unworn.

On her 80th birthday she went to Cartier and bought herself another diamond watch, the one Françoise had given her when they got married having finally stopped working for good. She had the old one put into a glass case and she set it on her dresser so she could be reminded each day of his love for her.

Chapter 35. Laid to Rest

Laura Celestina Boult Goldman died quietly in her sleep in 1960 at the age of 85. She had been active in show business for 65 years, having begun at the age of 20 and never actually ending her career, taking bit parts in the theater, the movies, and TV when such roles were offered to her, right up until the end.

Laura had told her family many times that she did not want to be returned to the place where she had begun life. There were too many painful memories there. She wanted to be to laid to rest in her adopted land where she had been so happy. Inside the city of Paris.

She is buried under a simply adorned headstone in the Père-Lachaise, cimetière de l'Est, the largest cemetery in the city. Père-Lachaise is in the 20th arrondisement where Laura had spent a great deal of her career working. It is said to be the world's most visited cemetery, attracting hundreds of thousands of visitors annually to the graves of those who have enhanced French life for over 200 years. The cemetery is on Boulevard de Ménilmontant. Laura is buried near a side entrance near the Père-Lachaise metro stops.

All of her older children, save one, had preceded her in death. Of the four oldest boys, only Hamp was alive. He was too infirm to travel to her services.

Marcella and Adrien were both there, as were many of her grandchildren. She had left instructions with Adrien and money in a bank account to pay for the transportation of all who wanted to attend.

After the funeral, there was an open house at Chez Laura!, again paid for by Laura, with funds she left behind for that purpose. Champagne flowed like water on that day.

Laura went out the way she had lived – with style and class.

ABOUT THE AUTHOR

Tracey Richardson was born Celestine Sands in 1947 in Marshall, Texas. She moved to Dallas as a single mom in 1970. She was always an avid reader, well rounded in various genres, especially historical novels. She has been writing since she was 16 as a way to cope under stressful situations. She has turned many of life's challenges into fictional works with strong leading women characters.

In 2010, knowing retirement was on the horizon, she started pulling together this body of work. It was at that time, she decided to undertake a major writing project involving one of her ancestors – Florestine Boult.

Florestine took two years to complete and involved many months of research, including a trip to Natchitoches and St. Maurice, Louisiana, to take a look at the place where Florestine and her family lived and conducted their business.

Tracey's second book is *Tomorrow Is Another Day* – Gone With the Wind fan fiction. An alternate account of what Scarlet O'Hara might have done and where she might have landed up after Rhett Butler left here that fateful day with the words, "Frankly, I don't give a damn." Oh, but he did. . .

Tracey's third book, *All That I Have to Give,* is an attempt to complete the book that her mother began before she became too ill from breast cancer to complete it. Tracey has it 3/4 complete and vows to finish it in 2013.

Laura! is Tracey's fourth book. It is a continuation of the Florestine story, taking up with Florestine's granddaughter Laura, not to be confused with Florestine's daughter Laura, Laura being an often-used name in the Boult family tree.

Made in the USA
Coppell, TX
11 April 2024

31156484R00125